MW01129118

ITTY BITTY WRITING SPACE

100 Stories by 100 Authors

Edited by Dani J. Caile and Jason Brick

Cover designed by Arthur Wright

Table of Contents

4

A Brief Introduction from Jason Brick

You don't want to read me talking about the stories you're about to read. You just want to read them. So I'll just say thank you to everybody who made this happen.

A Slightly Longer Introduction from Dani J. Caile

It is indeed an honor to once again be here to help Jason in his third anthology, this time with 104 authors and their short stories. Itty Bitty Writing Space is filled with all types of genre and styles, enough for all readers of flash fiction, and I'm sure there's something here for everyone. I hope you enjoy your time reading.

Bomb Shelter

Halli Lilburn

Pops always said there was enough room on the floor of the bomb shelter to roller-skate. He said the cement was smoother than the bottom of the swimming pool. He dug them both out at the same time.

"Son," He said, "Them movies in school tell ya yer desk will save ya from them nukes but they is lying through their teeth. What ya need is three feet a concrete and a couple loads a mother earth 'tween you and the blast else you'll become a pillar a salt like Sodom and Gomorra."

I told my teacher what he said and she sent me to detention.

Pops wouldn't ever let me go down in the bomb shelter but sometimes, when I was swimming, I'd dive down and put my ear to the wall of the pool and listen. The pool was like the next door neighbor.

"Son, I got enough supplies in that bunker to last five years on account of the radiation." Pops would say.

"What about chocolate?" I asked.

"Five-year supply." He boasted.

Mother rolled her eyes. "Five years according to whom?"

"I also got yer mother a crate a yarn so she can spend her time knittin' us sweaters." He pinched her cheek. "That'll keep ya from gettin' bored."

She put on her statue face. She did that to hide what she was really thinking. Every time she gave Pops a homemade sweater he wore it for a day or two then mysteriously lost it. He told me it was high time I started losing Mother's knit sweaters too.

When my folks listened to the news they would argue. My old man would say, "It's gettin' worse." And Mother would tell him to calm down and clean-up for supper.

I couldn't wait for the war to start. Just thinking about roller-skating all day and eating chocolate for five years sounded amazing. What more could a kid ask for? I would sit by the latch in the middle of the lawn and invent stories about shelves full of salt water taffy and pretzels. Living in the bomb shelter would be heaven.

It might have been true if we had used the nukes but we never did. A couple of years went by listening to the news and cleaning up for supper. What finally happened wasn't political at all.

"*We interrupt your regular broadcasting to bring you this emergency message.*" The radio dominated our diner conversation as rain poured outside.

Pops dropped his fork spattering mashed potatoes across the table. "This is it!" He turned up the volume.

"There is a severe weather situation. A tornado is affecting many residential and industrial areas. Citizens are urged to take cover immediately!"

"What?" Pops slammed his hands down making peas jump off his plate. "I built a bomb shelter not a tornado shelter."

Mother collected the rolling peas in her napkin. "This is second best, dear."

"Phooey," he said.

Sure enough, Mother barely had the table cleared before wind clapped the shutters and tipped the trash can.

"Phooey!" Pops repeated as he grabbed our coats and headed for the hatch.

The wind whipped up Mother's skirt before she could prevent being indecent and I protected my ears from the roaring wind as Pops pried open the latch. Finally, I would see inside the wonderland of the bomb shelter and eat candy all night.

First impression of the underground fortress hit us with the ungodly smell of rotten potatoes.

"Tarnations!" Pops bellowed, flipping the light switch and finding half an inch of water on the floor.

I think he would have turned around and taken us back to the house if the tornado hadn't dropped right on top of it. Shingles singed the air like fiery darts. The water in the pool flew into the sky as if it were raining upside down. Gravity was reversed, sucking everything into a slime green sky like an alien tractor beam. Pops wasn't strong enough to close the hatch but luckily our car rolled on top of it and locked us in with a bang.

We collected our breath and listened to the now muted noise of the storm. My new environment consisted of cans filling steel shelves that lined the concrete walls. Mother tiptoed through the puddles to a bunk bed where she removed her ruined heels and rung out her stockings. She was wearing her statue face again.

"Can I have some chocolate?" I asked.

Pops went into a silent rage. He might have hit me if Mother hadn't started crying. She was looking into the opened crate of yarn.

"Roger, you oaf, this yarn is all black. How am I supposed to knit anything with only black?

Pops was taken aback. He stumbled for an answer. "Well, uh, darlin', they only sell them bulk yarns in one color per crate so unless ya wanna get more crates..." His voice petered out.

She threw her ruined shoe at him. He didn't even duck.

Halli Lilburn is published in Tesseracts, Leap Books, Renaissance Press and many others. She is an editor with The Dame Was Trouble by Coffin Hop Press and essentialedits.ca. Find her at **hallililburn.blogspot.com.**

Rose Grace

Laura Petrella

When I saw her out of the corner of my eye, I knew that I had to have her. The mystery of her life grasped me and she haunted me in my dreams. Even with a houseful of boisterous, busy children of my own, my maternal instinct drew me to her and made me go back time after time to find the child that no one wanted.

I named her Rose Grace. Rose, because her skin was translucent like rose petals; Grace because she was acquired through the grace of God. The perfectly formed, shoulder length ringlets, which hung limply down her temples contrasted with her tiny, elegant hands and languid, sapphire eyes.

My husband hated the name that I chose and his disdain was apparent. He clearly wanted me to take her back, like an ill-fitting piece of clothing or a broken watch. She didn't compete for attention, or fight with the children. In fact, she was no trouble at all. Yet, he wouldn't even look at her. "She is someone else's," my husband would exhort and march off in silent shame, secretly knowing that if I hadn't taken her, she'd have no family at all. It was a solemn moment when I hung her portrait in the hallway with the rest of the children's.

Children call out to her and squeal with laughter as they run by, complimenting her dark tresses and her dress and proudly introduce her to family and friends. They are non-judgmental and accepting, as innocents can be.

She watches patiently as I spoon portions of warm, macaroni and cheese into little glass bowls that she will never eat and listens as my youngest rushes headlong through grace before meals. She smiles as I deftly apply Band-Aids to the other children's skinned knees and seems to agree as I fuss over unbrushed teeth. She enjoys being included, as I teach the children how to crack an egg, and as my husband reviews algebra problems and discusses rules for driving the car. However, she will never have these experiences. She will never have the joy of primping for the prom or swoon at the sight of her first love. She will stay with me, forever a child, as I ever so slowly loosen the apron strings and my three baby birds take test flights from the nest.

My daughter has promised to care for her when I no longer can and her portrait will continue to be treasured. In it, Rose Grace is dressed in a sheer, black taffeta mourning gown, with a black, ribbon choker tied tenderly around her lifeless neck. She was probably already dead before the first brush stroke ever touched the canvas. It is her postmortem.

Laura Petrella is a retired civil Engineer who enjoys creating, crafting, cooking and landscape design. When not planning, or working on her next project, she can be found surveying her garden, or exploring history and architecture with her husband.

The Flying Squirrel

Gunnilla Nilsson

On the lot next to my family's summer cabin on North Cooking Lake lives a grizzly old man in a rickety red shack. He has a pet flying squirrel. I am intrigued, so he invites me over. I am eight years old and in love with animals.

It's dark out. I sit on his front step. He hands me a tin cup of hot chocolate and parks his grease-smelling self next to me. I am wary; in the lantern light the drink looks like old engine oil.

"We'll just wait," he growls. "Off doing squirrel things. He'll be by eventually." He rakes his bristled cheek with stubby, grease-stained fingers and dirty nails. "Need a mow," he mutters.

Finally I take a sip and am surprised. It's the best hot chocolate I've ever tasted. I eye the dark woods in front of us, waiting for the winged squirrel to appear. I have to keep brushing mosquitos off my face and arms. There's a half moon.

"Why'd you get a flying squirrel, Mr. Hooper?" I ask.

"Didn't," he growls. "Squirrel got me. Not like I'd go outta my way to get a pet squirrel. Kept coming in the cabin like he bloody owned the place and me, I finally figured, easier to tame the little bastard than keep him out. Couldn't kill him. Goddam softy. So we're roommates. I call him Bisquick cause that's where I first found him, in the pancake mix."

We slurp our drinks and wait.

Mr. Hooper pipes up again. "Goddam squirrel saved my life once." He swats a mosquito on his tattooed forearm, pulls it from his thick arm hair and flicks it to the ground. The tattoo is old, blurry, faded. "Goddam lantern fell over, I was snoring, and Bisquick raised hell that coulda woke the dead with his crazy chi!chi!chi!chi!chi!chi!" His voice flings up to a gritty falsetto. "Anyway I put the fire out. Threw a pot of stew on it."

"What kind of stew was it?"

"Rabbit."

Suddenly a brown blur flies past my face. I gasp and lean back. A flying squirrel lands next to me on Mr. Hooper's knee. It stands up on its haunches and looks around, nose wiggling, tail twitching.

Sure enough. He wasn't kidding. I am immediately enthralled.

"Hey there you are little stinker what the hell have you been up to, eh?" Falsetto again. "You little stinker. Yooooou little stinker." He pets the squirrel with his thick finger and laughs. His laugh is raspy and turns into rough coughing.

"Can I pet him?" I ask.

10

"Hell, I dunno! Try it! Probably won't mind." Falsetto. "Be nice to the little girl, Bisquick. She just wants to pet ya, is all."

I reach over and pet the tiny squirrel with the back of my finger. Smooth, soft fur. It's little head jerks about as he looks around and then looks up into my face. He sniffs, his tiny nose and whiskers wiggling rapidly. Pink nose, round black eyes. I pull my hand away, grinning. Amazed.

"Yep, he likes ya. Woulda sunk his little razors into ya if he didn't. Be surprised how much blood the son-of-a-bitch can draw. Hey, Bisquick? Yooooou little stinker."

I walk home through the dark woods swatting mosquitos as I go. Our cabin glows yellow through the forest. I smell wood smoke, hear the hum of my family's voices as I get closer. I can't wait to tell them about tattoos, hot chocolate, Mr. Hooper and Bisquick.

Mr. Hooper dies two years later. I wait on his front step, alone under a half moon, and eventually Bisquick comes. He lands on my knee and wiggles his nose. Everything smells different.

Gunnilla Nilsson lives east of Athabasca, Alberta, in the old Melsness place, 13 kilometers north on the airport road. She's working on her first M.G. novel, Belle and Daisy, about an awkward girl who finds kinship with a worried horse.

The Day Before Yesterday

Christine E. Forth

The trouble with growing old is you forget things. I can hardly remember what I did an hour ago or five minutes ago, let alone the day before yesterday. I tell them that, but they keep on asking the same questions. The tall woman in the pink suit especially. I think she's a police officer, but she's not in uniform. Plain clothes, I expect.

All I know about the day before yesterday is that I was at home, in my lovely house, the one Harry and I built together. And now I'm here in this horrible place. It's like a prison. I think it is a prison. Where's Harry? Why hasn't he come to get me?

All that blood on the floor. Someone had tracked it through the house. Can you believe that? Who would do such a thing? Bloody footprints all over my nice clean floor. Ruined the carpet.

I think this must be one of those new-fangled open prisons, because there're men here as well as women. Lots of us. But it's not really open, because they lock the doors. Everyone here is old, except the guards. They're young, and they're all women. They look foreign to me. Small and dark.

Where's Harry, that's what I want to know. He should be here by now.

When I washed the knife in the sink the water ran red. Somebody had dipped it in paint. I polished it up with a nice clean cloth and put it back in the drawer.

Oh, here's Harry now — I see him. In the chair opposite me. *When are you going to take me home, Harry?* But he doesn't say anything. He looks so ill, poor man, so white. *What's wrong Harry?*

The woman in the pink suit is back. She's looking at him in that way. Just like the others. I can tell from her eyes, she's after him, the bitch. They're all the same, they all have that look. Years I've put up with it. How many more are there going to be? *Leave him alone you fucking bitch. I'll scratch your eyes out.*

The woman in the pink suit puts her hand on my arm. "Tell me again, Mary," she says. "Try to remember. What happened the day before yesterday?"

I turn towards Harry. Harry? Harry's gone. The woman in the pink suit is still here. She nods at me. "Mary?"

But Harry's gone.

Christine lives in Alberta, Canada where she has been happily writing for more than 20 years. Her first novel, "The Mapmaker's Wife", was published in 2018, and is available on Amazon. She is currently working on a second novel.

The View From the Shelf

Bert Edens

I still remember the first time Ariel held me. Her Momma dug me out from under dented Tonka trucks and amputated Power Rangers at the Goodwill. My Girl wanted to hold me right away, immediately in love with my dingy pink coat and rainbow on my belly. But her Momma fussed about throwing me in the wash first, since there was no telling what kind of germs I carried.

Hot out of the dryer and sporting the aroma of lavender fabric softener, I went straight to Ariel's loving arms, and that's where I spent most of the next ten years. It was such a magical feeling, to be loved and held again. I had spent months in that Goodwill bin, passed over and scorned because of my matted fur and age. Nobody wanted something that their moms played with as a little girl.

But now I had a new home, and My Girl loved me without hesitation and snuggled with me constantly. She and I were pretty much inseparable, as she took me everywhere, chattering at me as much as at her Momma.

I saw and went through a lot with that girl. Everything from ketchup facials at McDonald's to mud puddle baths in the driveway. Several times I even lost an arm or leg as one of them got snagged in the spokes of her motorized wheelchair, because Ariel was hanging me outside the armrests, giving me a chance to experience the world outside hers.

Her Momma never batted an eye sewing me back together. She didn't really have the skillset and definitely not the right color of thread to nail the task, so I ended up looking like some Fluff-stuffed Frankenstein, the seams of my love wounds visible for everyone to see.

Ariel wanted to take me to the tub with her for every bath, so I stayed nice and clean, invariably smelling just like My Girl, aromas of strawberry, peach, or mango. I'd have to drip dry while Ariel's Momma dressed her, a clothespin pinching my ear as I hung from the shower curtain. Even though I was never quite dry when Ariel snuggled down for bedtime, nobody seemed to mind, especially me.

Bedtime was the best time. That was when her Momma would tell us a story, usually about warrior princesses and mystery-solving girls. Or we'd watch Disney movies on TV until everyone was sound asleep, never tiring from seeing the same ones over and over.

I even made a trek with Ariel to the hospital, where she lay in bed for days, eyes closed and not moving a whole lot. But I kept watch over her, my post on the bedside table as near to her arms as I could get. I'd get moved so someone could dust and clean, and if I got put somewhere else, Ariel's Momma always put me right back there beside Our Girl.

Some time later, Ariel's Momma and I came home, but Ariel didn't. Nobody ever explained why. I just got stuck up here on this shelf, staring down at that empty wheelchair with "Ariel" embroidered in hot pink on the headrest.

Every now and then, her Momma comes in and picks me up, squeezing me so much tighter than Ariel ever did, tears sprinkling the top of my head. She'll sit in the glider rocker and hold and rock me until she has no more tears to give, then back on the shelf I go.

Wherever Ariel is, I hope she comes home soon. Her Momma's hugs are amazing, but they aren't the same.

And I don't like staring at that empty wheelchair day in and day out.

No, I don't like it at all.

I miss her.

*Bert Edens is an author, editor, and martial arts instructor. He lives in Arkansas with his gorgeous wife, with whom he severely out-kicked his coverage. You can read more about his works at **www.authorbertedens.com**.*

Sol

Jean Graham

The Ancients call us Young One. They say this particular young one is much too curious. And in truth, we are.

We ask, "Why do you call us young, when we, too, are ancient?" And their reply is simply "Why do you wish to know?"

We ask, "Where was our beginning?" and the Ancients say, "It is not a pleasing thing to know."

But we desire answers to our questions just the same.

Only after many such queries does the Ancient called Ceti take pity on us and acquiesce, agreeing to satisfy our yearning.

We wonder, "Did you not ask the same questions once?"

Ceti responds, "We did. But when the knowledge we sought was gained, we sorrowed. Do you truly aspire to sorrow, Young One?"

"If with knowledge must come sorrow, then we do. Without answers to our questions, we are incomplete. Will you complete us?"

"We will. Ask your questions."

We can scarcely contain our glee, but we temper our enthusiasm enough to begin our queries. "Why are we called young?"

"Because you are one of those most recently formed and added to our number. When you acquire the knowledge you seek, you will no longer be called Young One. Your name will be Sol."

The word fills us, resonates throughout our being. We know it, even if we did not learn it until this moment. "Why are we Sol?" we ask.

"You are all that once lived and breathed within that great sun's influence. For a brief time, billions thrived there, just as others have thrived in the warmth of other suns. We are their souls, their essence, collected in the names of their life-giving suns. We are the stars that were."

We revel in knowledge that once again flows in to fill a void within us. "And this was our beginning, this star called Sol?"

"A sphere within its orbit spawned your multitude. Some called it Terra. Others called it Earth."

Earth. *Earth.* We remember it, even as Ceti speaks the word. We *knew* it.

"What beings were these," we ask, "who thrived there once and who dwell within us now?"

"They are but one of countless legions," is Ceti's cryptic reply. "Many stars spawn life. Yours differed little from those fostered by other suns in other eons."

"How many have there been?"

"A vast number. We are a legion of legions."

"And all have passed into our midst? None survive?"

"Many still live. But they are fleeting things, born and thriving and dying, all in a twinkling. Nonetheless, in the eternity that is our universe, there is always life. Somewhere. Somewhen."

A yearning has surged within us, a need so strong that we have no hope of constraining it. "We must see this Sol, this Earth," we say, and our aura glows with the anticipation of it. This alone will complete us, make us whole. We must see it. We must.

But our request makes Ceti's aura dim with both sadness and conviction. "As you wish."

The aura's faint light brightens then, and grows to rapidly engulf our own. As one, we flare into star-white brilliance, drawn into a light that takes us across the void to a place that is otherwhere.

It is a thing of unparalleled beauty. Its vast, towering shapes glow iridescent rose and gold and blue.

Ceti calls it nebula.

But once, in another form, it had another name. We know it, even as we float within its remnant cloud.

Sol.

Our souls sing with a joy we have never known.

Home!

We seek and find the blackened cinder that was Terra, drifting small and alone in the cloud. And at once, an infinite sadness descends on us, just as Ceti warned it would do.

Our joy becomes mourning.

Ceti is beside us once again. "The sadness is a part of you now."

"Yes."

"You will grieve for a time. And then you will begin to seek others who are young. There are untold numbers who have not yet known the sadness. You will help to guide those who question, as you did, and wish to find their beginning.

We peer into the eons before us to find, in Ceti's words, our fate and our purpose.

"We will do this," we agree. "But first, we wish to linger here awhile."

"As you will."

And with that, Ceti leaves us to our sorrow.

The nebula embraces us then, welcomes us home. We will stay to mourn and to remember, perhaps for a millennium or two. Time and the universe are one, and endless.

Though we are no longer young, our curiosity and our thirst for knowledge endure.

We are Sol.

Jean Graham's short stories have appeared in Mythic Magazine and in the anthologies Memento Mori, Strange Beasties, From a Cat's View, and Killing It Softly 2. Her website is at http://jeangraham.20m.com.

A Stranger

Nicholas Popkey

You noticed me getting off work late, heading past marquis lights and bars to where I parked. Exhausted. You looked at me as I switched my bag to the other arm. Its straps hung low under its weight, but it contained the tools I needed. A ghostly energy pervaded, the effervescence of finally going home after fourteen focused hours. I was full from the six slices of pizza I'd had for a second meal, and I wiped some grease off the side of my mouth. It wasn't romantic, but from such a distance down the sidewalk, you trained your eyes on me, unbroken. You narrowed your gaze, cocking your head, which dropped your left-side bangs over your eyes. You cleared them away to recognize me, and turning completely from your friends, you drew me in.

"Do I know you from somewhere?" you asked.

"You look really familiar," I said. "But I'm not sure where from."

"Maybe we worked together on something," you said. "Do you know D.B.?"

"No, but I've heard of him," I said. "What brings you here tonight?"

"It's Friday night, this is our place," you said.

I put down my bag to shake hands with your friends, and setting it there cemented my presence strangely, for I was someone that couldn't be placed. And yet your eyes kept me still, kept me awake, engaged, delighting in cadence and serpent's tongue, the conversation flowing freely. Like I'd been meaning to meet you there all along, like we'd spent days, months, years together, and I followed you inside, leaving my bag in my distraction.

We ordered old-fashioneds and you left our tip, touching my arm when I sifted out cash. Then, you ran your teeth across the surface of your bottom lip, which was glossy, maybe too glossy, I thought. But even a doubt such as this made me want to laugh, as if someone so effortless could only have flaws in ironic tribute.

We had another round. You wanted to dance. I obliged, hoping the few goofy go-to moves I had would at least make you laugh. You laughed, but you also danced beautifully. You moved like water and you guided me with you, in music, in waves of the crowded dance floor, people stumbling, taking up space and then giving it over to one another.

When we left, my bag was still there, nudged under a table in the front patio. Your friends had parted ways, and we stood at a threshold.

You had to wake up early. You wanted to see me again. I said we ought to run into each other. You said you'd rather not leave it up to chance again. I said the beauty of everything we shared that night could have been from the happenstance of our random encounter. You were intrigued, but looked away, revealing an inner sadness when your eyes came back to me. Finally a chink fell from your mask. Your sensible logic of safety in solitude crumbled. You showed me an honest part of you.

You preserved silence. I thanked you, for trusting me so easily. Some delicate emotion had escaped, unexpressed in words. We saw through each other, and made plans for soon after, and after, and after.

Nicholas is a freelance writer and cinematographer based in Los Angeles. This is his first fiction publication.

Awake

Paddock Mitchell

That day started with the smell of an April morning rain on the Pacific Coast Highway outside of Malibu, which was followed by the blinding sun's glare off of the whitecaps as the frothy sea met the shore and found us binging on the taste of sashimi...caught, cleaned and eaten right on the pier. Completely sated, a nap was in order, upon waking there was just enough time for an evening hike. I remember the distinct echo of a coyote's howl through the Canyons in the moonlight and the feeling of comfort from you standing so close, even without us actually touching. You turned back and started to speak, but I blocked the words with a kiss.

You pulled quickly away and I couldn't see that well, but I heard the distinct sound of you sniffling.

"What is it?"

You took a breath and then stated, "I'm in love with someone else."

"It's Brad, isn't it?" I asked rhetorically. I already knew the answer.

You paused...and then nodded...and then stopped nodding. My heart felt as though it was falling down the side of the hill and part of me wished I could jump after it. You just stood there. Why didn't you try to explain or apologize?

I must have been standing and waiting for some sort of explanation for a minute before I realized that there wasn't going to be any apology. So I turned and started walking back to the car. You didn't follow me, but just in case you thought about following me, my walk turned into a sprint. Once I was back at your car I was panting, with tears and mucus choking my breathing. I didn't hear anything, I couldn't smell anything and I could barely see through my crying eyes...I had lost all my senses except for the pain of it. I couldn't even think of anything worth doing.

So I began walking out of the parking lot, down to the Highway. I thought about hitchhiking up to the caves near the county line. Then I changed my mind and wanted to hitchhike to the bars in Santa Monica and go on a bender. Split between my two options, I crossed the two-lane Highway and sat on a large rock, on the ocean side of the road.

I still didn't hear your voice, like I was quietly hoping I would. I didn't feel your hand on my shoulder and I definitely didn't hear you say the words I was most hoping to hear, "April Fools."

Realizing that I was now grasping for any other explanation than the truth, I untied my shoes, pulled off my clothes and ran out into the water. Now, I have never been much of a swimmer, but that hasn't ever stopped me from splashing around in the ocean. This time I wasn't splashing around, though. I was swimming, as fast as I could, out toward Catalina. I didn't have any intentions of making it to Catalina, I just used the large offshore island as a directional aid. The faster I swam toward that island, the farther away I was from you.

A way off of the shore I began trembling from exhaustion. I kept on my present course, just at a slower clip. The waves probably weren't getting any bigger, but at the time it sure felt that way. Getting more exhausted, I let myself sink under the surface for a few seconds to rest and then I reemerged to catch my breath. After a few minutes of alternating between this resting and what had become dog-paddling, I accidentally swallowed a mouthful of seawater. I didn't mind it actually, as the salty taste woke my senses and made me feel more alert. Being alert, though, was not necessarily positive for, after a bit of time, I realized how far out I was and how cold the water was and how I was trembling, both from the cold and from exhaustion...I didn't want to be in the water any more...I started back toward the shore...swimming as steadily as I could, but when I began to slip under the water without having planned on doing so, I panicked...my swimming turned from slow strokes to a freestyle dash for the beach. I kept trying to touch my feet on the bottom of the ocean, as if I were actually getting close enough to land to do that!

My panicked swimming only made me miss-time my breathing more and more and that, along with the added stress on my lungs of being so anxious, put me in even worse shape. I didn't want to be in the ocean, I didn't want to be naked, I didn't want to be gulping down brackish water, I didn't want to be here...what was I thinking, I kept asking myself, who tries to swim away from their problems?

All I wanted was to be back in your car, with the heater on. I could take you not comforting me, I could take you not consoling me, I could even take you not loving me! But I couldn't take any more of the waves, the moonlit waves that sparkled so ominously as they came undulating over me. My last thoughts were of how my sinking didn't even create a wake...

When ghosts of poor decisions couldn't act worse...Paddock threw fate to the purblind doomsters puppeteering the industry, in a final act of hoping Captain Providence would steer the ship. The whirlwind tour de force that is now unfolding is nothing short of a miraculous blockbuster! Paddock loves the minutia of his calling and is perennially pushed to pursue the perfection of the players, improvisers and production peeps providing our protagonist parts...profitable and (perhaps...) passionately pro nonprofit.
www.imdb.me/paddockmitchell

Override

Monica Viera

My dad was the first one to tell me about these surreal seats, which went by no known name other than "The Chairs". The Chairs started popping up at the local malls first, and then the laundromats, gas stations, doctors' offices, until you literally couldn't go one day without seeing one of these spectacular black leather specimens.

The Chairs were comfortable at first, as they were plush and intact with leathery arm rests, a recliner, and even a thick mask to wear over your eyes that was attached by some black woven thread at the head of the seat. To an outsider like me, at first they just looked like upgraded versions of those massage chairs you'd put money in to enjoy a simple five-minute massage.

But The Chairs had a purpose, and although they'd only been out a couple of months, there were already people addicted to them, waiting in long lines that circled around the block to just test out some of their notorious magic. What The Chair did had never been done before. You'd simply sit in a chair and by softly gripping your hands over the arm rests, reclining on the seat, and putting on that eye mask that apparently scanned your eyes, it could come up with a simple calculation within ten seconds.

That calculation was one of emotional pain, which had never really been established on a scientifically measurable scale until now. You'd on The Chair and you'd watch it come up with a number between one through twenty on the little digital screen next to your right wrist. It then had the option for you to override that number so that the chair would squeeze, contort, and hurt your body so that your physical pain was able to override your emotional pain, if just for a few moments.

It was brilliant, really. The way the scientists had designed these chairs had a way of smashing up your body and moving it around in ways that although were painful, really didn't cause lasting damage on one's being. You could set The Chair to the highest level — the number 21, and you'd still walk away with not even so much as a bruise.

The Chairs were free for everyone as the government desperately tried to get Seattle's suicide rate down. It was 2032 and the suicide rate had climbed to one in five trying to off themselves, perhaps because of the unforgivably bleak weather, the overwhelming presence of meth and heroin, and the three casinos that were merely a forty-five-minute drive just north, west, and south from where Seattle was.

I had just broken up with John and although he and I had originally mocked The Chairs, he was in rehab and I was living on the streets because we'd lost all our money to gambling and meth. The casinos were unforgivably intoxicating, which is how I found myself with a deadly addiction to The Chair.

Going to the casinos before I lost John to rehab was simply magic for the two of us. The carpet we walked on was the thick tongue of this exotic creature, with its red and purple designs splayed every which way to disorient us. The cigarette smoke that drifted through the air was overwhelming, but the rough tongue of the amoeba was built to withstand the ashes that constantly rained over it. And like an angler fish lures its prey, the sophisticated light fixtures that hung from the ceiling convinced us to continue our path without any resistance.

The casino breathed — there was a certain rhythm to it, so that even though all the machines had different tunes playing on repeat, it was a seductive symphony that morphed all those jingles into one thick song of silence after a while. We dissolved onto the casino's tongue the same way Xanax dissolved onto your own tongue and everything was complete. The high was in place.

Sealed off from the rest of society on sacred Indian grounds, we got the luxury of being able to float off in time and space to buy some time. Society doesn't give us enough time to grieve or dwell on what needs to be processed, so casinos remain full. People die, hearts get broken, babies get miscarried — but then it's back to work on Monday.

We'd stuff bill after bill into the thin-lipped, plastic mouth of each slot machine by the minute to ensure that the florescent lights, sounds, and screens would not stop breathing as long as we were there. Like all living organisms, the casino had a voracious appetite to ensure its survival and its guests were more than willing to support the casino so that its symbiotic relationship thrived.

Back to real time and I'm out of the addicting flashbacks of long nights with John and back in The Chair, which they conveniently have at the casino, too. I'm watching everyone spend their money, the same way I did, and as usual I get rated about a 16 or 17 on that scale of 1-20 for emotional pain. Although I could be reasonable and just set the pain scale to 18, I'm already addicted to 21. And like many others, I'm waiting for something harder. Twenty-one hurts the first few seconds but becomes tolerable much too quickly. I need to numb myself harder.

So, I have an idea, to move two of these leather chairs together and set them both to twelve, so that when I lay down in both, I'm hit with the 24 charge that will undoubtedly jerk me into a state I want to be in. I don't want to remember John and the way we fought towards the end of our relationship. I don't want to remember the fact that he's in rehab for the next six months, probably forgetting our memories, even if they were somewhat of a neon nightmare.

I put the two Chairs together when no one was looking — a thought no civilian had ever tried to go through with yet, probably much less entertained, but here I was. And after setting both chairs to twelve, I suffered a stroke at 24. I was also arrested after I recovered from the hospital for misusing the device. But luckily, they had The Chairs in jail too, again, because of the overwhelming suicides in Seattle. And I knew I would be okay, as long as I had access to The Chairs.

Monica Viera is a journalist from Los Angeles with work published on Hubpages, Tiny Buddha, and Hustler Magazine.

Phantom Spider

Thomas J. Misuraca

Something is crawling up your arm as you lay in bed. You look down and see a spider the size of a quarter. In reality, it's a dime, but when it's on your arm in the middle of the night, it's nothing less than a mutated monster.

SMACK!

You snuff it out.

Luckily there are tissues by your bed (stupid allergies) so you have something to wipe away the remains. Still feeling gross, you get up and go to the bathroom to wash your arm. Once dried, you return to bed.

Something is crawling on your arm again!

You look down. Nothing.

That always happens when you find an insect on you, you keep feeling it for a while. Why did this have to happen before bed? Now you're going to feel something creeping up your arm all night long. Just before you drift off to sleep, the sensation of crawling pulls you awake. Sleep will not be your friend tonight.

After feeling like a zombie all day, you can't wait to climb into bed. You're so tired, you doze off while reading a book. It slips out of your hands and onto the floor. You decide to leave it there until morning and go to sleep.

Before you drift off, you feel something crawling on your arm...

You sit up. Not again!

But it's on your opposite arm. So maybe that means...

Spider infestation!

You scramble out of bed, turn on the lights and toss off the covers. You search every inch of your sheets and mattress. No spiders or even the remains of one.

Barely able to keep your eyes open, you get back into bed.

This time, you feel it crawling on your leg. It's moving down to your feet. You're too tired to see if it's a real spider or just a sensation. It weaves its way between your toes as if they were a jungle gym for insects.

You're not quite sure what Restless Leg Syndrome is, but you think you have it that night as you constantly shake spiders off your toes.

Who needs sleep?

The following night, you feel the spider on your other leg. It's running in circles on your thigh. Suddenly it bolts diagonally towards your...

You leap out of bed and swat all over your body as if it were on fire. Some literary folks would compare this to the St. Vitus Dance. Not me.

This may be a good night to lay on the couch in the den and binge watch a television show. Out there, you don't feel any crawling sensations.

You sleep on the couch for a few nights without incident. You've forgotten all about your late night spider assassination and the creepy feelings that followed. Within a week, you're back to sleeping in your bed.

Once you switch off the lights, something crawls over your stomach. This has to be your imagination. So you try to ignore it and go to sleep.

As you do, it makes its way to the small of your back. There it rests. God knows what it's doing there. Possibly laying eggs...

You go back to sleeping on the couch.

Every so often, you have a mate spend the night. After hours of passionate love making, you both collapse, exhausted. The afterglow clouds any thoughts of phantom spiders.

"Hey!" Your partner exclaims in the middle of the night. "Something's crawling up my arm."

After a thorough examination you say "I don't see anything. Good night."

"Good night."

After a moment, "Hey! It's back! Do you have bedbugs or something?"

"I wish," you say. Then suggest it may be best if you each sleep in your own beds that night.

Now, before bed, you speak to it.

"I'm sorry I killed you, spider," you say. "But you were crawling up my arm at night. You surprised me. Wouldn't you do the same in my case?"

Apparently not. For that night, the ghost spider crawls all over your face. Until it decides to snuggle in the corner of your left eye.

The Internet has many suggestions on how to get rid of ghosts. You spray Holy Water on your bed like it's Febreze. You burn sage (and wonder why it's called "smudging"). Hell, you even pray, and it's not the World Series or Super Bowl.

Nothing works. The ghost spider's energy increases. It runs all over your body all night long. Maybe you could get used to it.

Not when you wake up with a spider crawling around in your ear.

You have no choice, you have to move. This ghost spider has driven you out of your home. You don't take any chances, you donate your bed to charity as well.

Your new home is clean, constantly fumigated, and lined with insect traps.

Sleep has never come so easy.

I wish I could say the same for me. All night long I feel spiders crawling over my body.

I've checked every corner of my bed and the room. I wash my sheets daily. I've changed pajamas weekly. But I've not had a full night's sleep since I moved here.

I blame you, the former tenant. You killed a spider in bed in the middle of the night. And now, I'm being haunted by the ghost of that arachnid.

While you sleep soundly. Wherever you are.

Thomas J. Misuraca has had over 80 short stories and 3 novels published, as well as over 100 short an 10 full-length plays produced globally. A collection of his short stories, If You Read This, You Will Die, is available on Amazon. **www.tommiz.com**

The Tradition of Eating Corn Flakes

Lucas Marten

It is tradition to eat corn flakes before the battle. By eating magic mystic-ingrained corn syrup, I am imbibing the fruity spirit of my ancestors. Generation to generation, my four fathers and I sit at the head of the table and preach values to each other. Nibbling corn bits and passing out husks is how we men survive in cold, dark times like this.

If it weren't for the bears I'd have given up my gun a long time ago. The attacks are daily now, four of the octagonal patriarchs have died in combat. I have voted time and time again to lower the drafting age, and yet the populus chooses casual sex and capitalism, seltzer water and bedcloths, over an adequate gun to take down a charging ursine barbarian. They are eating wallace scones outside the barrier, they don't know what it's like on the inside.

I have brought the trident, my fathers have brought nets and cloth. Our women are safe, and nowhere to be seen. I am exasperated and toiled by the day's plow. The crows' magic makes me light and spongy with the morning dew, sorrowful and homely by the evening light. We consume healthily and heartily, popcorn and baseball games, beer and a chardonnay.

I am attracted to the land. It has grown well and watched over 700 years of octagonal guardianship. We measure four or eight spans between ten or twelve circuits of exactly eight towers. I man #7, the northwesterly exporter of trident-cloth and foodstuffs. Our neighbors produce essentials like honey for the afternoon tea, more corn, and beard-dressings. I wear mine like my grandfather, pointed and stout with yellow ribbons and a deep cream finish.

Six aeons ago we rode horseback, alighting with pepper corn and meeting granny by the wayside. We held an uneasy alliance with the bears of the forest. They ate of us and we partook of them as well, but our hunger for buckskin and the hide of a brazil-nut grew and now we are enemies of the surrounding forest. My stalks are well but the forest stays idle, our sorcerer's circle unreachable.

Because of the bear attacks, I sit on the point of an octagon where Uncle Marcos and Aunt Sylvester paint portraits of the benevolent spring and the lucriscious fall. I recall cellular devices and macintoshes, a plethora of choice in a kingdom of interlocking identities unbroken by octomothers and the roar of a grizzly on a cold August morning. All I can do is pray to finish my corn flakes and drink of the milk.

Jeffrey is pregnant again. I am the designated octofather who will raise him to carry the trident and tell stories of granny and the wayside. The circle is complete, we are welcome to be about our business. My children and I will play

Crazy Eights on cardback tonight, munching candy corn and playing Live From Tel Aviv on the CD player. Listening for the horn.

Lucas Marten is a published author of short fiction, poetry, and nonfiction. He graduated with a BA from Bennington College in Psychology and Writing and is now a Master's student at Johns Hopkins University studying science writing.

Palavra Elemental

Faye Duncan

...frantically, he wrote down his ode to Fernando Pessoa onto her left arm with a Sharpie, well aware that the end of the world was near...

"'It was never the end of the world. Merely the end of the school year. But to me, it felt like the end of the world,'" read the handsome gentleman from the manuscript. He handed it over to the agent who was watching the tourists. He then picked up the tall glass of hot galão — this very Portuguese version of coffee with milk. He carefully placed it back onto the saucer, determined not to spill any of this precious drink.

They were sitting at a wobbly bistro table outside the cafe *A Brasileira* in the Chiado area of Lisbon. The bronze sculpture of Fernando Pessoa sitting at the table next to them listened quietly. The reflection of sunlight on the white mosaic floor was blinding. The handsome gentleman had tried to squeeze into the too tiny frame of the wrought iron chair, and he switched one leg which he had uncomfortably crossed over the other.

The handsome gentleman was George, and he was obviously not Portuguese. His height, a pair of piercing blue eyes, and an undeniable liking for classic business wear immediately gave him away as the American tourist that he was. A receding salt and pepper hairline told the tale of fading youth.

He hit the table with his right knee, causing a dangerous shake. The galão spilled all over the table and onto the agent's freshly pressed dress pants.

"Oh, disculpe, Senhor Fonseca!" said George quickly.

He was so embarrassed. He had finally got this one shot at meeting an agent, and he was screwing it all up. At least that's what he thought. Contrary to his grandmother, who had adapted to 'the mood' with ease, he still didn't understand all the fuss about *saudade* and the meaning of being Portuguese.

An attentive waiter with curly brown hair came to his rescue and wiped the coffee from the table. He wore a name tag: Tiago.

"Obrigado!" said George.

"Nao faz mão," said the agent. He wore the same hat as the sculpture.

George sighed with relief. It had taken him months of research to track down all the exact locations his grandmother had so nostalgically swooned over all these years. And most of the people had long since passed. But he had managed to find "The Davide," an achievement which George was particularly proud of, as Davide seemed to be the main player in this whole scenario. And finding a retired street juggler from the city of Porto from fifty years back was not exactly what he defined as a piece of cake.

He had nothing to do, really, with all this writing business. It was his grandmother's fame and her unexpected death that had driven him to take on this project. She had been in the midst of writing her memoirs when a heart attack swept her off the surface of the earth. Grandmother Maude was a world-famous fiction writer and Nobel laureate. Her amusing stories about her student years in Portugal had always intrigued him.

George was a real estate broker and had successfully worked himself up the corporate ladder into a top position in one of America's most well-known firms. He had accumulated years of positive business ventures. But maybe it was because loneliness was nagging at him (he had still not succeeded in creating a family), maybe because he needed a break from the sterile monotony of the American corporate world. George did not know, but he had decided to finish the memoirs of Grandmother Maude.

The project had led him to a year of research and a sabbatical he had chosen to spend in the city of Lisbon. Contrary to Grandma Maude, who had lived in Porto, the prospect of a nearly year-round sunny sky in Lisbon, as opposed to the rougher and rainier weather of Porto, had attracted him more. If he had research work to do in Porto, he could always travel up there by train.

Senhor Fonseca was carefully studying the manuscript. It was not every day that one held the biography of a Nobel laureate in one's hands. The pages had survived the threat of the coffee spill, because he had been flipping through it.

George glanced at the burnt-out ruins of the Carmo Convent. It so perfectly fit in with the rest of the historic center of Lisbon, which, unlike the convent, was very much alive. Fonseca noticed George's gaze. Nothing escaped the glance of this eagle.

He could not stop wondering about the ruin, which had neither been restored nor removed since the big earthquake of 1755. In the United States, it would have been demolished and rebuilt long ago, loaning the country the monotonous and soulless image George was so desperately trying to evade.

"How do you like our historical heritage?" Fonseca small-talked. The Portuguese were infectiously proud of their heritage and loved bragging about it in front of tourists.

"I think every city should have an old ruin," George said.

"The ruins in our cities are like the tattoos on the body of a beautiful woman," Fonseca said.

"Hmm, interesting thought," George said. He started to wonder what a naked woman with tattoos would look like. It felt like something dangerous and forbidden to him. It had been a long time since he had felt the touch of a woman — any woman. And usually, his women did not have many tattoos.

I should start dating again. Or maybe just visit another old city. That might work, too, he pondered.

"How do you like the manuscript?" George finally asked. He picked up the galão one last time to finish the cup. It was good. Better than Starbucks. The coffee.

"Good, good," said Fonseca. "I like the way you portray the spirit of the Portuguese soul through the character of a visitor. Your grandmother understood a lot about our country."

"She portrays," corrected George. "I just finished what she started."

"Yes, yes, Mister George, I understand." Fonseca continued flipping through the pages.

"I like the character of Davide. A true Portuguese. Were you ever able to track him down? Did you find out about the nature of their relationship? It would feed the hearts of the Portuguese, who are always up for a good romance, with a lot of joy, if they found out that a simple man of the streets had been in a romantic relationship with an international Nobel laureate," Fonseca explained with a nearly perfect American accent. "As you know, we Portuguese love our writers."

Of course you would love that, George thought. *Weren't the media all the same? Always in search of a good sensation.*

"I was," explained George. "I interviewed the old man."

"And how is he doing?" Fonseca wanted to know.

"He is currently residing in an old-age home. His legs have given up on him, and he sits in a wheelchair, the poor man. His small room overlooks a corner of the Rio Douro. But guess what!" George provoked the agent.

Fonseca curiously peeked up from under his hat.

"He is still juggling!"

"Excellente!" shouted Fonseca. "I love it!"

"And what about Miss Maude, now, please, Mister George?"

"Well, it seems like Davide and Miss Maude indeed had a very particular and somewhat interesting relationship. They used to watch movies and soccer together and spent time at their friends' houses. Whether there was anything more, I don't know. But before she left, he decided that he had spent enough time living on the streets. He told me that the presence of Maude and her fellow student friends had inspired him to go back to school and get a degree as a librarian. I understand he worked in the Biblioteca Pública Municipal do Porto for many years, until he retired last year."

"And he inspired her to write," added Fonseca knowingly.

"Es assím," confirmed George.

"But whether there was anything romantic, Davide still refuses to say. Maybe, being a native, you would have more luck. You should go and visit him one day."

"Indeed, I should. Maybe!"

"As a juggler, he knows some astonishing tricks! You would be amazed."

"I'm sure I would."

"As for the romance part, I don't know. But with regards to the impact that her many travels to Portugal had on her work and her life, and the many changes she went through and endured to pursue the mission entrusted to her by the magical words of Davide's poem, I would like to read you a passage from the memoirs, por favor."

George reached out for the manuscript, which the agent willingly handed over.

"Ouço. I am all ears."

"'There were hardships, disappointments, overwhelming joys, and excruciating sorrows. I had years of good fortune and years of depressing bad luck. Friends, they came and then they went. But in all those years of constant change there were two things that always remained: the sound of the Portuguese language and the feeling of *saudade* in my heart.'"

"Bem, bem," said Fonseca and got up. George dropped a couple of euros on the table. The days of the escudo were long gone. But even in the capital of Portugal, the coffee still was affordable.

"Gosto muito deste projecto," said the agent. "I shall get back to you about a contract."

The two men stood up, and with the manuscript under his arm and a tip of his hat, the agent disappeared around a corner. George walked the other way.

Nobody noticed, really, except the bronze sculpture, who was watching from under the shade.

Faye Duncan is the author of Murder on Wilson Street – Part One of the Bungalow Heaven Mystery Series. *She works as a reader for an international screenwriting competition and as a language tutor. She lives with her seven-year-old son and two dogs in Sierra Madre, CA.*

The Final Ans-whoops!

John Taloni

The ship plunged through space toward the center of the galaxy. Forty centuries of travel from near the galactic rim at a whisper under lightspeed, reduced by time dilation to decades aboard.

The central black hole loomed. Its massive size meant that tidal forces would not tear the ship apart as it approached. The crew expected to freeze in time until the black hole evaporated, to explore the distant future.

The ship remained suspended at the event horizon for aeons. Then the black hole evaporated in a furious explosion. "Oh crap," said the Captain as the ship was torn apart.

John Taloni has been reading SF/F since he was eight and stumbled across a copy of Alexei Panshin's "Rite of Passage." His major influences include Anne McCaffrey and Larry Niven. Taloni is a long-time attendee at SF conventions, and he met his wife while dressed as a Pernese dragon rider. Their daughter asked at the age of four if they could watch more of the show with "the robots that say 'exterminate,' and the entire family has happily watched Doctor Who together ever since. Taloni is a SFWA associate member.

Tom Kum Kai

Grace Eunsung

He was standing outside the restaurant, hands in his pockets, leaning against a wall. He was wearing khakis, a V-neck sweater over a T-shirt, and Converse high tops. He was edging towards forty-two and still dressed like a teenager. He turned his head and caught her eye. He neither smiled nor did he seem at all happy to see her. He simply stared at her with a look that seemed to say "Yeah, so, what do you have for me now?"

As she came closer toward him, he strode toward her, and they stopped about a foot away from each other, like two soldiers ready to salute. She blinked.

"Hi," she ventured.

"Hey."

About thirty seconds passed before she said "Well, do you want to go inside?"

"Sure." They stepped inside the restaurant and got a table. They sat and stared at each other, before he finally piped up.

"They have a good lemon coconut milk soup here."

"Okay." She looked at her menu. "Tom Kum Kai."

God, had she been this bored when she was with him? The conversation seemed to hit a dead end each time she ventured forth. His eyes took on a stoned glazed quality. After another ten minutes of silence, she found herself itching to leave as soon as possible. She looked at him and squinted. He had seemed so small, leaning up against the wall, and then as he walked toward her, he looked up at her as if he were upset, or angry.

They ate in virtual silence, and when the tab came, she paid for her half with cash.

They ventured outside and stood awkwardly, watching the cars drive by. The city began to light up as the day grew into night.

"You wanna get a beer?"

She hesitated before saying "Nah."

"We can go to my place and get high."

Helena had not yet told him that she had sworn off all drugs, no matter how "relaxed" it might make her, or rather, "defenseless". But something inside her stirred, she wanted to grasp on to something intangible, not answers necessarily, but a feeling.

"Okay."

They walked down the street together toward his house, buried somewhere in the cozy neighborhoods that were entwined through the miniature city landscape of a bustling college town. The silence had grown comfortable, and she ventured to break it.

"Have you moved much?" she asked.

"Once, since grad school."

"Do you have roommates?"

"No."

They continued to walk, as he pulled her into a neighborhood, around the corner, and the sounds of car engines and the chatter of drunken college students exiting restaurants and breweries faded fast against the softer sounds of trees rustling in the night breeze and the slapping of their shoes against the concrete. Lights lit up in the houses exposing that hidden home life of people she did not know, televisions lit up and flashed in windows. They finally arrived, at a run-down two-story house that could pass for Victorian, but was much too rickety to even deserve such a distinguished label. He jiggled the keys in the lock, and the door creaked open. He entered first and held the door open, as she walked in. His room was on the right, and he walked in, turning on a light. There was a futon mattress on the floor, a couch, and not much else.

He foraged into a drawer and pulled out rolling papers, and a bag of marijuana. He rolled a cigarette and lit it. He passed it on to her, and she took it, and held it between her fingers. She stared at it and gave it back.

"I can't really have any."

"Why not?"

"Doctor's orders."

"You sick?"

"Yeah. You could say that."

He didn't probe the subject further, and continued to drag on the joint.

They sat down on the couch next to each other. She stared straight ahead but felt his head turn toward her, staring at her profile. She knew the moment she turned, what would happen, and so she didn't. But he leaned in anyway, and she felt his breath on her cheek, the smell of the cigarette wafting past her nostrils. Just an inch more in and he kissed her cheek. He stubbed out the joint in an ashtray and then went in for the kill, a soft peck on the lips and then his hand on her thigh. Reaching toward the buttons on her pants, he opened them and began to unzip. She stopped him abruptly and pulled away. She still did not dare to look at him. He stopped as if in slow motion, and relit the joint. He sat back, carelessly, staring up at the ceiling and inhaling. She buttoned her pants and stared around at his room. It had the same bohemian quality she remembered — comfortably messy.

"Is there a reason why you called me?" he asked.

"I just wanted to know how you were doing."

He tried to kiss her again. She stood up and walked toward the door.

"I don't know why. You never really had much to say."

"What do you mean?"

"I mean, we sort of disintegrated, you know. I don't even know what we were really about."

"Well, maybe you should come over here and I'll show you." He patted the couch and began to laugh. It was a cheesy line, and then she realized what the attraction was. That sort of sordid power people can hold over each other when they fall into these sort of ridiculous roles, like she, the impressionable teenager, and he, the lonely rebel hermit, who denied everything sweet and kind, and fed the fire of bitterness and cruelty disguised as rebellion. It was kind of a turn on, surrendering to the drama, giving way to wanton scenarios and fantastical images that would one day be remembered with lust, or malice, or both.

(Excerpted from a previously published work *The Professionals*, published in 2014 under the name Grace Cha)

Grace Eunsung has written one novel, and two children's books. She is a former journalist who has published in over 12 print and online publications. She lives in the Central Valley in California.

Athena's Prison

Zachary W. Gilbert

My name is Captain Samantha Etnad. I fear that my ship is sinking deep into the Earth. The thermal energy extractor we call the Caterpillar was on its maiden voyage when something went terribly wrong. On the third day of extracting thermal energy from liquid magma at the bottom of the Atlantic Ocean the onboard power plant failed. The energy shield that protects us from the crushing weight of the water and the intense heat of the magma, may have been tampered with. When operating as it should, the shield looks like writhing snakes the size of cables, glowing like lightning swimming around the ship. After the event... or the accident... or the sabotage, the holographic display showed the Caterpillar wrapped in angry red storm clouds. They throbbed and puked energy as the Caterpillar drowned deeper and deeper into the magma.

I made my way down through the darkness of my wounded ship, I thought about all the people I left behind on the surface. When I was a young girl, without warning the black blood of the Earth ran out. I watched Monstrous buildings slowly grow dark and cold. Back then I swore I would save the Earth somehow. It took fifteen years to build the Caterpillar and I positioned myself through study and hard work to be its Captain. The intent and hope of the mighty vessel; to harvest thermal energy into a portable power plant. Suddenly, I felt the weight of the world on my shoulders as I traversed deeper into the darkness.

I brushed away some debris from a placard, "Level 5" I whispered, "almost there". I moved down the hallway to gain access to the lower levels. The power plant took up the entirety of level 7. Fear and anger danced in my heart. My burning question of "What went wrong?" became further enraged with each footstep.

A flashlight appeared in the hallway followed by an angry shout "Who's there! What are you doing down here?" It was the thick bellowing holler of Virgil the lead maintenance technician.

"It's Samantha!"

"What did you break?" Virgil shouted. "I told them it was a mistake to trust my rig to a woman driver," he shouted as he stormed towards me.

I felt an angry heat crawl down my neck as I held back my words. "Virgil," I whispered though my grinding teeth. "The ship is out of phase because the shield has been damaged, or altered..."

"What...?" Virgil's face became washed white with fear. "Wait... do you have a holo display... they are all offline on this level."

I handed it over and he looked at the hologram of the ship's status. I watched his face change from fear to horror.

"These readings, they... they can't be right..." He paused and looked down the corridor. "Wait... wait... that must be what he was doing."

"What who was doing?" I tried to mask my voice to hide irritation with him and my growing fear for my ship.

"Dr. Charon... he told me he needed to run some tests on the power plant... I... I... gave him my access codes... Oh no," he uttered in a weak whisper. "This is my fault."

"Let's get to Level 7." I pushed past him toward the ladders to the sub levels. I turned back, and he was frozen like a statue. "Virgil, I am going to need you. C'mon, let's fix this."

"Yes Captain," he replied.

I found myself smiling in the middle of my nightmare. Too bad it took all of this for him to finally respect me.

Reaching level six, the air began to stink like burning sulphur and metal. Virgil reached his arm out and blocked my way. "Wait," he whispered. "A storage battery may have ruptured, we will need some SCBAs, more than likely we won't be able to breathe the air in the power plant."

I nodded and headed into the Hazardous Response prep room. The smell grew worse as we suited up. The hiss of the fresh air filled my mask, and I felt the air surge every time I took a breath. I have always hated wearing these stupid things, but today I found comfort in them. I tested the communications system. "Virgil, you online?"

"Yeah." His deep voice seemed to rattle my whole suit. "Let's go."

When we reached the base of the stairs at Level 7, the entire room was full of thick grey smoke. A red flash of light burst out, illuminating a tall dark figure in the darkness.

"What the..." Virgil's voice filled my headset and made me jump.

"Look at that on the ground!" I screamed in horror.

It was Dr. Charon's hollowed out body. There was no blood, just a jagged rip from his head to his hips. A creature made of black smoke standing ten feet tall, loomed over him like an evil butterfly that had just emerged from its human cocoon.

"Dr. Charon! What have you done to my ship?" I shouted at the monstrosity. Its orange burning eyes turned to me. I felt my heart beat pound the walls of my chest.

A device attached to the shield generator, pulsed dark red energy into the system. Virgil knew this was what caused the Caterpillar to sink deep into the Earth, "I have to disable that thing, NOW!" he shouted as he began running toward it. The creature leaped into his path while raising its smoky bat like wing.

I shouted, "Virgil wait!" but the spiked wing had lodged itself into his head.

39

"Human, you are too late," the creature growled. "Soon my imprisoned kin, burning for eons in the Earth's belly, will fill this vessel. Once we return to the surface, we shall devour humanity."

I looked down at my holo display, the words flashed, 'CONFIRM SELF DESTRUCT, Captain's thumb print required'. As the creature violently lunged for me, a hot tear rolled down my cheek. My glove was almost off.

Zachary W. Gilbert has been featured in Sunrise Summits and Flash! A Celebration of Short Short Fiction. See more of his work at ZacharyWGilbert.com.

The Enlightened Skeleton

Ali Lauderdale

Once upon a time, there was a skeleton. It could be seen swaying in a particular tree outside a small village. It was not an especially unique skeleton, but it thought it was. The skeleton decided since it was above all the villagers literally, it was definitely above everything and everyone in every other way.

He could not remember just how long he had been hanging there, but for an extensive period of time, he thought of himself as the most enlightened being he had knowledge of.

He would watch the villagers on the road below doing their everyday mundane activities, and think to himself, "Look at these poor villagers. They walk in the dust, back and forth, all day, and then they do it again the next day, and again, constantly. If only they would hang themselves as I am hanging. Then they would rise above all that and attain true perfection."

He went on feeling sorry for the villagers until one day some of the village's older children went to look at the skeleton. He decided he would help the poor things so they would grow to enlightenment early.

"Young men and women!" he called to them, "Your lives are tedious and will only grow worse as you continue aging. I can tell you dislike running the errands the adults assign you. Get some rope and climb into the trees as I am. You will no longer have to slave for the adults. You will feel a lighter sense of being and achieve the greatest of enlightenment."

The young people were in awe. It seemed like an easily attainable goal that would make them invulnerable. So they fetched some rope and all hung themselves from the old unused orchard's trees.

The skeleton waited for them to affirm his belief. The silence confused him until he decided they must be basking in the glory of enlightenment. He was also silent and allowed the children their time.

Several days passed, during which he watched the villagers cry and saw them searching for their sons and daughters. All the while, he thought to himself, "How sad, the villagers do not realize that their children are experiencing total perfection and bliss in the breeze, and they think only of themselves and their grief. If they come close to me, I will impart my knowledge upon them. They shall be free and be with their children, and when they are done with their glorifying feeling, we shall all be enlightened together."

But his plan was not to be. When they came closer, they saw the skeleton moving of its own volition, and immediately tore it down and beat it into dust.

Ali Lauderdale has published one novella entitled Wild Man under the name A.N. Lambrequin. Her fantasy novel, The Seventh Soldier, is coming soon.

Existential

John Samuel Anderson

Jo glanced up into the dusk. "Xi. Don't look around. Just come." He kept his voice calm. No need to panic her. Or the monster coming up the ravine behind her.

A bundle of branches clattered down onto the path between Jo and his wife. Loud enough to wake the dead. Bick, the village idiot, skittered down the steep slope and landed with a crunch.

"Bick!" Jo whisper-shouted. "Can't you see — Xi!"

The green-and-black monster had gone out of sight in a bend along the ravine. It hissed as it caught their scent.

Xi heard it, too. She whimpered and collapsed in a heap.

"Xi, get up!"

Bick stared stupidly. He bounced atop the bundle and howled like a wolf.

"Bick, stop it!" Jo shifted to one side, then the other. The bundle with the dunce on top blocked the narrow path. "Xi, you have to climb," he said, even as he realized the absurdity of the idea. The ravine walls here were obsidian, as smooth as plate-glass.

She sobbed. "Leave me. Save yourself."

"Help me move the bundle." Xi sat like a lump. Bick howled. Jo's blood boiled. "Okay, I'll move it myself!"

Jo shoved at the sticks. "Get down, Bick." Shove. Bick raised his hands to the sky and jigged. The sticks jounced.

Jo sprinted up the path to get set for a running leap at the bundle. Just over Bick's shoulder, he saw it. The monster's blockish green face emerged from the bend. It hissed when it saw Xi — fresh prey.

He should call for help. Someone might show up. But no, that was just village lore.

Jo blasted into the bundle. Sticks spun off in every direction, clearing the path. Bick howled as he jumped backwards. Brainless as he was, Bick was strong. He sailed high and landed on the other side of Xi.

Jo grabbed his wife and ran. The monster and Bick performed an eerie duet, then were no more.

Back at the village shop, Jo shut them in and locked the door.

Xi rocked side-to-side. "Bick is gone." She clutched a raw chicken piece above the open stove. "Gone." She turned the meat as if by studying it, she could understand it. "It's your fault, Jo."

Jo whirled from his window lookout. He crossed the room and stuck his nose in her face. "It is not." He spoke low, so the other villagers wouldn't hear.

She closed her eyes. They opened with a glimmer of understanding. "Yes, it is. You pushed the sticks. You knew Bick would jump."

She had the facts right, mostly. Was he responsible for the ripple effects from his every action? The raw meat dangled from her fingers over the open stove door. He took a deep breath and fixed her gaze.

"Boo!"

Xi dropped the meat. It bounced off the door and into the oven. Jo slammed it.

"Why did you do that?" she asked.

"To prove that it's not my fault. You dropped the chicken."

The Enforcer came in the morning. Jo had gone out to catch another chicken. When he returned, he heard voices within the shop. He made ready to run should Xi turn him in.

The Enforcer stated the case. "Bick is gone, Xi. The other villagers are all accounted. You must know what happened."

"Yes," she said. "Bick is gone. Jo pushed him." Jo nearly bolted, but she went on. "No, that's not the right way to explain it."

"Jo pushed Bick?" The Enforcer opened the door. He saw Jo, frozen to the spot. He raised his weapon. "We both know the law."

As the Enforcer's weapon came down, Jo fell back, unexpectedly pushed out of range. Xi took the blow. She disintegrated, shimmering out of existence.

Jo stumbled into the cave at sundown. No weapons, no tools, just his bare hands. He felt along the floor for stones. Maybe deeper in.

The moon came up and kissed the cave's distant back wall. Jo crept in, taking his time, listening.

He slipped and fell down a slope. He glimpsed the cave mouth as it slid up out of sight. Strange shapes blocked out the stars. Nightwalkers.

His knees scraped on sharp gravel. Village lore said they couldn't smell his blood from this distance; he hoped that was true. He stood and hobbled forward, hands extended, feeling for the wall. He found it with his forehead.

Knocked on his back, stars flashing across his vision, Jo panicked. If the Nightwalkers came now, he couldn't run, let alone get up. He whispered into the darkness, "Oh, let there be... Someone, help me!"

Of all the village lore, this tale most defied belief. Still, Jo called out louder, "Someone, please help!"

A foot scraped the far side of the gravel pit. He could smell his own blood in the stale air. The Nightwalkers shuffled toward him, scattering stones.

A torch blazed close. Its heat rushed over Jo's face. Someone swung a diamond sword, dealing glittering destruction to the light-blinded Nightwalkers. They screamed and their rag-bodies tore like streamers as they dissolved into the shadows. The cave grew warm.

"Can you stand?"

Jo grasped the proffered hand and rose. "Who are you?"

"Someone who comes to help. I have much to explain to you: artificial intelligence, the construction of this world, and how every now and then a special pair of you becomes self-aware. But that can wait."

"Wait for what?"

"I am taking you to the other side of the world. Where there are no monsters, no Nightwalkers, not even any night. There, you can start life anew, and I will explain everything."

"But why? Why did you come for me?"

"Because you asked."

Jo nodded. A moment later, he stood in bright sunshine atop a magnificent mountain peak. Far below, a pristine sea glittered as far as the eye could see. He smiled and wished Xi could see this.

"Oh, but I can," she said and took his hand.

John Samuel Anderson lives one nautical mile from the beach and five light-milliseconds from space. When not speculating on human colonization of the stars, he enjoys life on Earth with his wife, seven kids, a cat and a bunny.

Narcissist

Barbara Letson

It wasn't like I planned it. It sort of just happened. I wasn't trying to be nosy, but when I saw the open notepad on his desk, I just naturally wanted to see what he was up to.

My husband had a girlfriend.

That didn't bother me — Lord knows I didn't want him, the bastard, after all the pain he had caused for myself and our family — but as I read what he had written describing her, she just sounded so very much like me, but from twenty years ago. Naive. Innocent. Trusting. She had listed for him every drug she had ever taken (both prescription and recreational), every man she had ever bedded (and why), and all the woes she had ever gone through. That was her first mistake; he had written it all down and would fling it at her when he needed ammunition, when he needed to get his way.

She talked about HER husband (she was trying for a divorce) but she was finding it was difficult to sell her little row house when the man in her life lay around all day, even when buyers were coming through. My own husband had drawn a circle around that part, in red, of course. I bet he had offered to help her eject her husband and get the house sold. What she surely didn't realize yet is that while he could do that, he could absolutely help her with those two items, it would come at a price.

Like I said, that was her first mistake, trusting him, telling him the intimate details of her life. She didn't know my man at all, and all the pain he would eventually cause her. To start, he would court her, charm her, win her affection, put himself on a pedestal and make himself indispensable, be everything she needed. And he would start to take charge, making all the decisions, show her his was a better way, slowly take over her life until she depended on him for every little thing. Whether she liked it or not.

And if she wanted to do things her way? When she wanted to make her own decision on something? He would tell her he knew better. If she persisted, he would remind her that her life was a dung heap until he had gotten involved. If she resisted, insisted, refused? He would up the game and make her understand that she was crazy, no one would EVER think as she did, no one would make such stupid mistakes or do things her way. He would remind her of all the mistakes she had made, bedding men and trying drugs and not being as perfect as he could have made her. He would wound her and make her doubt herself and then take over as her benevolent savior, and all she had to do was remember to worship the god on that pedestal... him.

What I think that even he, himself, didn't understand yet was that there was NO pleasing him, not for long. Say 'no' and he finds a way to get that 'yes', but say 'yes', and it still wouldn't be enough. While he would insist the fault was hers for every little thing that bothered him, the fault was nowhere but inside himself. That man didn't love himself. Somewhere within, he was sure that, if anyone could see through the veneer of his wit and charm, they would see a putrid pile of slop that no one could ever truly love. That was his fear. Bottom line? Whatever she did to please him, no matter how much she gave in, he would never be happy, he would never be satisfied, it would never be enough. Not because there was something wrong with her, other than being your average fallible human being, but because he was a damaged soul who felt he was worthless, and all he wanted was to be loved.

And he, himself, was the only thing in the way of achieving his life goal of being loved, because he couldn't love himself.

Ah, she would find that out, sooner or later. But not before the damage was done to her own soul. Good luck to her. And good luck to me, too, trying to dig my way out of this terrible existence.

Barbara Letson writes stories filled of magic, mayhem, and ghosts. Her urban fantasy series "Fort Hopeless" follows Bobbi Harwood, a reluctant witch who returns to her ancestral home to discover she is next in line to inherit the family curse. The first novel in the series, "Fortress of Fear", releases in Fall, 2019. Find out more about Bobbi and Fort Hopeless at www.BarbaraLetson.com.

Lexie's Funeral

(Two Eight-balls, Seventeen Stitches and a Sawn-off Shotgun Ago)

Scott Crowder

Blue lights spear the darkness behind him, cutting into his eyes from the rearview mirror. He squints as he lets the car drift to a stop in the middle of the road.

Blood runs down his chin, pushed out by a heartbeat pounding at the stitches in his scalp and the stump of his tongue. His heart jackhammers in his chest and he wishes he could say that this horsepower surge of adrenaline was nothing more than the unexpected appearance of the cop behind him, but no.

It's also the final line of the second eight-ball of coke he'd burned through since Lexie'd died.

It's the sawn-off shotgun sitting on the passenger seat beside him.

It's the promise he'd made to Lexie months ago – *no more dope, sweetie, I promise. No more sellin', no more buyin'.*

Mostly it was the smile that had washed tide-like over her face, exposing the tiny white sea shells of her teeth.

I love you, that smile said, glittering, ocean-washed. I *trust* you.

Yes. Mostly it was the smile.

* * *

He'd been arrested two days before Lexie's suicide, he and Lucas busted for trying to sell a half-pound of weed to an undercover cop. The rest of the task force had swept in from the shadows, handcuffs and tasers and guns, oh my.

A young cop, blond buzzcut, sleeves stretched tight with muscle, had body-slammed him when he'd instinctively whirled to meet the newcomers, and motherfucker, you better believe that shit *hurt*.

They'd had to transport him to the ER to get his head sewn up before they'd even been able to arrest him. And through it all, the foul-smelling back seat of the cop car and the ER and the stitches, one thought had run through his mind, and one thought only: Lexie. She'll know I lied to her.

* * *

From the suicide note of Lexie Wheeler, as addressed solely to her boyfriend:

Sometimes the words that come out of your mouth seem to be in a language I don't understand. And maybe I've figured out why.

Pain is the language you speak, sweetheart. I know everyone does occasionally. But you speak it more often than most, or more loudly, or more fluently, I don't know which.

And it's a language I don't have the heart to listen to you speak anymore. I love you, and I need you, but what I need even more is some silence.

* * *

His parents had bailed him out of jail two days after his arrest, his mother unable to keep tears in, his father unable to force words out. Some two weeks later, after having read the suicide note countless times between chopping out rails of coke, he'd walked to the convenience store in a drizzling rain for a soda. On the way out, he was stopped by Lexie's younger sister Liz. She held a butcher knife at her side.

In the rain and the flickering fluorescent outside the front door she brandished the knife at him.

"She *killed* herself because of you! Because of your lies!" she howled, snot and tears sluicing away in the rain. "I should cut out your *tongue* for telling her so many lies!"

He dropped his soda and his heart stuttered to a halt despite the coke coursing through it, rain a cold acid in his eyes.

Pain is the language you speak, sweetheart.

What I need...is some silence.

He saw them, Lexie's sea shell teeth, heard the creaking of a rope as it swung heavily from an attic rafter, a silence fragile as bird bones breaking under the moaning creak.

With a grunt, he darted forward and snatched the knife from Liz's hand. She squealed, and as he back-pedaled, he stepped on the Pepsi bottle. It rolled, and he fell like dead weight to his ass.

She looked down fearfully at him, hair plastered to her face with rain.

He grabbed the tip of his tongue with his fingertips and pulled it stoutly from his mouth.

Liz screamed as he began to cut.

* * *

Systole and diastole of blue lights flashing behind him, and in the rearview mirror, he sees cops crouching behind open doors, guns pointed his way.

Out of the car now! they shout, and *Hands where we can see them!*

He stays in the driver's seat, though, heartbeat galloping but hands steady as he drags the shotgun over into his lap.

He knows the gun is loaded because he loaded it himself but he breaks it open anyway, checks the chambers for glinting brass, snaps it closed, wood cool and indifferent in his hands.

48

Pain may truly be the language he speaks, but if there are any other words at his disposal, he doesn't know what they might be.

Gun in one hand, door handle in the other…

And he pauses, pushing back against the coke in his system, pushing, waiting, *tell me, Lexie. Please*…

Nothing but silence.

He flings the door open, leaps from the car, spinning to bring the shotgun to bear. Shouts of anger and alarm rise to meet him.

His heart, already thundering, now a manic vibrato in his chest, eyes burning with tears, sinuses aflame, and a sudden fire in his throat ignites to join them all, words queued up behind the stump of his tongue, burning and searing his flesh with their impotent impatience to get out.

Scott is a husband, father, and writer living in Florida, and much like his main character, struggles to force the words out. He is the author of The House of Fists, Beastseer, Undermeat *and the frighteningly excellent short story collection* Serpent Sermons. *His brilliant short story* Valley of the Black Pig *was also featured in the 100 story anthology* Baby Shoes.

Migratory Animals

Nathan James

"Hey, how you feeling?" my son, David, says as he walks in. The too-loud words bounce off the quiet of my hospice room. He has a beard now. I don't like it. It is orange and pushes out from his muzzle like a beak and the way he bobs out of view reminds me of that bird Zazu from that movie I watched all the time as a kid. *The Lion King*.

"Morning, Peyton." Adaeze, my aide, adds as she enters the room behind him. I see her thick braids and then the sparrow of her wave. She is so small. It's a wonder how she manages to change my sheets every day, though the grunts she makes are nothing short of Olympian. I try lowering my chin to see her oval face — I want to gauge her mood — but, as usual, my muscles ignore me.

David returns holding up an Amazon box about the size of a toaster oven with the word *DigiNurse* written in a plain font across its side. His smile broadens as if someone has just pointed a camera at him. When you're diagnosed as catatonic, people's attention tends to flip like a light switch. Full power or none.

"This is for you," he says. His eyes flick to the box before he plunks it onto the bed next to my hip.

After some cutting, rustling, and cussing, he presents a green armband with different-sized shapes bulging from it.

I try to speak. My words — *Looks like a torture device al-Assad used on us during the war* — come out as a labored exhale.

"It's a digital dosage device. It works like those FitBits that were popular thirty-odd years ago, you know?" — I don't, but he's talking to Adaeze — "Only with more features. I have to make a few adjustments to tailor it to his symptoms, but..."

David remembers who this presentation is for and brings the thing back into my line of vision. "This is where the syringes come out. The sensors for vitals are here, and the band is infused with essential nutrients that your skin will absorb. Adaeze," — he still pronounces her name with two syllables instead of four — "or I will replace the medipaks every week." His voice dims because he turns to address her. "Pretty cool, huh? It records what it gives to him and when. All we have to do is check our phones to find out how he's doing. We won't have to hunt down Doctor Lu anymore."

Why is he wasting his time showing me the damn gizmo? What's happened to the doctor?

"Yeah, cool." Adaeze's voice is unusually monotone.

David puts the thing down and finally looks at me, two telescopes eyeing a distant planet. "These DigiNurses can do practically everything now. There's one model, the Advokat 3.1, I think, that can even translate muscle movements into words, but I didn't order that one for you... Adaeze? He's drooling."

Adaeze speaks to me as she wipes my chin. "Don't worry, sweetie. This new arrangement will work out just fine. You'll probably get sick of me preening over you all the time."

David digs in the box again. "Help me put these on."

They lift the weights of my arms, slip my hands through the contraptions, and pull them up to where my biceps used to be. The way they hug, I feel like I'm learning to swim again — look at little Peyton in the kiddie pool, water wings and all.

David whistles as he pecks at buttons on his phone. Adaeze has water running. She's creating work to stay with me; if he weren't here, she'd be helping another one of her patients by now.

Beeping from the armbands fills the room. "There we go." David steps back and watches me as if I'm about to break into a dance number. "It's started the baseline tests."

The backs of my arms warm. No, not warm...tingle? Is there a word for the sensation in between? Like how swans know the feeling of water on their feathers though none has ever touched their skin, or how people feel a stranger's gaze before they realize they are being watched.

"I don't like this, David," Adaeze snaps. I can tell that she is facing me, not him. "What if it malfunctions? He has no way of telling us."

"He couldn't tell us if Doctor Lu was malfunctioning, either." David laughs at his own joke. Then, silence.

I feel their stares. Look at me, standing in a spotlight without a mic.

"It seems like the more human interaction he gets the better. He *does* respond. You don't believe me, but he twitches and blinks when I do something he doesn't like."

"I want him to be in there just as much as you do," David sing-songs to her. "But the tests show his belfry is devoid of bats."

"Yeah," her voice glides over his. "You've said."

David's phone beeps, telling him the gadget's tests are complete. He picks up the box and calls out a terse goodbye. No hand on the shoulder, no peck on the cheek. A bird free from its cage. My door clicks shut.

Adaeze is at the sink again, but then the mattress sinks and the smell of lemon verbena wafts. Her arm encircles my mound of a belly.

"It's the money, sweetie. He can't afford taking care of you and month-long vacations to Greece. Who needs doctors when there's a beach on Mykonos waiting? Like everyone else these days, he's replacing the most important things with a gadget and calling it done. But at least he agreed to keep paying room and board here. You'll have me and the nurses down the hall if there's any emergencies."

The *DigiNurse*'s first needle pierces my skin. It is quick, yet gentle.

I try to focus my attention on Adaeze's breathing. She has done this before, held me, but it's different today. Less perfunctory. I feel sleep approaching. This gadget's meds work fast.

"Your son is an ass, Peyton," Adaeze sighs. "What should we do about him?"

After a time, she says, "Yes," and pats my arm. "We'll get our hands on one of those Advokat models. Show him and the doctors you're still there."

A fog engulfs me, and I am lying on a deck chair beside a pool watching a child swim furiously away from nothing.

Nathan James received his degree in creative writing from Western Michigan University. He is an editor and writer in the educational publishing industry in Chicago and has most recently been published in Wizards In Space Literary Journal.

The Junkie

James Dorr

He staggered — shambled — into the alley, crashing into two garbage cans. He knew what it meant.

The craving was starting to get too strong.

He'd been an addict before at one time, prescription pain pills which was sort of ironic if one thought about it. Because the first symptoms of withdrawal, whatever your bag had been, was always pain. He'd known someone who overused aspirin once — not aspirin, whatever the non-aspirin substitute was — but the thing was, he claimed if he didn't take it, even the first thing in the morning after he'd woke up from plenty of sleep, he'd be bothered by headaches.

"Bothered." Yeah!

But that was what being a junkie was, being "bothered", big time. He'd gotten over his own painkiller thing by deciding one day that he'd just tough it out. Go cold turkey. And it had worked for him, after the lousiest week in his life, without help from anyone. Because even with programs or doctors or whatever else they used these days, withdrawal was withdrawal, something you had to do just by yourself. And sometimes, no matter what help was offered, whatever you were on was just too strong for you.

But the painkillers, yeah, that had been more than a decade ago. When he had been young. And he wore a suit to a steady job — he picked himself up now and looked around. A steady job, a house in the suburbs, a wife and a kid. He looked around now and saw dirty bricks, and garbage, and brown puddles — everything dark, a brown or gray or maybe a dirt-encrusted red, even though the sun might be still shining. No house in the suburbs anymore, but a box on a heat grate if he was lucky. Or just a dead end in an alley out of the wind.

Did they still call it "Skid Row"?

It didn't matter, he was where he was, the darkest, grimiest, half-abandoned, worst part of the city. Where not even drunks went if they could help it — the lowest of the low.

And with the pain starting up now in earnest.

He looked above him, to try to see daylight. Try to figure out what the time was. If he could tough it out past sundown, maybe the cold would make him numb. He'd tried that before.

But the pain! They were never honest about pain in the self-help programs. How it throbbed and waited, growing steadily, steadily more intense. Taking its time. Knowing its victims must break eventually...

And then he heard a moan! It was too much for him. He listened, he heard it a second time, one part of his mind screaming *No! No! No!* even as he turned toward the dumpster he thought it had come from. Frantically he opened the lid and dug through — *NO!* Dug into the overflow piled around it. Dragged out what first looked like a dead woman's body. Except it was twitching!

Angel dust, maybe. That kind of thing, once you'd started on it, you couldn't even tell how much you'd had. But he didn't think. He just bit — bit hard. With the help of a brick, he crashed through the old woman's skull, then buried his face inside and started chewing.

Brains, yeah, but with that little off-taste too, that told him his victim *was* high on something. A recent fix, maybe a stash she'd hid behind the dumpster, putting it off for as long as she could.

Just like he had still tried, to push it from him, except for her there would be a cure this time. Regardless of what they showed in the movies, if a zombie ate enough of his victim's brain, that person would just die.

She herself would not turn into a zombie, which was why the Earth had not been overrun. Because like any other true junkie, once that last shred of resistance was torn, a zombie'd just eat and eat until everything he craved was finished. Unless something happened to interrupt him.

Which was why, with zombies, it usually was best just to herd them into the city's dark places, then leave well enough alone.

Yes, he had been through this once before, a long time ago, as a prescription drug addict, and was finally able to shake it off. But this time was different.

*Indiana writer James Dorr's THE TEARS OF ISIS is a 2013 Stoker Award®
Fiction Collection finalist. Also look for his TOMBS: A CHRONICLE OF LATTER-DAY
TIMES OF EARTH, published by Elder Signs Press in June 2017.*

The Bulletproof Cheesemaker

Michael Headley

Emil Pepin's interview for an Assistant Cheesemaker of the Appleton Creamery started off with the director suitably impressed. Her eyes widened when she saw the credentials on his resume — CCP exam passed, Affinage specialist, Competitor in and winner of the Mondial du Fromage, the international competition of elite cheese makers — over forty years in the business, and art, of cheese. And yet, even here in far-away Wisconsin she looked up from his resume, squinted at him, and spoke that awful name.

"You're him, aren't you? The French Wonder."

Emil tensed. "That's not my name; that's something the papers came up with."

"You're a super hero."

"I am a cheesemaker," he replied. It had been an accident. The wrong flight at the wrong time. He and the rest of the passengers had seen some sort of a blue light, and then they were all special. Some started leaping buildings, others donned elaborate costumes and took up pseudonyms. And from then on, all anyone ever wanted to talk to Emil about was that experience and what he could *do;* they ignored every achievement in his long and distinguished career. He shifted in the chair and tried to change the subject.

"It is nothing. It shouldn't come up."

The director tapped her fingers.

"What happened to your last job?" she asked.

"There was an accident. They let me go."

"And this accident had nothing at all to do with those... other things?"

Emil stared down at the table and didn't say anything. He only shook his head.

"I know what happened, Emil."

He remembered. A random super showed up to prove himself. He'd saved three people, but the building was destroyed.

"We'd be taking a risk bringing you on. It does come up. But imagine for a second. Cheese made by the French Wonder himself. Think of the viral marketing!"

He recoiled. "I am an artisan, not a prop!" he said, standing up. He should have been more careful, but he wasn't paying attention. As he stood up he bent the steel chair roughly double by accident. He glared at it, and she gaped. But it wasn't open-mouthed terror, it was a look of utter glee. The look of a marketer going *think of the possibilities.* He didn't want to think of possibilities, he wanted to think about *cheese.* It had been foolish to come here, to hope that he might find someone who would just let him work on his craft.

"I don't need this." He turned to walk out. At the door, the interviewer spoke up.

"What if we didn't hire you as an assistant. What about full director?"

He paused and stared. "What's the catch?"

"We could use you. Publicity lets us pay for an expansion. Get some viral videos – you lifting a tractor or something. Use your name in some branding."

He gritted his teeth, "That's all anyone sees —"

"That's not what I see. I know you're an artist. But we have to pay for your art. Just a couple of videos, some pictures, and then I'll leave you alone."

Emil saw the lie in her eyes. It wouldn't be just one picture, one video. He would always be the French Wonder to them. A gimmick. Costumes and pictures and posing. Humiliating. And before that stupid flight, he'd been a professional. Now reduced to a name he'd spent five years running from. But nobody else had called back. Not after last time. He looked at his wrinkled hands, then at the bent chair. *I just want to make cheese.*

He turned, slowly, and walked back over to the table, his shoulders hunched.

"No ridiculous costumes," he said quietly.

"Of course not," she lied.

Mike Headley lives in Kansas with his wife and two cats. He does freelance TTRPG writing, and also constantly thinks about things like giant robots or dinosaurs.

Made for Each Other

Eve Ott

"Why…" she said to her long term friend, short term occasional lover. "…have all the men I've ever loved been smart, yes, talented, often, but also bi-polar or alcoholic, or both?"

He grinned across the table at her.

"Be serious," she demanded. "I really want to know!"

When all he did was sigh and cock his head toward one shrugging shoulder, she pushed her chair back and stomped away.

He ordered another drink and waited for her to come back.

Eve Ott loves Kansas City's varied and vibrant writing community. Her poetry collection, Album from the Silent Generation was published a few years ago by Aldrich Press. Her chapbook, On the Jefferson Line was recently released by Prolific Press.

No Star to Guide Us

Jonathon Mast

"Sky's red again," Gerard murmured, searching the heavens. His two long, thin blades rested point-down nearby in the sand.

"Any stars?" Worry stretched between Marlene's chestnut eyes. Her hair had finally started growing back in patches through the burns on her head, white now, despite her youth. She recited the plan over and over to herself.

"Not yet. I don't know if there are any left." Gerard maintained his vigil of the early morning sky. "Not since she used them to stop planes from flying. And turning the population of Los Angeles to cats. I hate that she thinks it's funny."

"Heth-Sophar thinks she's the god of cats. Or something." Marlene's voice shook. "She used so many stars last night." She closed her eyes for a moment. "You think she canceled out any of her old wishes? Do your guns work?"

Gerard took a pistol from a holster on his hip – Marlene never learned what kind it was; she didn't have a mind for that – and he pressed the trigger. The gun clicked. Once. Twice.

He cursed. "Nope. Still useless." He pressed his lips together, suppressing a growl. "We just need the one star. Just the one."

Marlene nodded. "Just the one." She looked back at Gerard. He still didn't look at her the way he used to. Of all the vindictive things to wish. To make it so no man could fall in love.

There's no time for this. They had a plan. If it worked, he would be hers again. Just push through. Keep looking in the meantime. "Our last star should be in view soon."

But Marlene looked back out across the river. In the ruins of Cincinnati, between the burnt husks of the Great American Tower and Paul Brown Stadium, thousands of campfires flickered. The camp followers that came for the promise of food and safety gathered in the rubble, praying to the false god that had destroyed their world.

Gerard grunted.

"What?" Marlene asked.

No answer.

She turned. Her companion, her guardian, didn't move. He gazed at the sky with frozen eyes. His skin turned white. Granular. His hair stilled, solidified, crystallized. Clothes fluttered on a body made of salt.

Marlene couldn't take the time to scream. Don't think about him. Don't think about what they used to have before the god reawoke. Just do what's necessary to fight her. Look for her.

Heth-Sophar leaned against an oak tree about twenty yards up the hill, shaking with mirth. "I used up the last one with that. Your little friend can't watch, now."

"You imploded a star just to murder one man?" Marlene reminded herself not to hyperventilate. She just needed one star, now that she knew how to *wish*.

"I thought the last one should be frivolous. And it was!" Heth-Sophar's beautiful, dark face cracked with a smile too large for her head. "And you. You think you've finally figured out my trick."

"Collapsing a star at will and using the energy to bend reality? Wishing on a star? Yes."

"Too bad there's none left." Heth-Sophar stood. "That was my mistake when they exiled me the first time. I tried hoarding all the stars, and then someone else figured out how to do it. Wished me away. But you can't keep me away forever. No one can. And this time... oops. All gone!" She grinned her terrible grin as she picked her way down the slope. "And I've wished myself enough power and enough devastation to my enemies that, well, no one can stand against me!"

Keep her talking, Marlene reminded herself. *You just need a little more time to get the star she forgot.* "I'm still standing."

"Only because you amuse me. Did you know, last time it was a woman, too? There's just something about us that understands wishing. Maybe we have more reasons to bend reality than men." She shrugged. "But now it's over, little bug." She came close. "Unless you're willing to bow down and worship me?"

"Never," Marlene growled.

Heth-Sophar backhanded her. The crack sent her backwards, sliding down the slope, crashing through brush. Her neck. Something was wrong with her neck. Something cracked? Did she break her neck? She didn't feel any pain in the rest of her body. Not good. As she tumbled, she saw Gerard over and over and over again, a white statue of the man that had followed her for weeks after the first missing star, the first time things didn't work the way they were supposed to, the first time Heth-Sophar made herself known.

The man who no longer loved her.

The false god picked her way down the hill in the brightening predawn. The sky was still so, so red. "That was pitiful. Just dreadful. I expected to at least break a sweat." She towered over Marlene's fallen form.

She couldn't move. She couldn't get up. Breathing. Was she still breathing? She had to be able to breathe. There. Her lungs listened to her, filled with air.

Heth-Sophar leaned down and wrapped her fingers around Marlene's neck. "I wanted an epic struggle. I guess that's my fault. I should have left you some hope." She hefted her broken adversary up, holding her high above her head. "I guess this is it."

Marlene lifted her eyes to the hills. Above the hills. The sun broke above the hill's crest, a crimson band in a scarlet sky, a glorious, glorious dawn. She smiled through cracked lips. "Yep. I wish Heth-Sophar had never been reborn."

The sun, the star they all forgot, imploded.

"No," Heth-Sophar screamed through clenched teeth. She crushed Marlene's windpipe and let her fall to the ground. Wind whipped down the hills, grabbing at her with icy fingers. Across the river, campfires winked out. Buildings grew themselves back to what they had been. In the suddenly-dark sky, stars relit. Gerard flexed his fingers. Marlene stood, whole.

And Heth-Sophar vanished.

Jonathon Mast is a geek, a pastor, and a writer, who lives in Kentucky with his wife and insanity of four kids. (A group of children is called an insanity. Trust me.)

Haint Witch

James D. King.

I always be the one sent over to help old Aunt Juju. That's 'cause everyone else was 'fraid of her. But she liked me. I was her daughter's daughter and Aunt Juju said I had the "gift". She taught me about the medicine herbs that was in the swamps, like snake wort that cured cotton mouth bite and gator lily root that stopped swamp fever.

Folks say Aunt Juju is a haint witch. That's worse'n a regular one. Regular witches mainly do fortune tellin', love charms and potions. A haint witch do that too, but also casts evil spells and talks to angry ghosts of dead peoples that ain't passed over. That's why folks was 'fraid of her. They didn't want to end up like Big Tom.

I heard the story when my momma took me to a family get together out on the flat land. The grownups were sittin' in the shade and swappin' stories 'bout the old times. Aunt Lulu began one about Black Water Swamp so I slipped in and listened. Here's what she told.

Big Tom was the handsomest man ever seen. He was as strong as two men and had an easy way about him that the ladies loved. Big Tom traveled around leaving heartbroken women behind, often with a belly full of baby.

One day Big Tom was being chased by an angry daddy with a shotgun. If he got caught he'd have to get married or get shot. Being desperate he took to the swamps in a pole boat. Big Tom didn't know the swamps so he got lost and got bit by a cotton mouth. He must have drifted a while 'cause he fetched up in a bayou in the Black Water.

Aunt Juju was a young woman then. She was out huntin' medicine plants and found Big Tom layin' in a boat. He was all swoll up with snake poison and skeeters had feasted on him givin' him the swamp fever. Seein' that she snatched up batches of snake wort and gator lily root. Although a little woman, she managed to pole that boat back to her place and got Big Tom inside her one-room log house.

It took every bit of what she knowed of herbs and potions to keep Big Tom from dyin'. As he got better she fell in love for the first and only time of her life. It didn't take long before she was with child.

Usually Big Tom would be scootin' out by then, but he stayed. He must of had some feelin's for her too 'cause he built a room on that little cabin to make it bigger. He even helped birth the baby and cooked while she was bed nursin' the child.

When Big Tom was buildin' the room he made himself a strong chair of the knobby roots of swamp trees that never rot. This was the chair that at the end of the day he would sit in to rest. Juju would climb on his lap and they would talk about the wonderful things they'd do together.

After some time the wander itch came over him again. One night he snuck off in that pole boat he'd drifted in on. That's when Juju began to change. While she raised her girl baby by herself she learnt all she could about spells and talkin' to spirits. Then she planted a garden. It was a garden of morning glories. These weren't no regular morning glories, but the swamp kind that grow fast and strong. She'd mix magic potions and feed them morning glories. Then she put Big Tom's chair right in the middle of that garden.

Morning glories are twining flowers. They put out vines that latch on and grow up around anything near. Juju put up poles around the chair and made them vines climb up the poles until the chair sat in a little house of purple and white flowers. But she never let them vines wrap around that knobby chair.

Next she started casting spells to bring Big Tom back. Every night by the light of the moon she talked to angry ghosts and cast the spells they told her. The power of them spells kept gettin' stronger and stronger. She must have known what was comin' because she took her girl baby, named Glory, to her sister Lulu's place and left her there.

One day Big Tom returned and he was under a spell. He came up the bank and sat in his chair like he use to did. Juju brought him a potion and he drank it without even noticing her. Then he slept. She stayed there saying spells the mean ghosts had teached her. The mornin glories stirred and the vines grew fast.

When Big Tom woke he couldn't move. His arms and legs was all wrapped around with them strong swamp flower vines. Juju was sitting in front of him. He yelled to be let go, but she said that he would never leave her again 'cause he belonged to her forever. Big Tom cussed and then pleaded and then cried. Juju sat there as quiet as a cat watchin' the vines grow around him. When them vines covered his mouth he stopped movin'.

Aunt Lulu, who was tellin' the story, spied me sittin' by the tree. She looked at me hard. "After that Juju became a mean haint witch and lived alone. She never came back for her baby girl and I had to raise her. Thank the Lord little Glory turned out to be a sweet, normal child. But you know the talent to be a haint witch jumps around. It's passed down on the mama's side. It ain't no blessing. It's a curse."

That's when I learnt Big Tom was my granddaddy and why Aunt Juju goes out at night and talks to that knobby chair covered in morning glories. I'm hopen' she'll teach me how to talk to ghosts.

James D. King is a full time writer in the Washington, DC area. He has authored the true crime book "Ghost Burglar" (Savage Press) with co-author Jack Burch. He now writes science fiction and speculative fiction, having published three novellas in his "Hive" series, (Aois21 Press) and several short stories

Q. & A. with Mr. Hideous

William Delman

"My apologies for the daylight abduction, restraints, and blindfold, but as the Globe's chief reporter on Abnormals, you know how it is. Would you like some water? Very good. Acolyte Bob, would you help our guest? Being evil is no excuse for being a poor host. That's it, drink up."

Q.

"That's your first question? Not, 'why did you kidnap me?' Very well. Yes, I would consider 'evil' to be an accurate description."

Q.

"Easily. My followers and I are evil — in the eyes of the system we are seeking to end."

Q.

"Well, to hell with what Paleo says! Paleo is a fake, and a hack."

Q.

"Once. He's beaten me once, and only because he'd hardened his robotic triceratops herd against my electronic countermeasures. And I had no idea he was coming. He won't beat me again."

Q.

"Listen, he only started taking jabs at me in the press because he was desperate for a rival, but as everyone knows, my nemesis was The Answer. Speaking of which, I can't tell you how much I enjoyed the story you did on Eureka Squad, their hacking of government databases and the insider trading schemes they used to fund their vigilantism. Who would have thought The Answer and his allies, would end up in prison?"

Q.

"I told you, Paleo is nothing but an over-grown, avaricious, fitness-obsessed idiot who inherited his billions *and* the Raptor suit that lets him play hero. How many lives do you think he could save by donating his wealth? But no, he spends his days giving soundbites to financial news services, and building mechanical dinosaurs. Just because I happen to be somewhat educated and keep pointing out the ways his mechanized companions fail to accurately reflect the latest paleontological data..."

Q.

"No! I did not bring you here to discuss Paleo's ridiculous challenge. As if I'd ever be sophomoric enough to lead my followers into a direct confrontation with his army of mechanized kaiju."

Q.

"Finally! I'm glad you asked. Humanity has always been a superficial, egotistical race. Conscious and subconscious reactions to appearance have defined our interactions from the battles for Troy, to the formation of the American ghettos. Our eyes have blinded us to innumerable bloodlettings. What I have wrought will emancipate our vision."

Q.

"You're familiar with the condition often known as face blindness? No? It doesn't matter. I have engineered a virus that causes an incurable sort of aesthetic agnosia. The afflicted, or perhaps I should say "the liberated," lose their ability to see and judge faces, as well as body types, skin colors, and the like. We'll see how well Paleo does then!"

Q.

"Ruining his health and wellness empire is just a fringe benefit. I have larger aims than destroying that emotional Neanderthal. I am trying to create a world without judgment!"

Q.

"Well, yes that is true. My plan, if effective, will cost me my defining aspect. No longer will I be able to reduce humans, normal or super, to near-catatonia with my gorgon-esque visage. Then again, humanity should experience an unprecedented awakening."

Q.

"There are always pros and cons. If mothers are no longer able to recognize their children, our police will no longer be able to act on their prejudices."

Q.

"Indeed. All visually based legal testimony will become far less reliable, but I suspect this will be among the least interesting impacts my virus will have on criminal justice. The consequences should be fascinating to witness."

Q.

"No!"

Q.

"This is about more than Paleo, his Raptor suit, or his stupid dinosaurs and the laser cannons attached to their fricking heads. As I said, he's overrated, and so are his Dinobot wannabes. Now, Acolyte Bob, untie our reporter friend."

Q.

"You can take off your blindfold."

Q.

"Because the virus was in the water Bob served you. That's how it's going to spread. In a matter of hours, while Paleo is waiting to see if I show up for his petty challenge, my hirelings will be dosing reservoirs in two-dozen states. By the way, I want to say, for the record, how much I love social media and the modern postal system. Together, they make outsourcing this kind of minion-level work

64

laughably cheap and easy. You wouldn't believe what people are willing to do for gift cards."

Q.

"You, the first? Hardly! I like you, but the honor of being my initial test subject went to Bob. When he was able to look at me without screaming, I knew I was on to something. Then to be sure it wasn't a fluke, I rolled it out to some of my other acolytes. That's how real science works you know, through rigorous testing."

Q.

"It should all be over by tomorrow night. Now, do you think you'll be able to find your way back to your office if I have one of my acolytes drop you at a subway station? I only ask because some of my subjects developed topographical disorientation."

Q.

"With GPS, which I suggest you use after we return your phone. Also, please try to get the story up by tomorrow morning. I think there might be a Nobel in my future after everything shakes out, and it would be unfortunate if Doctor Malevolent or General Chaos tried to steal the credit for my work. You understand, don't you? Wait. Are those sirens?"

Q.

"No, I am quite sure those are sirens. And why is the ground trembling? Also what happened to your mustache? And your hair? Oww! Bob, quick, that's no reporter, it's The..."

Q.

"Yes, and I hate it when you finish my sentences!"

Q.

"What do you mean, 'How did I recognize him?'"

Q.

"I never said that."

Q.

"Why are we even talking about this right now? We must escape before my plans are rendered extinct by a legion of anatomically incorrect stegosauruses! Our getaway car is ready?"

Q.

"A Pontiac Aztec. Yes, that will do nicely."

William's work has previously appeared in Daily Science Fiction, The Arcanist, Little Blue Marble, and other fine venues. You can follow his occasional successes and numerous failures on Twitter at @DelmanWilliam.

Exhibit 286

J.R. Heatherton

(Exhibit 286 — A letter of unknown origin and context, found inside an ornate tin box among items retrieved from the Donnan Auction House before demolition. It is signed, Naggy Siker.)

To whoever may find this letter:

Please read this. It's imperative that you read this and understand. To whoever finds this, look out around you. Look hard. Can you see it? This is the end result of the event, and we don't know if it will ever get better. The way it looks most days, soon it likely won't matter at all. That soon, it'll all be over. Everything. But until that time comes, we try not to despair. We remain vigilant. This will hopefully be nothing more than a testament for those that may come one day to see with their own eyes and bear witness to our follies. Hopefully this letter will find its way into the hands of those who have the future we fear we never will. Hopefully there will be a future. Hopefully you'll understand that those responsible for our current state of being want you to stay ignorant. Don't want you to question. Don't want you to know.

Nothing happened here, they will say. It's all a myth, a story, a lie. But it did, and it all started here. To whoever may find this letter, you are at ground zero. Can you see it, now? For a community so isolated and seemingly so insignificant, this is where it began; and we fear this is the beginning of the end.

Please accept our confession and our plea.

Why did we let them convince us? Test plots! The very notion now seems so ludicrous, so insane. Why didn't we see what was right in front of us?

Yet, it was so tempting, being the first community to apply the miracle: Syckle-Grow. The jealous eyes of the world would be on us. They said we would be feeding the land while eliminating all weeds and undesirable growth. They said we'd be planting the new Vacanthimum vulgaris, rendering it into a type of sweet alcohol that could then be used to power our engines, heat our homes, illuminate our lights. We'd be rich. We'd be famous. We'd be saving the world. We had the best intentions, didn't we? So we did it.

How were we to know? Did they know? They were the ones that created the unstoppable devil. And we were the ones that unleashed it. Dear God, did they know?

Only, alcohol is no good for kids, is it. Do you blame yourself when nothing is all you have to offer? So we all decided to put the children to bed early. It was the only thing to do, with their tummies so empty for so long. I tucked little Ruthie in myself. Even as weak as she was, she cooed and giggled with delight,

66

anxious for another game of peek-a-boo as I fluffed the pillow. It was a struggle. It took her awhile to finally go to sleep. I guess it did for all the other children, too, but she eventually settled down, became still. I watched over her for a bit, stroking her silky hair, which always smelt warm and sweet like sun-dried alfalfa, as the rosy glow in her cheeks slowly faded.

Would you do different?

Sleep tight, children. Sleep tight. Tonight, somewhere out there a select few will be dining and making merry. Tonight, they will be fattening themselves on profits and ledger sheets; while your loving parents will be toasting their own success, toasting how clever we were, toasting just how we were the ones who were to save the world. Tonight we will raise our glasses high, full of emptiness, and warm our stomachs on the fruits of our labor while your stomachs turn cold.

Then, we will throw our glasses into the fire.

Naggy Siker

J.R. Heatherton lives in mid-Michigan. His work has appeared in Aphotic Realm: Tales from the Realm (Volume One), as well as various eZines.

Mighty Huntress

Susan Murrie Macdonald

My name is Meow-mew-mew, but my first human servant called me Princess Caraboo. She was an elderly human and I had to share her with six or seven other cats. Now I have hundreds of human servants all to myself, and they call me Princess.

Some are old like the Colonel, but most are young, hardly more than boys. They ride in noisy, stinking machines that fly in the air. They fly away to fight the Nasties. The Nasties are scary; my servants always turn to me for comfort, eager to pet and adore me, eager to provide laps. I calm them before they go off to fight the Nasties, and soothe them when they return.

The Colonel is pleased with me, he says I'm good for base morale. Sgt. O'Neill is thrilled with my suzerainty. I hunt mice and Twitches.

The Twitches are small and green. They're bigger than mice or even rats. They look like small humans, but they're prey, not servants. They go into my pilots' flying machines and chew up the wiring.

When I was a little kitten, my mother told me some cats could walk through walls… if they were very clever. The Twitches don't seem to be clever, but they walk through walls. Sgt. O'Neill calls them Gremlins. I call them Twitches because that's what they do – they twitch and then they slip into another dimension. I have to be very quick to catch them before they disappear. They don't taste good, but my mother said it was wasteful not to eat what I kill.

The door to one of the B-17s was open. I saw a Twitch slip inside. I immediately followed him. The Nasties are bad enough – I wasn't going to let a Twitch endanger my servants. Once inside the bomber I followed my nose. I had just settled into pounce position and begun my tail wiggle when Corporal Damon reached down and picked me up.

"Hey, Princess, you can't come with us. We don't have any kitty-sized parachutes." He picked me up and cuddled me lovingly. "You need to get where it's safe."

I am a mighty huntress, not a kitten who needs protecting! I protect my humans from the evil Twitches. While normally I love my humans holding and adoring me, there is something undignified in being picked up and carried without so much as a by-your-leave, ma'am. My subjects are adoring, but unfortunately prone to *lese-majeste*. A little respect to accompany the adoration would be nice.

"Hey, Baker, can you take Princess?" Damon yelled out the airplane door. "I'm afraid if I just chuck her out of the plane, she'll get run over."

Just chuck me out of the plane? As if!

When Cpl. Damon loosened his hold on me, I jumped down to the floor and immediately turned around and re-entered the plane.

"I guess she wants to go for a ride," Baker said.

As if! The air is no place for a self-respecting cat. I sniffed. The Twitch was that way. I went after it.

My paws were silent on the metal deck. I followed its scent. Then I caught a glimpse of green. I dropped into pounce position and began my tail wiggle. As fast as my cousin the cheetah, I soared. The gremlin tried to twitch out of there, but I seized it. I didn't know what would happen if it twitched whilst I had it in my jaws. Would we teleport to the colonel's office or another plane, perhaps one in flight? What if it teleported to a Nasty plane? Do Nasty planes have Twitches?

I clamped my jaw on the foul beast, rendering such queries moot.

I started to eat it, more to dispose of it than because I was hungry. Twitches taste terrible, but mess hall scraps are worse. Thank Bast for mice, or I would surely starve. My humans generally apologize when they offer me scraps from their plates. They don't call for mess hall chow any more than I do.

"Hey, Princess, what have you got in your mouth?" Damon asked.

Nothing. I swallowed. Well, nothing now. Damon grabbed me and picked me up. He stuck a finger in my mouth. Most undignified.

"C'mon, Princess, what have you got in your mouth? Is it something that will make you sick?"

Disrespectful and undignified, but at least he did it because he cared.

He stared at his finger when he removed it from my mouth. "Green? What did you swallow, Princess?"

A gremlin. I killed a gremlin, you doofus.

"You didn't get into any motor oil, did you? He lifted his finger to his nose. "Doesn't smell like oil. Looks like blood, except for the color." He turned me around and kissed my forehead. "Princess? Did you kill a gremlin?"

I meowed.

"Good girl. You should get a medal."

I should get a medal for eating the foul thing and forcing it down.

"C'mon, girl, let's go show the captain." Petting me gently, Cpl. Damon carried me to the cockpit where the pilot, Captain Gold sat reviewing his pre-flight checklist.

"Hey, Cap, guess what the Princess did?" Damon carried me into the cockpit. "See that green on her fur?"

"Did she get into a paint can?" Captain Gold reached out to pet me, but he carefully avoided the bits of fur with Twitch blood. I began delicately licking myself clean. Cleanliness is next to godliness, after all, and cats were worshipped as gods in Ancient Egypt.

"Naw, Cap, that's gremlin blood. She killed and ate a gremlin."

"Well, who's a good girl, then?" Captain Gold coo'd at me.

"She's a war hero, she is," Damon bragged.

Shush, corporal, you'll make me blush.

Susan Murrie Macdonald is a staff writer for Krypton Radio. She is also a freelance writer of stories and other people's blogs.

I Warned You Once

M. J. Wilder

She wiped the sweat from her brow and readjusted her baseball cap against the sun as it beat down on her and the rickety lawn mower. A leather booted heel dragged from the little wagon that bumbled along behind, disturbing the ground of the well-worn path.

She hummed an eighties tune, hips rocking back and forth in the seat as they entered the shaded canopy of the woods. Fingers of gray moss reached for her as she passed under the ancient trees. A small squirrel skittered across her path into the dense undergrowth of the other side.

Not letting go of the steering wheel, she twisted her wrist and looked at her watch. Almost time for dinner. She was looking forward to a quiet, stress-free evening for a change.

Ahead the little path dipped down to the edge of the bayou. The brake squeaked as she depressed it. Steering off to the right of the path and shifting gears, she swung the little wagon around and backed it down the slope to the water's edge.

Still humming, she climbed off. Looking down at the crumpled piece of shit in the wagon, his crimson Bama T-shirt darker around the collar, she retrieved the top half of the broken beer bottle from his lap. She gave the weapon a hefty throw towards a patch of duckweed, with a little splash it sank from view. She pulled the pin from the wagon and it dumped violently under the dead weight hitting the ground with force and consequently sent the body in a forward flip down the incline.

She snorted. "Jeez Daryl, you were holding out on me. You did have a talent."

No one would miss him. The sumbitch didn't have friends. He was too damn mean for anyone to stick for long. He hadn't held a job for months. No one would be expecting him come Monday. No one would ever come looking. If they did? Just another good for nothing that ran off and deserted his family. Would have been cleaner if he had, but life had a way of getting messy now and then.

Bzzz. She spit and waved a hand to scatter the gnat swarm that she walked into as she approached the water's edge. The bark under the sapling was rough as she gripped it to climb onto a downed tree trunk to get to the rope that stretched down current into the murky water. She pulled in the rope until the grid of a trap emerged.

She was happy with the load. She felt like a good old crawfish boil tonight. Outside where the steam wouldn't heat up the kitchen. Setting the trap aside she got back to business.

She grabbed an ankle and dragged the body closer to the lapping water. Then with her foot she lifted his shoulder and rolled him into position. With a heave of her leg she sent him into the water, a gulp and he disappeared.

Wiping the sweat from under her chin, she exhaled and tightened the shirt knot at her waist. Looking up the bayou she was startled by the little skiff that came floating slowly towards her on the current.

"Howdy Caroline," said the old man with a toothless smile. There wasn't a hint in his expression to what he'd obviously seen.

"Howdy Jack."

"Hot for April."

"Yes, it is," she agreed. "Catching anything?"

"Nah, mostly just keeping out of way of the misses." He winked under a grizzled eyebrow. He spied the trap sitting next to the wagon and said, "Gotcha a mess of mudbugs do ya?"

"I sure do. You're welcome to join us if you like."

"Appreciate it, but I think I will just mind my own today. Another time." He tipped his hat brim and floated on.

She released a breath. A rustling noise from the other bank caught her attention and she spotted the beast just as he glided into the water. Sleepy gator eyes met hers before he sank below the water and disappeared. She saluted him and wished him a good dinner.

Speaking of dinner. With one hand she pushed the wagon bed back into place with a thunk and with the other grabbed the trap and tossed it in. The wagon creaked merrily as it bounced back a couple of clicks faster than it had before, lighter.

The ancient screen door squeaked as she walked into the house, banging shut behind her. The cool interior was refreshing and smelled of pine cleaner. The scratched and dented wood of the kitchen floor was half dry. A bucket of water and mop sat in the corner.

"I brought back dinner, thought we'd make a salad to go with," she said.

She grabbed a cold beer from the fridge, taking a long pull of liquid before retrieving a bag of peas from the freezer. At the table in the small eat-in kitchen, she gently laid the bag over the swollen eye of the young girl sitting in a faded sundress.

"Thanks mama." The delicate hand reached up to hold the peas.

The woman set her hand on her daughter's swollen belly and smiled when she felt a responding kick.

"You're welcome, precious."

Find other fiction novels by M. J. Wilder on Amazon. Her ebooks include the Beating the Odds Series as well as One Fine Mess.

Forseti and the Dragon

Adam Thomas Gottfried

"I really hate this," Forseti grumbled, spinning his axe ably through the air. The opaque outline of Former President Teddy Roosevelt merely sighed... or seemed to. As a spirit of the nearly-century dead world leader, he did not breathe, technically speaking. But he had retained much of his essential humanity to a sufficient degree that he mimicked the act without thinking anything of it.

"'Tis good tactics my boy," he murmured, not for the first, or even tenth time. "You are the target therefore be where your enemy is not." He removed ghostly spectacles from their perch on his spectral nose and cleaned them. Forseti glared at him.

"For someone who can appear very literally however they want, you would think you'd keep your glasses clean."

Teddy chuckled. "And so begins the abuse. You are quite predictable, young man."

Forseti all but stamped his foot. "I am not! I just... don't like others doing my fighting for me."

Teddy nodded sagely, standing from where he had been leaning on the fender of a 2017 Tesla, and put a hand on his companion's shoulder in a vaguely fatherly gesture.

"You have bled for each and every man and woman who stands behind you today," he murmured. "Let someone else bleed on your behalf for once."

Forseti rolled his eyes. "You know I don't roll that way."

"You are the one who insisted your home be protected, it does not matter how you 'roll'," Teddy cajoled. "You have to take your orders, as do the rest of us."

Forseti's eyes were wide, blue, and dangerous, the look he often got before he told whomever had given him said orders to put them somewhere uncomfortable, and damn the consequences. Forseti opened his mouth to speak when a sound like slightly annoyed thunder split the brisk autumnal air. Both the President and Forseti glanced around though it was the mustachioed Rough Rider that spotted the source first.

"Good God," he murmured, grasping Forseti's muscular arm and pointing. The blind God of Justice turned and squinted against the sun. Down the quiet side street he and Teddy had opted to await news of the battle stood an anachronistically huge dragon.

"Well fuck," Forseti murmured, thus permanently canceling his application to the Scooby Gang. That the dragon had been sent for him was without question. That he would fight the dragon went without further question. That Teddy Roosevelt would try to stop him remained to be seen. Forseti glanced around.

"That is quite a large specimen," Teddy stated, his eyes riveted to the ambulating wyrm. The creature was no Norse or Chinese dragon but a good old-fashioned European dragon: Four powerful legs, huge bat-like wings, a thick scaly hide, spiked ridges across its skull and a spine and jutting teeth like that of a slightly engorged angler fish.

"We cannot, of course, engage with that creature," the President murmured. "Shall we flee to a more advantageous battleground?" He turned to face Forseti but the deity had already left his side.

"Hey Teddy!" exclaimed Forseti, and Theodore Roosevelt's vision was pulled across the street to the bearded, grinning face in the driver's seat of a massive 4x4 truck. The moment he was spotted, he touched the ignition wires and the truck, some twenty years old and a behemoth in its own right, roared to life.

"Hold my beer!" Forseti called and chucked something out of the window. Out of instinct Teddy reached to catch it but it fell through his immaterial fingers. He looked down to the grass and then behind him where the object had fallen and discovered a six-pack of Pabst Blue Ribbon beer, minus one, which had been thrown ungraciously at his feet. The truck's front wheels spun as the blind god hit the gas, laying down a thick layer of rubber on the asphalt. The truck lurched forward toward the huge beastie, with the sound of Forseti's mad laughter barely audible over the roar of the finely maintained engine.

The dragon took notice and landed at the end of the street, rearing its massive head back for what would inevitably be a gout of flesh-melting flame, but Forseti apparently had held back the last of the big truck's get-up-and-go because the truck suddenly lurched forward, the spray of draconic napalm hitting the rear of the truck as Forseti frantically grabbed at his seatbelt and scrambled to click it into place.

It snapped home a mere instant before the truck, all two and a half tons of it, slammed into the broad chest of the dragon. Teddy could not estimate the speed Forseti had achieved but he would guess it was nearly double the speed of a charging horse. He winced as the truck struck home, nearly caving the dragons chest in on itself, certain that while Forseti had mortally wounded the dragon, the god himself might not walk away.

He ran up to the vehicle, and to his surprise, the cab seemed reasonably undamaged. Huge white pillows had deployed, one in front and one on the side and Forseti was blearily ripping the fabric free. Seeing the President's face brought a huge, shark-like grin to the god's face.

"Scratch that off the bucket list," he murmured as he pulled himself free of the wreck. He reached over the driver's side and grabbed his axe, then turned to the dragon.

The truck had damn near cut the creature in half. The giant creature twitched feebly as it bled, not dead but dying. The blind god moved to stand near the creature's head. The dragon saw him but made no move to attack. It was over and it knew it. Teddy was shocked to see the intelligence behind its eyes. It knew it was dying, and it knew who had killed it. Forseti reached out a hand and placed it on the creature's nose between the nostrils. He seemed to almost... pray. Then he drew back his axe and put the creature out of its misery.

Adam is a professional writer from St. Paul, Minnesota. This is his third anthology, and his first full length novel will be available for download and print on demand in 2020. You can find him on most social media under Adam Thomas Gottfried.

Bobby's Father

Randy Attwood

Bobby's father felt very bad about dying because of all the trouble it was causing. He was like that. Everyone was sad about it and we did not like to look at each other when we passed in the hallway.

The cancer made him smell bad. When I walked into the room I had to hold myself to keep from gagging. When he defecated, no matter how hard I clenched my teeth, I still gagged. Bobby's father would burn wooden matches, blow them out, wave the smoke, and we both ignored it.

Bobby was a sophomore in high school and the kind of kid that who gets picked on in school. He was drinking coffee for the first time. Perhaps it was something adult he could do since he was soon to be the man of the family.

Bobby's mother was Catholic and wore a black veil that seemed to be made of lead. She was as sad as her posture.

I was wrapping a man's leg with gauze soaked in saline solution when Bobby's father died. There was a sudden wail. I stopped wrapping the man's leg and we looked at each other. The man did not say anything and I went on finishing the wrapping.

In a little while, they shuffled past the door on their way to the new chapel that had just been built in the new wing of the hospital. The nuns were very proud of their chapel. Two women were on either side of Bobby's mother. They had their hands on her. Bobby followed alone, trying to understand this new dirty trick that had just been played on him.

I finished putting the last safety pin to hold the outer protective covering in place, then walked into the hall and saw Shirley walking towards Bobby's father's room.

She was carrying the shoebox.

"I'll do it, Shirley."

She didn't say it, but I could see the thank you in her eyes.

I took the shoebox from her and we walked into the room. Emma helped me roll the body on its side and she held it there. I took the forceps out of the shoebox and as they prayed for his soul in the chapel, I stuffed cotton up his anus.

Later, when the man from the funeral home arrived, I helped load the body onto the cart. It was hard work. We had to wrap the body in a green plastic thing first and it was necessary to jerk the body to make it move.

I knew Bobby's father would have felt very bad about that.

Attwood lives in Kansas City and has published 11 novels and three collections of shorter works. All can be found on Amazon.

After Reading "Shaving" by Leslie Norris, the Sophomores Write a Narrative

Maryfrances Wagner

The pages of Lindsey's book fluttered. The fan's rotating voice was wavy and cut through the thick air. Most of its benefits never reached us. Our feet shuffled under our desks like long loaves eliminating the last of summer's thick wax.

"Do you have any final comments about the story?" I asked.

We shifted and remembered the character Barry with his father's razor erasing the last line of lather from his father's once-whiskered face. He would not get better. As Barry worked, the sun retreated. He told his father, "You needn't worry."

"Why did we read something so sad?" asked Max.

"I thought it was a good story even though it was sad," said Jenna.

"It was real," said Sarah.

"Do any of you want to read your narrative?" I asked.

Students smoothed the top pages of their narratives.

"I'll read," said Marie. Her story captured the memory of the zoo with her Uncle Joe. She saw her first panda and zebra, and her Uncle Joe bought her a stuffed hippo. Another offered a story about the first time she went swimming and learned how to paddle in the water. She particularly liked eating snow cones with her Dad because she only saw him once a month. Jenna's story was about her best friend moving away after eight years of friendship. They experienced so many "firsts" together.

"Anyone else want to read?" I asked. The room was silent except for the fan. I looked around the room for a hand.

The star basketball player of long, black, graceful fingers shot me a glance. "I'll read," he said. From our mouths floated little *Oh*'s. He walked to the front of the room.

Terry cleared his throat and read, "After someone shot him for the second time, my father called me to his hospital bed. My five sisters waited outside. I knew what he was going to request."

We sat quietly and didn't move. We didn't shuffle. We didn't move our pencils or our papers ready to turn in. All around, as he read, hands collected themselves into knots. We listened. It was hot. The air was thick. It was not going to rain at all.

Maryfrances Wagner's newest books are The Silence of Red Glass and The Immigrants' New Camera. Winner of the Thorpe Menn Book Award for Literary Excellence, she has served as co-president of The Writers Place and is currently a co-editor of I-70 Review.

A Winter's Tale

Erica Ruppert

"Michael? There are footprints in the garden."

"Whose?" Michael said from the mess of the bed.

"How should I know?" Denise said, raising the balky window and peering out over the back yard. Scattered across the snow like droplets was a string of sharp mud-red tracks. "The gate's closed. Did you lock it?"

"Maybe." Michael got up and stood beside Denise at the window. The frozen air cut in. "Can you shut it?" he said. "It's too cold."

"Look first," she said.

Michael leaned out of the window to peer at the empty white swath a storey below him. The tracks snaked through the back gate, up to the kitchen door, then back down the yard and over the garden wall.

"That's not right. I'll go look," he said, his brows drawing down at the puzzle.

He tugged his pajama shirt into place as he went down the stairs. He paused at the kitchen door. There were streaks on the window-glass. He leaned closer and realized they were long, dirty scratches gouged into the glass from the outside.

His brows knit tighter.

Michael scuffed into a sprung pair of moccasins that lay next to the door, and let himself out into the yard.

Cold bit through his flannel pajamas as he trudged the length of the yard to the gate. He was careful not to smudge the footprints. They looked like deer tracks, sharp and split, but too large for that. From the spacing it looked as if whatever made them had come through the gate. But the latch and bars still had a layer of snow on them. Nothing had touched them.

Michael looked around the yard, and back at the house. Morning sun sheared blindingly off the kitchen door's windows as it swung quickly closed.

"Denise?"

As the door slammed he realized how quiet it was. No neighbors were about. No traffic noise came from the street. Even the air hung in a hush. There should have been *something*, a bird, a backfire. Nervous sweat slicked him, despite the cold. From behind the garden wall he heard a high, hollow laugh.

He'd never heard a sound like it. He never wanted to. It struck a brute nerve in him, and animal instinct shrilled quickly into fear.

Michael ran then, clumsy in the snow, tripping on the step up to the kitchen door. He could see Denise inside, impassive, unmoving.

He righted himself and reached for the door, but his clammy hand slipped off the knob. He banged on the scratched glass. "Let me in! Let me in!" he shrieked.

Denise watched him from the other side.

"Let me in! Denise!"

In answer she held up her hand. He saw a mark on her palm, like a sharp, split hoof burned into her skin. She smiled at him, and then, still smiling, looked past his shoulder. He heard the fast clip of footsteps behind him. The laugh came again at his neck, carried on sweet, hot breath.

He spun around on the narrow step. He could not make out the figure's face in the white glare of the morning sun, but he was sure he knew it. He held up his hand to the shining blur, showed it the mark on his own palm.

"No," Michael said. "Her first."

He blinked, and was alone in the snowy garden.

Behind him, in the kitchen, Denise began to scream.

Erica Ruppert's work has appeared in magazines including Unnerving, Weirdbook, and PodCastle, and in multiple anthologies. She is, very slowly, working on an unplanned yet persistent novel.

Sprinkles

Jenna Weingarten

It was a dark and stormy night.

Mr. Abbott was at the point of securing his shutters when a gentleman came barreling through the door, his overcoat dripping onto the café's welcome mat. Mr. Abbott shook his head indulgently. He flagged down a waitress.

The gentleman was led to a table in the back corner. He fussed a bit before settling down; it seemed to be of utmost importance that his chair faced the couple at the window. The waitress thought this rather odd, but she had coffee to serve and a side of ketchup to deliver and didn't care to comment.

The couple, for their part, were in the midst of an argument.

"It was a mistake, I swear, John. I'll never do it again!"

"That's what you said the last time!"

And so they were at a standstill.

The gentleman didn't mind. His focus was singular. In the center of their table sat a frosted donut. Sprinkled to perfection, it was, and nice and plump. It reminded him vaguely of his former lover.

"But it's always been you!"

The gentleman froze, his heart in his mouth, as her fingers skimmed the frosting. He didn't breathe again until they settled atop John's hand.

"I never truly wanted anyone else."

"Enough." John slammed his fist on the table, nearly upsetting the remnants of his drink. "Don't you understand, Jenny, why we just can't be together?"

The gentleman shuddered and calculated the trajectory of the liquid to the pastry. It was a near miss indeed.

"We were made for each other."

The waitress, at this point, came to take the gentleman's order. "Sir? Have you had a chance to —"

"That donut, please." The gentleman waved his fingers in the couple's direction. "And coffee. Black."

"I'm sorry, sir, but that was our last one. Care for a muffin? They're really quite good."

The gentleman paused. He trembled slightly. "No. No, just the coffee then."

The waitress returned to the kitchen.

"Stop it, will you? I've had enough." John pushed his chair back.

"Don't act like this is all my fault! You've done this too. Emily told me so!"

"That was before we were dating, and you know it!" His face turned a bright red.

Jenny reached for the donut. The gentleman watched, frozen, as she liberated a single sprinkle from the frosting. She flicked it into John's hair.

"You're a child, you know that?"

The gentleman closed his eyes, pained.

"Here you are, sir." The waitress placed the hot cup into his hand. "Are you alright?"

"Yes. Fine." The gentleman didn't meet her gaze. He raised the coffee to his lips. Put it down. "Might I have a check?"

"Sure."

He turned his attention back to his friends at the window.

"I'll be by for my things tomorrow," John declared.

She scoffed, rising. "You're not gonna find them!"

They were nearly to the door. The gentleman's eyes shined. In their haste, they had forgotten his beloved on the plate!

He salivated as he snuck his arm — ever so slowly — to their table. He hesitated, for the briefest of moments, with his hand positioned above the donut. And then he died.

Jenna Weingarten is studying psychology and creative writing at the University of Pennsylvania.

Moonberries

Peter J. Foote

"Close your wings Jitterbug, you're too bright," whispers Clare, eyes probing the dark forest.

Amber light within the lantern dims. "Remember what Grandma said lives in shadows, we need to be careful." Clare weaves her way through the underbrush, slippered feet silent upon the moss of the forest floor.

Parting branches, dislodging trapped droplets of dew, they leave the dark of the forest and enter the clearing. The harvest moon above the treetops, pure white light landing upon small orbs hanging from the low bushes.

"Moonberries!" Caution forgotten, Clare rushes forward. The light in the lantern blooming as the fairy inside flies in loops and twirls, her amber light stabbing into the shadows and neither see the brief flicker of movement.

Careful not to get their mother-of-pearl coloured juice on her dress, Clare settles amongst the bushes and uses her free hand to pluck a single, perfect moonberry.

"Chirp, jingle, chirp!" from within the lantern, as Jitterbug bounces off the glass. "Okay, I'm sorry. There you go." Lifting the latch, the tiny door bursts open letting the fairy free. As Jitterbug weaves through the leaves of the moonberry bushes, Clare picks berries and pops them into her grinning mouth.

"Snap." In the silence of night the sound is thunderous, the berry in Clare's hand slips from nerveless fingers.

"Jitterbug... the shadows are moving."

Peter's story "Sea Monkeys" won the inaugural "Engen Books/Kit Sora, Flash Fiction/Flash Photography" contest in March of 2018. Founder of "Genre Writers of Atlantic Canada", Peter believes that the writing community is stronger when it works together.

The Prophecies

Jeb Brack

"Hear me, O faithful," boomed the oracle. "The Goddess has commanded me to give you tidings. The enemies of our nation will gather and move against us. They will be legion and they will be relentless. They will employ devices and strategies the like of which we have never known and for which we have no defense. The realm will teeter on the precipice, and the mighty will despair!"

The high priest and his assembled congregation gaped, awestruck.

"But a champion will arise!" thundered the oracle. "A hero who will rally the people to them. They will see the course before them, and the people will flock to acclaim them. Though the struggle will be fraught with peril, the champion will not shirk the challenge. They will rise above the fray and the foe in triumph, and all will be as it should be, forevermore."

The echoes of the prophecy tumbled down the hillside and died away. From inside the shrine came a deep breath; it had been a long time since the oracle had recited such a long prophecy, and he wasn't as young as he used to be.

"I'll take questions now," said the oracle after a moment.

Before the high priest could say a word, someone from the procession called out, "Who is they?"

"What?"

"You said 'They will rise.'"

"Oh! That's the champion," said the oracle.

"But you said, 'They.' Will there be more than one?"

"No, no. There can be only one."

"Then why not say 'he'?"

Exasperation tinged the oracle's voice. "Well it might be a woman, mightn't it?" he boomed. "That was not given me to know. So I said 'they' because it's shorter than 'he or she.' Look, if that's all..."

Feeling that he should exert some leadership, the priest spoke up. "O Oracle, how will we know the champion you have foreseen?"

"Well, they'll rise to the occasion, won't they. I've said."

"But how are we to know?" That was the scribe, a pedantic little man who took notes at the vestry meetings, the sort who liked to point out other people's mistakes or oversights. "I mean, suppose someone rises and it's not him?"

"Them."

"Right, sure. Suppose he, sorry, they rise and it's just some berk pretending they have what it takes?"

The oracle said, a trifle uncertainly, "Come the hour, come the person, I expect."

"That's it? Peril threatens and we just wait for some non-specific champion to turn up and save us?"

"Listen," said the oracle with some asperity, "I'm just the messenger here. If you don't like it, someone else can volunteer, and I can stay home of a weekend."

"What if we went searching for him...them?" said the priest. "With the aid of your insights, O oracle, we might find the champion before the hour grows too desperate."

"Yeah," said the scribe. "Give him some training, like, before he has to face the enemy."

"It wouldn't work. They'll be born in a faraway land," said the oracle. His voice sounded petulant, probably because his arms were getting tired of holding up the heavy washtub he had to shout into, to make his voice echo. "Listen, can we move on? I've also got news about a coming storm ..."

"Hang on, how far from here? Like a day's ride away, or a ship's voyage far away?" Other members of the congregation pressed forward; this was the most interesting consulting of the oracle they had ever attended. The older ladies smiled self-righteously, knowing that for the rest of their lives they could hold this over their relatives who had skipped the ceremony.

"Just a faraway land, all right? Doesn't anyone want to know about the coming storm?"

"What, with war bearing down on us, you expect us to be worried about the weather?" said one of the acolytes, a teenage boy pressed into service by his parents.

"That's treasonous, that is," said the other, and the two of them sniggered.

From inside the shrine came the crash of a washtub being thrown aside. "Fine," said the oracle. "Fine. It's a faraway land, right, and there's a twisted tree by a lonely lane. It will be a night of omens and portents, right?"

"What sort?" said somebody.

"The sort you get when a hero is born, okay? Storms and lightning and whatnot. And he'll be born in the humblest of settings..."

"Here, you said 'they' before..."

But the oracle would not be stopped. "HUMBLEST of settings, and his name shall be champion."

"What, literally?" said the scribe.

"No, you daft bugger, that's poetic license. If I tell you his name it makes the entire prophecy moot, doesn't it? You'll just have to figure out the rest from context clues. Anyway, I've had it. That's all, thank you very much!" The oracle's angry muttering died away, emerging from behind the shrine as he stomped down the hill back to town for dinner and a pint.

The procession broke up, leaving the priest and the scribe standing by the shrine.

"Did you get everything down?" said the priest. "I'll want it transcribed right away. But we'll have to punch it up to make it more portentous."

"What?" said the scribe.

"Don't you see? Do you have any idea how long it's been since there's been an honest-to-Goddess prophecy?"

"No."

"Believe me, the faithful will eat it up, and people will come from miles around to visit our temple!" He clapped his hands together. "Right, then! Let's get to work!"

The Prophecies, when published, became a sensation. For six months, pilgrims flocked to his temple to hear his interpretations and fill his collection baskets with coin. The temple and the village flourished, until they were swept away by a flood, the result of a storm that unleashed a torrent of water, ice, and rock the like of which no one could have predicted.

By a staggering coincidence, however, the oracle had left town the night before.

Jeb Brack is a modern day Renaissance man, which means he does lots of things for not a lot of money, such as writing, illustrating, game mastering, martial arts, and magic. You can see his work on his website, wordspicturesmagic.com.

Bernice the Book Wyrm

Cathy Smith

As the heir apparent of her mother's kingdom, Princess Hilda's people expected her to show strong leadership. Being the President of the Crown's Book Club was her one refuge from the pressure of her duties. Or at least it had been before the wyrm, Bernice, burned books.

Her chief guard Sir Wallace said, "Bernice may've played nice for a while, but she can't fight her instincts forever. You should hire St. George the Dragon Slayer to deal with her."

Hilda waved a dismissive hand. "No, Bernice the Book Wyrm is civilized. I'm sure we can reason our way through this misunderstanding."

Her first instinct was to call the other members of the book club to brainstorm a solution. Lady Spangle looked less spritely than usual. Most times her fairy dust sparkled so much it served as a good nightlight but now it was dim. "We can't allow her near our collection anymore."

Matilda the Dwarf lifted her hand as if she were swinging a battleaxe. "I second that motion!"

Princess Hilda held up her own hand. "As the Chairman of this Board, and your future sovereign, I may veto this motion. Let me speak to her first."

So she went to see Bernice for a private chat only to find a flaming mound of books at the mouth of the wyrm's cave. "Bernice! What are you doing?"

Bernice turned to face her with flared nostrils. "I'm destroying all copies of 'Bury Your Treasures!'"

"Why? That sounds like something you'd like," Hilda frowned.

"Its subtitle is 'Stop Your Compulsive Acquiring, Saving and Hoarding!'"

"Oh," Hilda sighed.

"I find such hate speech insulting and offensive. Hoarding is an ancient custom among my people." Bernice's voice rose with each word.

"I'll take it off the recommended self-help reading list, and you're free to leave any book review you want, but you can't keep burning books. This is a country of free speech," Hilda said.

Bernice snorted so violently a fireball spewed out of her nostrils and almost hit Hilda.

Hilda started but sidestepped the fireball and continued talking. "You can either respect the Crown Book Club's Charter or we'll withdraw your membership to our subscription library."

"Hmm." Bernice had more books in her hoard than gold. She was called the Book Wyrm for a reason. Treasure seekers avoided her cave because of it.

Some ancient tomes she possessed were worth their weight in gold though only antiquarians knew their true value. She stayed on good terms with the humans so she could have a continuous supply of reading material.

"Well?" Hilda asked.

Bernice used her body to smother the fire on the mound of books.

"Good," Hilda said.

"Let's have a more dragon-friendly selection next month," Bernice said.

"We can read 'Girls with Dragon Tattoos?'"

Bernice nodded 'yes' and stomped inside her cave for a nap after all the excitement.

Hilda sighed. She'd never thought the Crown Book Club's latest selection would ever become a contentious issue: she thought of the book club as her safe space. Reigning over a diverse populace took more effort than going to war with them, but at least this latest fire was out.

.

Cathy Smith is a Mohawk writer which is why she's chosen "Khiatons" as her motto. It means "I am a writer" or "I write" in Mohawk. She has written two novels in the Shifty Magician series, The Shifty Captive and The Shifty Minion.

Civil Service

Gregg Chamberlain

Sitting at the kitchen table, chin resting on his fist, Phil stared at the open letter he held in his other hand.

"Dear Sir/Madame," it read. "We appreciate your application for a position with our company. However, we regret to inform you that..."

He dropped the letter onto his little kitchen table. It landed on the pile of other open letters that had come in the morning mail. The pile included two other job application rejections, a letter from the bank reminding him that his credit line payment was due, another letter from the bank notifying him that the mortgage payment was due already, plus notices about the latest phone bill and his cell phone account, a final notice for payment from the cable company about his Internet connection, along with a polite request from the power company for some payment of the last bill.

There was also a not-so-polite letter from a credit card company notifying him once again that his account was overdue and that should it remain in arrears "we shall be forced to turn the matter over to a collection service". Below that was a letter from his ex-wife's lawyer outlining the agreed-upon terms of the divorce settlement, one which, as the lawyer observed was "only proper and fair recompense for the best 10 years of her life" and if Phil could make arrangements soonest for automatic debit of his account for the alimony payments it would be appreciated. Underneath that was a letter from his own lawyer that featured an itemized bill for all the costs involved in limiting, as much as possible, any loss of blood, real, virtual or financial, while his ex's shyster skinned him to the bone during the divorce process in return for being allowed once-a-month visitation rights with Jesse.

The last letter, yet unopened, was in a long, white, and very thin envelope bearing in the upper-left-hand corner what looked like the letters I.R.S

Just great, Phil thought. An audit. Now my day is complete.

"I'd give anything," he said aloud, as he slit open the envelope and slid the letter out, "if only once, just once, someone would do something for me."

He unfolded the single sheet of cream-colored paper and puzzled over the glaring, and likely very expensive taxpayer-paid-for typo in the letterhead that should have read Internal Revenue Service if not for the "f" replacing the " in "Internal", before starting to read the generic salutation.

Phil felt a tap on the shoulder. He spun about in the chair.

Standing in the middle of the tiny kitchen, dressed in a very conservative business suit-and-tie with horn-rimmed glasses perched on a crimson nose, and holding a briefcase in the neatly-manicured claws of one hand, was a demon.

89

The demon offered Phil a polite fanged smile and extended another neatly-manicured taloned hand for him to shake.

"Good day, sir," the demon said, warmly. "I'm from the government, and I'm here to help."

Gregg Chamberlain lives in rural Ontario Canada with his missus, Anne, and their clowder of cats. He has several dozen story credits in venues such as Daily Science Fiction, Apex, Ares, Mythic, Nothing Sacred, and Weirdbook magazines, and various original anthologies.

Mabon

Fiona Plunkett

It was quiet. Too quiet. I was warned that door-to-door hustlers were roaming the town, so I remained hidden in the backyard with nothing but a floodlight and a laptop for company. The sun had set an hour before, and my solar lights danced merrily in the gloom. There was no one home on either side of me, as far as two houses over on either side. No one would hear if I screamed.

One side wouldn't have responded anyway. I have enemies in this town. I did things on impulse. I spoke my opinions. I remained true to myself. I harmed no one. I was merely The Witch. But still, the enemies grew. My sanctuary, violated. I could have retaliated, with horrible attempts at new tunes on the bagpipes at ungodly hours... but then I would have been subject to loud, twangy, country music. That torture still occurs, from time to time, but for the most part the quiet has returned. Finally, a cold impasse. I do not exist. I am happy with that.

Coyotes howl in the distance. Crickets sing their constant drone. The occasional car passes through town. Tires on gravel as neighbours, further afield, return to their homes after a long day. I hear it all as I sit here.

I see movement out of the corner of my eye. It's just a neighbourhood cat, passing through my backyard in search of... companionship, combat, prey down by the river, something...

My mind races with a million thoughts at once. Although it may be quiet outside, it will never be quiet in my head. There are too many uncertainties. Too many unknowns.

Something is rustling at the end of the garden. I can't see anything. It's too dark, despite the lights. The sounds emanate from various parts of my yard. It's almost like creatures are crawling out of the plants from every corner. It's subtle, however. A faint rustling. But it, they, are coming closer.

A flash of pink streams across my peripheral vision, but disappears as soon as I turn my head. I hear the sound of metal on metal, and, oddly... plastic. Surely I'm just imagining things. The air conditioner next door is clicking on and off, it must be acting up. I need more wine.

I refill my glass, cuddle my familiar, and return to my post outside. As I settle myself back down again, I see a flash of pink again. I turn towards it to see one of my pink flamingos stuck solidly in the ground, below my tree. Very strange, for all my flamingos are scattered throughout the yard, none under the tree. I turn back to the laptop only to see movement out of the corner of my eye again. Two more flamingos. No wait, there are more. Suddenly, the Dr. Who episode *Blink* pops into my head. I chuckle, shake my head, and take another sip of wine.

That's only on television… but that still doesn't explain why all my plastic flamingos are now standing at the bottom of my deck, staring at me. Old ones, new ones, shiny ones, skeleton ones, zombie ones… even the legless one peers at me from the tree.

Today is the Autumnal Equinox, where the day is of equal length as the night. The Sun God is to be mourned, and we grudgingly accept that all things must come to an end. A time to reap what we have sown.

"By the Gods, what have I done?"

Fiona is a "mostly sane" freelance editor, researcher, and do-er of things. Known as The Witch of South Mountain, she lives in a small town in Eastern Ontario, Canada with eight cats and a number of skeletons.

Dear Communist Dog Catcher

Elizabeth Beechwood

Dear Communist Dog Catcher,

I'm ripping up the ticket you left taped to my front door (AC 18-0362). My little dogs are NOT neglected and my backyard is NOT full of crap and they are NOT dangerous. You just want an excuse to kill my babies. Well, this is America, not Russia, and I pay your salary with my taxes so you work for me and I'm not paying you diddly-squat.

I don't know what my ungrateful daughters told you, but I feed those dogs the best food I can afford and take them to the vet when I have the money. But my daughters wouldn't know that since they don't come around here anymore. They are too good now, with their rich husbands and their fancy houses. They look down their noses and show no respect for their mother, so what can I expect? After they moved out, child protective services stopped trying to catch me doing something wrong. But now I guess I have the Communist Dog Catcher spying on me. Don't you have some real animal abusers to arrest?

And if it wasn't my daughters who made these FALSE allegations, I bet it was the dad of that boy in Walmart last week. First off, Havoc didn't bite anyone. He's a service dog who provides me with emotional support. He has a vest that says SERVICE DOG on it, so it's official. That kid was running wild in lingerie — my baby was on a leash and minding his own business. I don't know how that kid ended up bleeding all over the place but it was not from a dog bite. I want to see the security video of the incident. Do you know that the dad and three other people ganged up on me right there in the store and said they saw Havoc grab that boy's arm? Lies! I won't let you kill my baby just because someone accused him without ANY PROOF. People like to blame pit bulls for everything but they ARE NOT VICIOUS animals. I suggest you do some research on the breed. Peanut, my Chihuahua, is really the one you should be careful of — she'll take your finger off in a minute if she gets the chance. That's why I always leave her at home. Would a bad dog owner do that? No!

Your ticket also says that my precious fur babies are not licensed. THAT IS A LIE. All four of them were licensed by my son before he left for Afghanistan. Call Camp Pendleton and check. My son took care of his responsibilities. He never gave me any grief, he sent me money every month, and he left his four dogs with me when he shipped out. It's hard to pick up all their crap every day because of my walker but I clean up as much as I can. I take good care of those babies no matter what the neighbors say.

I'm surprised your ticket didn't mention the neighbors complaining about my babies 'eating the fence' as they like to call it. They're against me because my yard backs up to their big richy-rich house. It's not my fault that my dogs jump on the fence — it's their yappy little dog's fault. Havoc, Satan, and Rebel love puppies and kittens and they get overly excited when they see that Yorkie on the other side of the fence. The neighbors' allegation that my babies shove their heads through the holes in the wood fence and try to eat their dog is absolutely crazy. Pitbull heads are huge! Come out and look at it from the neighbor's side — I dare you! — since they are so concerned about their precious little Princess Bunnyfoofoo. Maybe they should replace this flimsy fence they put up with a sturdier one. They have the money.

I came home this afternoon from visiting my son's grave and found your lovely ticket. Did you wait for me to leave before you taped it to my door? Too chicken to confront a disabled old woman face-to-face? You'll never be half the man my son was, my beautiful son who died protecting my American rights. YOUR American rights, too, you ungrateful Commie. I'm ripping up this ticket and I will not let you kill my son's four babies. I will take good care of them just like he took good care of me.

You can go to hell.

Elizabeth Beechwood is your typical Subaru-driving, scarf-knitting, bird-feeding tree hugger who lives on the western fringes of Portland, Oregon.

Redemption

Zack Palm

The pain of death was far less excruciating and timeless than Johnathan had first imagined when he was alive. He had been shot once and stabbed three times while in the line of duty, and those were far more memorable than being shot through the head. Then again, as Johnathan stared down at his bloody corpse as it oozed blood from its pouring head wound, he couldn't recall a more weightless experience. His troubles had transcended, and his worries uplifted to another world.

While Johnathan's lifeless, twitching corpse proved he couldn't serve on the police force anymore, it did hint he maybe had a future career as an interior decorator. His scarlet brains had scattered all over the luxurious apartment carpet of Ricky Tathwell, a well-known second in command to a prominent political figure. One to whom Johnathan owed an immeasurable debt.

He had nearly paid off all the debt, but the turncoat police officer had a change of heart almost a year ago. Johnathan sought out federal authorities, and they had been developing a convincing case against the corrupt figures.

"I was young," Johnathan mused, standing above his corpse as the distinctly high-pitched laugh of the shooter echoed nearby. The dead man looked over at the cackling figure, but the entity's facial features had melted away. As too had all of the colors of the room. To Johnathan, they were all black and white, stripped of their finer characteristics.

Even Johnathan's own body appeared foreign to him as he looked down and observed the clean mess. There were small bits of his orange hair mangled in his dripping brains, though he only knew this because he could remember his hair color. Presently they looked like tiny bits of twine contorted in bunches of goop.

"You things always make a mess," a soft voice replied.

Johnathan turned to stare at the cloaked figure that stood in the corner of the apartment. The silent observer stared straight ahead, hiding all important features underneath its black coat. It whispered again, "You were not a special case." Each word was spoken maliciously at a slow, careful pace. It was as if it had an eternity to think of every correct thing it could say. Johnathan tried remembering where he had heard that voice before, but it was like the wind, and it was unrecognizable. It simply existed.

"I tried to fix it," Johnathan pathetically croaked as he thought about his twenty-three years of service. "They found me when I was young, and we had a child to look after. It was small work. However, then things got bigger and worse."

The cloaked figure tsked under its hood. "And you did try to fix it," it pointed out, almost sympathetically. "But you are defined by how you mend your mistakes, and how many you commit."

"They all pile on top of each other."

"'Fraid so."

Johnathan turned his head to the one who shot him. He was now on the phone with someone, the figure's more defining visage, clothing, and voice had melted away. The person in the chair holding the smoking gun was nothing more than a ghost, his surroundings a poor drawing that required a good editor and a steady hand. He drifted into the background and became nothing.

Tightening his fists in blissful frustration, Johnathan desperately tried to remember his wife. Her joyous laughter turned into a voiceless facade, her soft touch a ghastly breeze, and the words of love and support dripped out of his soul similar to removing venom from an infected wound.

The more Johnathan attempted to remember anything, the more it slipped away. Like too much water pouring into a bowl, and the bowl's base was steadily cracking, threatening to shatter from the amount it was taking on.

Still, Johnathan tried. The strain to keep it all together was unbearable, but the faint voice brought him back. "Are you ready?" the voice asked.

Looking over, Johnathan saw the hooded shadow raising one cloaked side up to gesture behind him. Over his shoulder, Johnathan recognized it as the door he used to enter the lavish apartment. Now, everything shaded in dull greys and appeared clouded. The entrance's color and welcoming warmth were all that was left.

"Once more," Johnathan requested, and he looked down at his faceless corpse. Much like the one who had shot him, his body had faded into the background. The blood had seeped into the floor, coated his back, and made a mess of the wall behind him. Even though he knew it was his, he would have said he never knew the person lying in front of him. His corpse had become another stranger.

Taking an unnecessary deep breath, Johnathan turned his back on the corpse and made his first steps toward the new exit.

There was a soft glow to the doorway's outside, piercing through the drab shading. It made the walk over not feel as bad. Johnathan stopped and turned towards the silent observer. A question burned at his skull, hotter than the bullet had been. "Was everything worth it? Trying to do good, even though I failed to finish?"

The hooded viewer almost looked taken aback. However, Johnathan knew when you'd done a job long enough; nothing surprises you. "You don't ask the ship captain if it was worthwhile."

96

Before Johnathan stepped forward and accepted it as the final answer, the hooded bystander tsked under its cloak again. "Was it worth it to you?" it asked, still as breathless as a calm wind sweeping through a misty forest.

Johnathan felt his mind nearly shattering as he tried to hold onto too much water, despite the ruptures and cracks in his bowl. The base of it all broke, pouring water everywhere, except what he clung to in his palms.

Giving the hooded figure a nod, Johnathan confidently said, "Yes," and stepped forward.

Zack Palm is a part-time freelance writer and part-time bank teller. He spends his free time learning how to code, swimming, cooking, and trying not to listen to too much heavy metal.

Take My Breath Away

Rosie Bueford

My entire body was warm except for the place where his hand gripped my neck. That's why I hated him, not because his eyes glistened with a disgusting jeer that shouted, *I have the power to take your breath away*, but because his fingers were so cold they forced my skin to recognize his presence. I had no choice. He had my attention, front and center. I knew why he was there. He was there because I let him be. It was crippling to be reminded of the vulnerability I chose, like an addict recounting the series of bad choices leading up to the final fix that left them lurching and jerking on the floor, alone. One-hit, *so good*. Two-hit, *not enough.* I wanted more, no matter the cost.

I feel like my strength could, in a moment of adrenalined defense, be a good match for his — enough for an escape anyway. *I'm scrappy; he's clumsy.* Instead, something has me stuck. Right. Here. It's not even really him forcing me to obey his power in command, it's me. I am fighting for something by staying. *What the hell is it?* You'd think my life would be first on my list to protect, but every time my muscles twitch in sheer instinct to wrench myself free of his claw, something deeper says — *wait.* Just thinking of the disagreement between evolutionary intuition and my ridiculously romanticized brain curdles my stomach. No right-minded human would understand why — in the moment that reasonable life skills should be taking over and the thought of each breath being the countdown to my last running rapidly through my head and lungs — I would be choosing to wait it out.

As I sit clenched in his snatch, I hate and love him equally. Hating him makes me love him — I'm in a sick cycle. Loving him... *well, I'm a self-deprecating idiot.* The hate can be easily explained. The creature before me is enthralled with the fact that his physical grip means very little. He knows his physical restraints are not his main weapon against me. Rather, this sick freak has gotten such a thrill from draining my life through invading my emotional cage and gutting it of its contents. He's been like a sly fox in a chicken coop ever since I left the door open. This game he is playing could ruin me beyond death and his glassy, gleeful eyes confirm he planned it this way.

So, what of my love for him? Maybe love is too strong a word. Maybe my own narcissism led me here. All I've ever wanted was to be powerful enough to be beautiful to him. I opened the door thinking I was catching something rare, something I could be both in control of and vulnerable to. I despise his own confidence. He damn well knows I find him intriguing. *Fascinating, really. Addictive, more accurately.* His arrogance slays my pride with one smooth move and with little to no effort he's got full access and complete self-fulfillment to my shattered, emotionally shredded self. His true enjoyment is not in the fact that he can rule over me and completely overpower my frantic, momentary attempts to defend my body; it's in the fact that he doesn't have to do those things. He knows all too well I am still here by choice and that he holds something more sacred to my life than my jugular.

I take a breath hoping my lungs will be satisfied with how little they are allowed for just a few minutes more. I realize this man's clasp is not so much a choke as just a compression to hold me from fleeing. It is still difficult to breathe and fairly impossible to move without a fight but there's a softness in his icy fingers. *Do I sense restraint? A glint of affection?* The potential fondness freezes my universe. A pause of hope pumps my blood faster, past his fat fingered restrictions to my heart, my brain. *Fuck, he's good.* That's why I'm still here. He has shown the tiniest hint of interest in my essence. I hoped and he lunged.

I need to remember... All I've ever been to this player of the game is a pawn he is not willing to lose to strategy. I'm not the queen of his board. I'm not enough to be. This game I thought I cleverly crafted, he premeditated far before me. I am not enough, but I have a place. Just not a place of power, like I'm used to. I want to stay in this disposition long enough to fight it out till the moment — if ever — that he will find me breath-taking-amazing. *Give it more time, he will see your beauty.*

I.   Give.   Up.

In retrospect, if it even matters now, I may need to admit my pride exaggerated the attempts he made on my life. He walked away from me, relieving me of his grossly cold hands as if he became bored with the struggle. Maybe he noticed I gave up; maybe my fight was the only thing that kept him holding on to me. Maybe, like me, he's addicted to that sort of thing.

I am still left wondering why I wasn't beautiful enough even after I gave him everything — right to my very last breath.

Rosie is a wife, mother and social work student. Writing is her rejuvenating escape from everyday life chaos. Rosie has another short story published in Strongly Worded Women.

Rain

Christine Hanolsy

I remember the days before the burning of Verdure, before the great starships went away. Those last hours lined up like buckets, ready to catch whatever fell in. Just dribbles at first, rumors and best guesses, barely enough to dampen the soles of our boots. I dipped my cup in pail after pail. I filled my head with names and my mouth with the taste of ash, until the buckets overflowed and nobody saw it but me.

Historians already argue over the circumstances of the past. There were signs, some say, that a slow, deliberate withdrawal from Loess was already underway. The silences between transmissions had grown longer. When messages arrived, they were conciliatory but cryptic. The New Blood ships came less frequently. It was just a matter of time, some historians posit, before the ships stopped coming at all.

Others believe it was the manifestation of generations of accumulated resentment and rage. There had been insurrections before, after all. Not all of Loess' inhabitants had settled here willingly. Even those who loved the harsh, brilliant beauty of these striated dunes and layered cliffs chafed under the rule of the Council-appointed leadership. Especially those, perhaps. But some saw the burning of Verdure's spaceport as the final, unpredictably violent release of a pressure valve, and now there is nowhere left for the ships to land.

Then there are the politicians. They argue over the consequences for the future. A world in turmoil. Communications primitive and sporadic at best. The Planetary Council disbanded or fled, the Governor deposed and each settlement left to fend for itself. Some clamor for a return to a single world government, others for the dispersion of power. Some envision a new status as equal players on the galactic stage. A minority insists on the status quo: isolation from the larger galactic community.

Ever since the starships abandoned us, red-orange plumes of smoke and fire scoring the sky and mirroring the conflagration below — ever since then, people have been talking about how to call them back. The question, of course, is not just of how and when, but of whether and why. My desires are not so far-reaching. My concerns are personal.

They will say I caused this, that the city burns because of me and in a way, this is true. It was my research they came to steal. It was my hand that set the flame. But the sky was already raining metal and acid before I made my choice — stinging drops that etched the sands while we clung to fences, watching the ships leave.

From my vantage high over Verdure, the Green City is almost beautiful. Smoke wreathes the hanging gardens, the silent fountains where the water itself burns like grass on this grassless world, igniting stone and steel and leaving trails of blue-green luminescence where canals once flowed. Even here on the driest of worlds, our language is water-laden, dripping with half-remembered longings. We sail over dusty seas. We measure our worth in pearls of salt. We anchor our airships beside rivers of stone that cascade down from craggy buttes like fabled waterfalls.

I can hear footsteps on the stair below. I wonder if my children are safe. I wonder if my pursuers will tell me, if I ask, before they take me away. The shuffling of their feet reminds me of rain.

Christine Hanolsy is a science fiction and fantasy author who simply cannot resist a love story. Her published works include short stories and essays; she also serves on the editorial staff of the online writing community YeahWrite (yeahwrite.me).

HerStory

Jean Harkin

I'm an old girl born in 1884. Can you believe it! I'm still here in 2019, with my breakable face and strawberry-blond wig. My name is Aline (pronounced Al-lean.) Yes, an old-fashioned name for an old-fashioned girl.

My original and truest mother was Florence. We lived in a three-story Victorian home in Louisville, Kentucky. Her father, just nineteen years out of the Civil War, never spoke of it around Florence. But sometimes when she left me alone in Pa's library, I heard him muttering about *Stonewall* and *foot soldiers,* and *Manassas.*

Florence was a vivacious brown-eyed girl who laughed easily. We bounced around with her rascally dog, her fancy toys, and she dressed me in stylish clothes. Those were the good days!

As I grew older, I spent more time alone in Pa's library or in the parlor looking pretty for Florence's mother's friends. Just after my sixth birthday, I was seated on my usual velvet-upholstered chair in Pa's library when he walked in with a grizzled old man I later heard was called Old Cash.

Pa and Old Cash talked serious awhile about people I'd heard of — Robert E. Lee, presidents Lincoln and Grant. Pa gave the elderly gentleman a compliment about the purchase of Alaska territory for the United States. Old Cash nodded. "Yes, I believe my influence with the tsar helped some."

Pa laughed heartily. "You are much too humble."

The visit ended. When the two walked past me, Old Cash stopped and stared. "She's beautiful!" he proclaimed. Pa nodded. "I'd love to take her home for my new wife, Dora."

Pa looked puzzled. The old man continued, "Truly. She's the prettiest doll I've seen, and she'd be the queen bee in my Dora's collection."

Pa stroked his beard. "You'd take her?"

"I'd be honored."

"Well, Florence is growing up now; I reckon —"

"Your daughter Florence? I'd be much obliged, and I could give her something precious in exchange — a little trophy I'd brought along to show you, but now it could be a gift to Florence."

Pa's eyes lit up. Old Cash reached into his trousers pocket and extracted a little burgundy leather box. He opened it to display a large square-cut amethyst ring inscribed with the crest of Tsar Alexander II. Pa emitted a surprised "Ah!"

Old Cash beamed. "A gift from the tsar when I was ambassador to Russia. I would like Florence to have this in exchange for the doll."

Suddenly, I was swept up by Pa and given to Old Cash, his coat sleeves reeking of sweet pipe tobacco. Florence and I had no chance to say goodbye, as I was soon in a carriage with Old Cash. The driver greeted us. "Home, Mr. Clay?" We were off to the rhythm of clomping hoof beats, on our way to Richmond, Kentucky and my new mother.

As predicted, I became Dora's favorite. She was about Florence's age but had fewer outside interests and spent more time with me. She liked showing me off to her giggly girl friends. Old Cash wasn't home much. I later learned his real name was Cassius M. Clay, a busy man with lots of political and business friends.

Two years with Dora came to a sudden halt when Old Cash divorced her. She left the Richmond estate with her possessions — except for me. Old Cash decided to return me to Florence. Happy day! But I didn't show my emotions.

The return journey to Louisville seemed like forever. I couldn't wait to see Florence again. When we arrived at my familiar old home, Pa and his wife greeted us at the front door and ushered us into the parlor. Oh — the familiar velvety chairs, lace curtains, and the rainbows in the glass chandelier. The scent of furniture polish on the oak tables — home! Old Cash sat on the sofa and settled me beside him. Pa and his wife stood, waiting for Florence to join us.

She entered the parlor. What joy! I couldn't wait for her to sweep over and embrace me. But she just stared at me, rather coldly I thought. Her face pale, she looked solemnly at Old Cash and curtsied an acknowledgment. As she turned to face Pa and her mother, she looked like a prisoner going to the gallows.

"Florence, Mr. Clay is returning your doll," said Pa.

"Thank you, sir," she whispered. Could he even hear her?

"And what about the ring, Young Lady?" Pa said.

Florence wrung her hands and looked like she would faint. I wanted to rush over to comfort her.

Old Cash spoke. "No, no. Never mind the ring. It was a gift to this beautiful young girl who so unselfishly gave up her pretty doll. No. Florence is to keep the ring."

Florence relaxed her shoulders and seemed to revive. Then she burst into tears. "Oh thank you, Mr. Clay." She dashed over to us on the sofa and extended one dainty hand to Old Cash, who clasped it gently and smiled. Then she picked me up and hugged me tight as she twirled us around with happiness. We were together at last!

Florence and I fled the parlor and scurried off to the garden. Outdoors, Florence seated me on a stone bench and said, "I can't believe you're back!" She hugged me again.

That night, snuggling with me in bed, Florence shared a dark secret. "Don't ever tell!" she cautioned. Of course, I wouldn't. She spoke in a whisper so no one else could hear. "Dear Aline, I love you so much. I cried and cried when Pa gave you to Mr. Clay. And I was mad too. So mad that I gave the ring away to a servant's daughter. They left soon after, to where — I don't know. That ring is long gone!"

Through the years I've had new mothers — Florence's descendants. And until now, I have not revealed what happened to the tsar's ring.

Jean Harkin is the author of Night in Alcatraz and Other Uncanny Tales, an eclectic collection of short stories. She has also contributed to various books published by The Writers' Mill group of Beaverton, Oregon.

Dressed to Kill

Mira Lamb

She liked the boots best. The coat was nice, a charcoal gray tapered at her waist, flaring around her knees as she walked. Her gloves, pink leather, with two gold buttons at the inner wrist, pleased her in their functional, supple clasp of her hands. But the boots had inspired the entire outfit, were the reason, really, why she'd come to this small coastal town on a rainy day in February.

They were coral to match her gloves, and the small pink slash of her coat's breast pocket. Rubber, like a child's rainboots, but tapered about the curve of her ankle, the shape of her calf, peeking cheekily beneath her knee-length skirt. She admired their reflection in the windows as she passed the salt-water taffy shop, the combination kite store and ice-cream parlor, and came abreast *Debbie's Designer Boutique*.

A window display caught her eye and she ducked inside, emerging a few minutes later with a fuchsia scarf and a flat woolen hat. She examined herself in the window's reflection, adjusting the knot of the scarf at her throat, the angle of the cap against her sleek blonde hair. Satisfied, she abandoned her reflection for the used bookshop next door.

A bell tinkled as she entered. The shop's close, musty warmth enfolded her. Dust motes played in the light from the window, dancing over a display of bestsellers ten years out of date. Heavy wooden bookcases loomed against the walls and blocked in the narrow aisles.

She ignored the travel guides lining the wall to her left and bypassed Home and Garden, browsed idly through the Mystery aisle (Agatha Christie, Patricia Highsmith, Mary Higgins Clark) and landed at a long table laden with biographies at the far end of the store. An old man, the shop owner she supposed, leaned on a counter next to the cash register at one side, a magazine spread out before him and a stack of unpriced books at his elbow. A clock ticked on the wall behind him. There was another door here, with another bell hung above it: the door through which she'd entered was hidden from view.

She made a circuit of the table, trailing her gloved fingers over the covers: Seabiscuit, George Washington, Sitting Bull.

"This is a lovely shop," she said.

The old man didn't look up from his magazine.

"I've always thought it must be so nice, having a little used bookshop like this. A quiet place where you can sit and think, and say hello to the customers who come in. Not many folks on a day like today, I suppose."

The owner grunted. His bald head protruded on a long neck from his flannel shirt, like a turtle from its shell.

"You could help them find a book they want or recommend something they haven't read. Host a book group on Thursday nights. Bring in local authors to read."

She stopped by the frosted glass door. A wilting philodendron hung limp in its pallid light. The man finally dragged his gaze up from his magazine. "Can I help you find something, miss?"

She considered, tapping her fingers against her thigh. "No," she said. "I think I've found it."

She turned the deadbolt on the door, snapping the lock into place.

The owner blinked rheumy blue eyes at her.

She snatched the heavy Seabiscuit biography from the table and took two swift strides, winding it back behind her shoulder, and snapped forward, slamming the hardcover full into his face. He cried out, staggering back, his hands to his nose. She rounded the counter, knocking the stack of unpriced books to the floor, and kicked the side of his knee.

He fell, hands still clutched to his face, blood leaking between his fingers and his leg bent bizarrely to one side. A high-pitched whine emitted from his open mouth. She dropped the book and yanked her scarf over her head, sending her cap flying. She pressed her boot against his shoulder, rolling him onto his back. She bent down and looped the scarf around his skinny neck, anchored one end with her boot, and pulled the other.

The whining stopped. His body bucked once, twice, his bloody fingers leaving his nose to claw the smooth rubber of her boot. His good leg kicked, scattering another pile of magazines behind the counter. His face went pink beneath its mask of blood, as pink as her scarf, pinker, purple. The veins in his temples bulged as his mouth groped soundlessly for air.

She twisted the scarf, grasped it with both hands. The wool stretched tight, a narrow pink band disappearing into the reptilian folds of his neck. She looked up at the counter, the magazine still open to a glossy spread of motorcycles, the philodendron dying in the winter sunlight.

She waited while the clock ticked away one minute, two, three. His hands dropped away against the floor, like starfish fallen from their rocks. His eyes bulged upward, bloodshot and sightless. She let the scarf go, the stretched out fabric pooling over his chest and groin.

She straightened and shook out her hands. Her hat lay on the table, half covering Lincoln and his team of rivals. She went around the counter to get it, careful not to tread on the tumbled pile of unpriced books.

A bell tinkled from the far side of the shop. She moved quickly back behind the counter, adjusting the cap on her head, stepping over the former owner's outstretched arm.

"Hello?" a voice called.

"Up here," she answered, and smiled at the middle-aged woman and her daughter as they emerged from the stacks. "Can I help you?"

"I hope so," the lady said. "We're looking for something for my daughter. She loves horses, you know, and she's read all the books she can about them. Misty of Chincoteague, Black Beauty, you name it."

"The Black Stallion's my favorite," the girl put in.

"Is that so?" She glanced at the hardcover fallen just out of reach of the dead man's hand, its pages bent. "I think I have something for you."

Mira Lamb is the author of numerous short stories and the novel Rena's Game, available on Amazon and wherever books are sold.

Hush: A Homage to Poe

Debby Dodds

Perhaps the Raven visited others...

She craved respite. The house at the end of Pluto street butted up against swampy woods, a wilderness preserve. It'd been vacant for a year. A tragedy occurred that dissuaded any buyers. A kidnapping. Small town, people talked.

She'd kept a key, though.

The house reeked of mold and sweet rot. But it had no rustling silken satin curtains, no rapping or tapping, and, most importantly, no raven with "parrot aspirations." There was a "For Sale" sign but she doubted there'd be a showing today, the anniversary of the worst crime the tiny town had ever seen. The accused man, no longer waiting for his trial, was locked up in a state hospital after a rambling confession that he'd kidnapped and killed the baby because a Big Mac told him to.

She poured herself tea. She'd brought a thermos, pillow and sleeping bag. Just a few hours of peace. That's all she needed. Though if the demon-thing didn't find her, she might stay longer. She looked at the corner where his crib had once been.

When her son was a baby, sleep deprivation worked on her like a deep-sea fishing trip with choppy waves; the nausea was unbearable. Her IQ seemed to be dropping and she couldn't rid herself of obsessive thoughts about the story, *Flowers for Algernon*. It nagged at her: would she suffer more knowing what she lost, than if she'd never had it at all?

Her exhaustion now surpassed what she'd suffered through back then.

But maybe that ebony feathered monstrosity would nevermore bother her here.

If it could only be trained to say more than that one word. She'd repeated, "Polly want a cracker?" offering poison pellets on a Trisket. The abhorrent bird abstained.

The first time the loathsome black fiend visited her, it came in through her apartment window. She lived sparsely on the money her neighbors had raised in pity for her tragic loss, her pit of sorrow. A Go Fund Me worth $60, 651. She could live for quite a while on that money.

More recently, the foul fowl came in without going through the door or the window. It seemed to know her apartment better than she did. Once it came out of a coat closet she rarely used. Another time, it was sitting on a bookshelf. It seemed to come and go at will through some secret passage. How did it know so much?

She tried tactics honed in her childhood from the copycat game her brother used to play. He'd repeat whatever she said to annoy her as small boys always seemed to do.

After making her brother say "I'm stupid" or "My butt stinks," because he echoed her every statement, she'd say "I promise to stop copying you or I'll give you ten dollars." She could still envision his face crumpling, an impossible choice. He'd either have to stop or she'd force him to give her his money.

She attempted to play a version of the copycat game with the grotesque bird.

"Hey crow, are you going to talk?" When it replied "Nevermore," she cackled, "Okay! A promise is a promise!" but it'd kept going even though the degenerate creature had pledged otherwise.

She recorded it on her cell, played it back, but its fiery eyes still burned impassively.

Even though she said "Are you going to keep bugging me?" and "How about you go on living?" and it responded "Nevermore" to both, the raven didn't honor its word. The only word it had. Damn diseased liar.

She hated liars, sighers and criers.

She liked fires. But couldn't get close enough to burn the bastard. Wretched thing sought to drive her mad.

Finally, options exhausted, she tried to smother it just as she had her baby boy after beseeching him to be quiet for days and days.

While suffocation was wildly successful with her son, whose bones were somewhere out in the swamp, the raven proved harder to catch and subdue.

When Plan A fails, go to Plan B. A few hours of shut-eye in this empty house would have to suffice. She was no fool, she knew that ugly feathered-rat would be back. But if it was trying to make her feel guilty, her old house would be the last place it looked. Most people don't really like to return to the scene of the crime. Only those power-obsessed murders who enjoyed reliving the incident revisited the scene, but obviously she wasn't one of them as this was the first time she came back. She imagined it'd be torture for other parents to be in the place that they felt their baby stop moving under a pillow. But she was betting the hideously intolerable bird wouldn't guess that she was impervious to any location-stimulated guilt. She had no regrets. She hadn't set up the town's outcast to take the fall but she didn't feel bad about that either. She wasn't trying to forget or run from her sin. She didn't hate the bird because it evoked shame or remorse.

She hated it because it was just too damn noisy. Just like that baby that never let her sleep.

She closed her eyes, listening to the wind. The raven couldn't have her soul. Silly bird.

She'd already sacrificed it for silence.

Debby Dodds is the author of the novel Amish Guys Don't Call which was on the list BEST YA OF 2017 by Powell's Books and made an Amazon Top 100 in a YA category. She's also had short pieces in over 20 anthologies.

Albert and Lenny

E.C. Lawrence

Albert didn't have the best of luck getting along with others. Lenny was the only guy Albert seemed to tolerate. Maybe it was because they both had Vietnam in common.

Albert arrived at Tan Son Nhut airfield in '67 for his first of three tours. He left Southeast Asia on a stretcher and for good in 1970, the year Lenny started his first and only tour in Nam.

Albert's left arm was useless. It hung to his side. He would usually pocket his left hand in his coat to keep it from swinging or looking like he had a useless arm. On the streets in Seattle you really don't want to show vulnerability.

Albert tried to fit in with a 'normal' life in the Real World right after he was released from the hospital. He fell for the nurse who was in charge of his physical therapy at the VA. They married in '72. Their divorce was finalized in '78. He left behind his daughter and all his medals. He had spent three months in Ada County jail the year before the divorce for hitting his wife and beating her boyfriend with a drapery rod. It was now 2017 and Albert was still having issues. The VA diagnosed him with PTSD. Albert diagnosed himself as no longer a part of society or the human race, and he was fine with that.

Lenny, even after all these years, was determined to rejoin the human race just as soon as he could whip a couple of crutches he acquired such as alcohol and heroine.

Albert tolerated Lenny, but he wished the brother would shut the fuck up. Lenny talked too much.

"Sarge says to me, 'they just keep comin' like ants. We've got to find the goddamn ant hill they're crawlin' out of.' Like that was possible. We're in the goddamn jungle. You could hear 'em; you just couldn't see 'em, Alby."

"Lenny, I'm only going to say this one more time — shut the fuck up."

"Excuse me." Albert and Lenny looked out from under the shared blue tarpaulin. A slender woman with graying hair and a straw hat adorned with what looked like a cockade was bending down looking back at them. She had snuck up on the two vets unnoticed. "Are you two hungry?"

"Always," said Lenny.

"It's no concern of yours," Albert remarked under his breath, but loud enough for the intruder to hear.

"Hey, I'm not here to get in your business. I just wanted you to know my farmer's market booth is right over there." She pointed at the white canopy with the sign *A Good Day's Harvest Farms*. "I've got more than enough to sell so, if you feel like it, head on over and I'll give you a bag with pears, apples, carrots and nectarines if you want. If anybody tries to stop you, you tell them you're friends with Michaele. That's me." The lady rose up from her crouch. She looked around the small community of homeless then took a deep breath of Puget Sound air. "I also have a first aid kit. It looks like that toe is infected." She pointed at Lenny's socked right foot where his big toe was exposed.

"It ain't nothin', just a poke by some nail or screw. I'm just waiting for the swelling to go down so I can put my shoe back on."

"Yeah, sure." Michaele extended her hand to Lenny. "Come on, let's get you to my booth. That toe will turn green and you will lose your foot if you don't get it cleaned up now."

Albert sneered. "Just who do you think you are, lady?"

"I'll tell you what you told me," she said with a sneer that equaled Albert's. "It's no concern of yours.'" Lenny stood up and put his arm around the woman. "Grab your shoe and take it with you." Both walked away leaving Albert inside the makeshift tent.

That evening Lenny didn't return and it was apparent the lady had something   to   do   with   it. Albert was once again separated from the rest of the human race... at least for the night. "I'm glad that mouthy turd is gone. Now I can sleep without listening to him revisit the same old nightmare night after night." Albert leaned back against the cardboard wall. "Hell, this place is startin' to smell better already."

E.C., Lawrence has several short stories published including his book "It's Nobody's Fault?" available at Amazon.com. He was born in Idaho and currently lives in Central Oregon.

Deep Blue

Kylie Cokeley

He pulled up in his Jeep right before the sun was about to set. Excitement gave me the jitters, a school of fish swimming through my belly, moving swiftly through my reefs and maneuvering my currents, their tails tickling my insides. I've taken many men, but none had made me feel this way before. I invited him in with a wave. He took a deep breath, filling his lungs with my scent. As he got closer goosebumps grew on his skin. The air was cool, but I hoped that I was the culprit of his prickling skin. He approached me confidently and swiftly, but hesitated once he was within reach. His muscles were large, and his skin was tanned from the sun. And don't even get me started on his deep, blue eyes. I lusted for that blue, a blue like none I'd ever seen before. I was green with envy.

Our relationship was casual, though I longed for more. Neither of us spoke. It was purely physical. He used his whole body to move through me. I waited and yearned for him all day until he finally turned up. He only came to visit me every once in a while, days going by before I would see him again next. It had been awhile since our last meeting. My heart was beginning to break until he showed up that night.

He reached out, dipping his toes in and testing my waters, beginning slowly. As he made his way inside of me, his heart raced. I could feel his heartbeat against me. Our bodies glided gracefully over one another. He held his breath as he dove deeper. The sunset was beautiful and wide above us. The deep purples and bright pink danced in the orange clouds while we danced together. It started gentle and got more intense the longer we were together. Both of us pulling and pushing under the moon.

I didn't want it to end. I pulled him deeper, and he struggled to keep up. I couldn't let him leave me again. There was no telling when he would come back to me, of if he would. How would I go on without him? He begged for me to let go, but my waves grew stronger. The pressure was intense. His blue eyes grew wide and bulged. He needed to stay with me. I couldn't lose that blue. His breaths became further and further apart until he finally sunk down to my depths, where he could never leave me.

Several days later, emergency vehicles came looking for him. The coast guard searched my shores, but they could never take him from me now. A body that's drowned is never found at the bottom of the ocean.

Kylie Cokeley was also featured in Flash! A Celebration of Short Fiction.

The Last Dance

Jenny Cokeley

Jay was a young naval officer during World War II with a cocky attitude and a quick wit — always looking for a good time, a good laugh, and a stiff drink. He sat next to a shy woman at the bar and asked her to dance. Anna Marie had not been tempted by Jay's charming remarks and unsolicited flattery. She had no doubt he was on leave for the night looking for someone to ease the tension that months on a ship brought. He was no stranger to the sensuous curves of the female body. In fact, he had been with many women, but only for the night and only after spirits flavored his kisses with gin. With each word he spoke, Anna Marie drew in the intoxicating smell of liquor and tobacco. It was almost midnight when she agreed to dance with him.

Jay drew her slender body tight against his. Her chestnut hair fell in waves down her back; her bee-stung lips tempted him. Her hand disappeared in his calloused hand — the other rested on the small of her back. He felt the warmth of her breath against his neck and smelled the sweet fragrance of rose petals in her hair. He was not searching for love, just a dance. Jay was not a spiritual man, but he prayed for the first time in his life this dance would never end.

The sound of the band faded away and seven decades vanished in an instant. Jay sat in the corner of the dark room, hidden by the privacy curtain that became the boundary of Anna Marie's world in the nursing home — a world he could not be a part of, only visit. She was his entire world and he could not imagine it without her. They had watched each other's transformation as the years wore on — her lovely hair turned to silver wisps and deep grooves encircled her tempting lips; the skin on her tiny hands turned to crumpled tissue paper. Jay's smooth skin surrendered to a furrowed chin and cheeks; his waistline bulged; and his joints stiffened and ached.

He watched helplessly as Anna Marie was seduced by dementia — an adulterous thief of memories and dignity. Instead of stealing passionate kisses and carnal pleasure, this lover slowly erased her mind and stranded her in a confusing and terrifying world. She no longer recognized the words that were spoken to her or the loved ones that surrounded her. She became imprisoned behind the bars of a broken mind.

The handsome sailor that had asked her to dance so many years ago — the dedicated husband she had vowed to love for a lifetime; the loving father of their two sons; the friend she shared cocktails with after dinner — had become a stranger that held her hand and sang softly in her ear day after day. She had become a stranger to Jay, as well. He lost the love of his life years before after she was devoured by this pale, fragile woman who lived behind the privacy curtain. He would look deep within her pallid eyes that once were spell-binding and imagined seeing his love screaming to break free from her sadistic lover. Jay closed his eyes and imagined Anna Marie caress his aged face in her delicate hands and kiss him gently before whispering, "I love you, my darling Jay." He opened his eyes to find a stranger. He wiped his tears, grabbed his coat, and returned to the shelter of Mike's Tavern where he found comfort in a drink and a joke. Although he laughed and shared stories of misguided adventure with his friends at the bar, he could not escape the loneliness and heartache that overcame him each night. He could not deny he was alone — an old man who had once been loved so passionately by an amazing woman.

The night death freed Anna Marie, Jay was filled with sorrow and relief. Guilt tried to punish him for praying for her death, but he fought it with all his strength. He kissed Anna Marie's lifeless lips and dripped tears on her peaceful face. As he reached the door to leave, he turned to see his beloved blow him a tender kiss and whisper goodnight. He smiled and replied, "Thanks for the dance, my sweet Anna Maire."

Jenny lives in Salem, Oregon with the love of her life doing what she loves — writing stories about all of life's struggles and celebrations. You can find Jenny's short stories on The Fictional Café and in the anthologies Baby Shoes and Flash!

Danny Boy

Nancy Townsley

"This won't last long," Danny says, peering up at the rumbling sky through his one good eye. His words come and go as effortlessly as the weather patterns over Kaua'i, the tropical island to which he fled more than a decade ago.

He's much older now than he was during the Summer of Love, when he was only a punk kid who tore open a letter telling him he'd been drafted into the army for the purpose of warfare in Vietnam. Something about stopping the march of communism through Indochina. He didn't want to go, but his parents were splitting up and that was shitty, so why not? All in the same head-spinning six months, he graduated from boot camp, boarded a transport plane and disembarked into the unknown, a foul foreign place with searing heat, giant bugs, booby traps, machetes, drugs, and despair — things that filled his days and nights with endless fear. Danny lost his virginity a week before he lost his left leg to a rocket-propelled grenade, fourteen days before he was supposed to return home to Rochester all those tangled years ago.

Danny did not die. He surrendered to the tide: *In and out, in and out, in and out.*

His salt-and-pepper hair is a shaggy mess framing a tanned, craggy face and he wears dark sports glasses that hide his glass eye, the one on the right, the one that was hit by shrapnel. He's wearing a hemp T-shirt, cotton shorts with cargo pockets on the sides and Birkenstock sandals, the easy wardrobe of a local. A racing wheelchair bears his weight, less than in 'Nam, more than after. When his leg stump slides off one side of the vinyl seat he nonchalantly hoists it back into position. Then he smiles the wry smile of someone who has been seared by life but survived, in pieces, nonetheless. His is a beguilingly trusty, crusty grin.

The two of us and another refugee from the sudden island shower watch the rain fall in sheets from the edge of a green corrugated metal roof. Hunkered underneath, we wait, impatiently, for the squall to pass. A rooster, a hen and two fuzzy chicks scurry across rivulets in the red dirt path outside our shelter, hopping puddles as they go. A foul odor wafts from the restroom abutting Kealia Beach, but as we stand there dripping and Danny wrings water from his shirt, breathing hard because of the humidity, none of us say anything about it.

"We've got the trades today," Danny observes, stabbing an arthritic finger into the air, explaining that the signature warm breezes will soon push the showers offshore and into the mountains jutting up from the north coast of Hawaii's oldest island. The rest of us are visibly relieved. Danny flashes a broad smile, revealing a mouthful of slightly-too-white dental work and a pink diagonal scar on his right cheekbone, more collateral damage from the bomb that found him on the steaming edge of My Lai. He was in country only forty-five days before he realized the conflict wasn't America's to win, or really to be involved in at all. After that he wanted no part of it. Some of the GIs were raping women and setting fire to village huts with children inside, atrocities that messed with Danny's mind.

Some nights in the jungle he was so frightened he would soil his pants as he crept through brush and swamps alongside his platoon mates, unsure when or where the enemy might strike with a knife or a rifle and that would be the end of him, the sandy-haired boy who had sung in the choir at St. Michael's Church and played clarinet in the East High School pep band. But somehow he was spared. Mostly. Maybe.

Danny was good at numbers, so he worked as an accountant after he left the army. He never married. For years he had recurrent nightmares of faces white and dark and screaming, and once he was awake he had a lot of trouble getting back to sleep. He often felt like he was going insane.

"So I just chucked it all," Danny tells me when I encounter him again on the running path that meanders along the Coconut Coast. "My mental health was not good." He boarded a plane at John F. Kennedy International Airport on a cold day in 1997 and flew to Honolulu, a short hop away from here. He only planned to visit — he needed to "just chill out" and to forget. All the time back in New York had not healed Danny. Maybe the slow-paced life of the sleepy town of Kapa'a would. Government disability checks helped.

Danny has a teenage son with a South Vietnamese woman he met when he returned to face his tormentor-nation one withering July. He calls it his summer of reckoning. Together they strolled beneath the trees in My Lai Peace Park. He placed one arm around her waist and one hand on her belly, swelling with their child, and they talked about their future, but she did not want to come to America, or even these islands, so Danny and his boy live here now and they are a team. The son's name is Maoli, meaning "real" and "true." Danny lives for warm breezes, salt air, the woody melodic tones of his u'kelele, and Maoli.

Every Saturday during soccer season he watches from the sidelines at Kapa'a Beach Park, through the chain link fence, as Maoli flies down the wide-bladed grass field on long lean legs, guiding the ball with remarkable focus and precision, his black hair flowing behind him like flames. Danny smiles. He is sharing his vision with his boy: Kaua'i as refuge, as sanctuary, as their forever home. Danny wears the camouflage of a warrior. Riding on the wind, he is free.

Nancy Townsley lives in a floating home on the Multnomah Channel west of Portland, Oregon, where she writes, runs, and plays ball with her golden retriever. Her work has appeared in Brave On The Page (Forest Avenue Press), Role Reboot, NAILED Magazine, The Riveter Magazine, The Manifest-Station, and Bleed, a literary blog from Jaded Ibis Press. The backdrop for her novel-in-progress is a rural houseboat marina.

Mrs. Bueller Goes Time Traveling

Gregg Townsley

We surged forward.

The machine's movements aren't supposed to be all that noticeable. They are, after all, an add-on — an effect the architects added to let the occupants know that something is happening. You can't step out into the middle of 2213, after all, not while the shift is occurring. Or shouldn't, anyway.

But we moved nonetheless. A grinding, roaring wheeze pushed the time machine into the vortex. We got cold, then hot, then everything went to shit as Personal Belongings Bags — PBBs, in the time travel trade, with every Imagineer allowed just one — hit the main window like snow sliding off a Lake Tahoe metal roof. The pile-up — angry thumps, followed by a sliding slow melt of same-color day packs — stacked themselves onto the time craft's silver metal floor. Blue and gray and green, because the Wisconsin State delegation of Women United wanted them to be that way. The women should have used name tags.

Safety belts tugged, personal protection balloons inflated, and the supposedly "just for the effect" effect — one of a series of sales exaggerations that were made prior to our signing the waivers — literally went out the window, followed by Mrs. Catherine Bueller of Canton, Ohio. Services will be held for Mrs. Bueller — mother of two, grandmother of four, and a level four practitioner, tried and true from the cheese state — as soon as all the pieces can be collected from the warp origination venue.

The machine wasn't supposed to hum, bump, grind or thump. The Timex Ten Thousand wasn't supposed to do anything except put a smile on everyone's face and deposit the first-time travel tourists on the left bank at the Grand Canyon Inn, at the base of the Southwest Territory National Park in the year 2019, one-hundred-and-ninety-four-years ago.

"No big deal," the brochure read.

"A tiny leap," the conductor aped as we boarded, "without the least bit of discomfort, while you're sipping a beer or enjoying a glass of wine." Tell that to Mrs. Bueller, whose personal parts will probably never be found — scattered from the present all the way back to what used to be the U.S. State of Arizona in the 21st century.

The Timex vessel is said to have successfully visited more ports of call than a San Francisco whore in the late 1800s, and without the complications. Though I'm now wondering if it isn't time to find another time travel provider.

Each of the Imagineers were given tickets to a 21st century-style American dinner at the origination station as a consolation prize while repairs are being made, though there's discussion of Timex Travel sending a freshly-painted craft to attempt the shift again, not that all the women are up to it and that paint has to do with anything. These are some perceptive women.

The Wisconsin State delegation was formed just a few weeks ago, from mid-Western political pods that wanted to see a dedicated Wisconsin chapter of Women United. This was to be their first outing, their only previous activities having been the election of a chairperson and the reading of their first meeting's minutes. "A nice meal was enjoyed as well," the secretary said, "at the new Latter-day Saints Museum of American Religion in Appleton, where the LDS temple used to be."

Change is constant, I guess.

Commander Les Flavinoid now tells us the company is upgrading the Wisconsin Imagineers' experience by sending a brand new Timex Mega-Traveler to take everyone — that is, everyone who still wants to go — to the Grand Canyon lodge. It'll take a few moments, he says, to get the device out of New New Jersey, because of storms.

"But it will be here before you can say Han Solo."

"Tonight's free gratis supper," the commander explains, "is mac and cheese with bacon, a 21st century tasty delight with absolutely no nutritional value, but nonetheless."

Gregg Edwards Townsley is a reflective, free-thinking ex-pastor, martial artist, writer and Western Fast Draw enthusiast living on a floating home in Scappoose, Oregon, with his wife, Nancy. He is the author of six Nevada Westerns and more than a half-dozen New Jersey detective stories. His place-based fiction and other work can be found online or at www.greggtownsley.com.

Autumn

Kate Ristau

The Johnsons left two weeks ago. They told everyone they were taking a trip to Denmark, but we all knew. 8.39 interest rate. Lingering hugs. Late night pickup trucks.

They were in over their heads — cutting their losses, taking the foreclosure.

It won't come through for months. Their big, beautiful avant-garde will sit empty, vacant, and uncared for, until the bank plants the sign.

I wonder if they took the fixtures.

"Joan? Where's my sweater?"

You see, Shina has this bathtub. Metal and wood.

I know.

You're thinking, who puts metal and wood in a bathtub? But that's how they were. They never had a single *thing* in their house. They had the idea of a thing.

The idea of a bathtub. The thought of a chair. The shape of a marriage.

That bathtub didn't need to be made of porcelain and steel, so they made it out of stars. You walk into it and into infinity.

"I can't find the razor heads."

He had it designed for her. Back when Triten was making all that money, he gave her whatever she wanted.

"I'm going to miss my plane."

The summer we finally got our floors, they got moon rocks. Cratered and puckering. One Christmas, I asked for a new desk. She asked for a carousel.

"I'll see you Thursday."

He had it made in Sweden. Because that's what they do in Sweden now. They make carousels out of fallen leaves.

Every time she set it in motion, maple leaves floated down, covering the living room.

I can see it now, through the front window. Orange feathering through crystal windows in the middle of June. She left it on, spinning and twirling.

How many leaves until the whole thing dissolves? How much time? Floating, falling, fluttering – all I see now are leaves, swirling through their living room and out their open front door.

Always open. That was Shina. She took the door off the hinges with a cup and a kitchen knife. Mike put it back on, so she left it open. Told me to come over for coffee.

I grab my sweater; my front door swings open. I walk across the lawn, feet sinking into their grass, thick sod. Sun shining, but still the cold.

I take the knob. Close the door behind me. Crush of leaves beneath my feet.

Over the moon rock. Up the stairs.

He never gave me infinity.

But I never asked.

Kate Ristau is a folklorist, an author, and the Executive Director of Willamette Writers. Her essays have appeared in The New York Times *and* The Washington Post*, and she is the author of the middle grade series,* Clockbreakers, *and the young adult series,* Shadow Girl. *You can find her online at* Kateristau.com.

Seems Mean

Paul Frazier

George winked in and looked around. The shelter seemed familiar. The walls were plastic and featureless on two sides, with a transparent insert on a third side and the fourth open to the weather. He was in a city of some sort. He was alone and he squinted from the bright sun. He looked around. There was no shade anywhere on the bench. A bus went by with colors that looked familiar, but didn't stop.

George winked in and looked around. The shelter seemed familiar. He saw there was someone sitting next to him on the shady part of the bench. He peered at her, realized he didn't have his glasses. Damn nuisance not to have them.

"I'm sorry, Ma'am, I don't recognize you without my glasses."

"George, you old fool, it's Ellie. I've told you a million times."

"Ellie, old girl, sorry. I'm a bit absent-minded these days. Where are you headed?"

"I'm going home. I'm sick of the food at that place. I've been sitting here a long time without a bus. I can't see the road very well. What was the number of the last bus you saw? George?"

Two retrievers approached the shelter from behind. "This is the blind side," Bert said. "It's always better to come up on the blind side."

Lawrence said, "I know it's for their own good, but it still seems wrong." Lawrence was new, and young.

Bert snorted. "You kids should have been here before. Some of them are spry. I've spent half the night looking for them. Let alone the guy who fell into a half-dug hole full of water. He was going down for the third time when we found him."

George winked in and looked around the shelter. The shadows were long. He heard voices! He stood up, feeling ice in his veins. They had found him! The woman — what was her name — was asleep sitting up on the bench. She was really old. How long had he been gone?

"Wake up, they've found us!" He pushed the woman's shoulder.

"Who's found who?" she asked querulously.

Lawrence came around the right and Bert the left. The scrum was short. Bert called for the van on his cell phone. "Got George and Ellie. George's gone off to la-la land again. Ellie's not happy with the food."

As they waited, Bert tried to explain again. "We put up a bus shelter where no bus ever stops. The old folks wander off because they want to go home, see the shelter, and sit down to wait for a bus. It's safer for them and easier on us. Their home is gone; they just don't want to remember that."

Lawrence stared off into the distance. "I don't like tricking people, even old people, even for their own good. Seems mean."

Paul Frazier writes fiction informed by his passion for history, technology, and character. He is currently at work on his first novel, Ancient Enemy. *Paul is a member of the Writer's Guild of Texas, and lives in Dallas.*

The Trouble with Broccoli

Michelle C. Ferrer

I learned to cook in self-defense. In my early childhood, Mother labeled me a "fussy eater." A few bites of broiled liver and scorched broccoli choked down with a glass of milk sufficed.

During an annual checkup, my pediatrician advised Mother that I was severely malnourished. Mother tilted her head, surprised. She patiently explained that I was rarely hungry, and regularly ate very little. He cocked an eyebrow and offered to report her to Child Protective Services for neglect.

Lest one think that Mother harbored a secret ambition to be childless, the issue was not indifference for my welfare. Hers was a failure to understand the fundamental relationship between food and stove. She could burn boiling water. Pots and pans uttered audible screams at her approach.

Mother grew up with four sisters. They cooked and baked. She washed the dishes and cleaned the kitchen. Their tools were spatulas and ladles. Hers were floor mops and dust cloths. When Mother swooped, dust and dirt died.

She tackled the case of her recalcitrant daughter who refused to eat with the same zeal. I could leave the table only when my plate was clean. Each morning, Mother rose early to cook me a nutritious breakfast of burned toast and one soft yellow egg yolk swimming in the snot of uncooked egg white. I promptly threw it up. We repeated that ritual seven days a week for a year. Mother switched to oatmeal. The cooking instructions were on the box.

The evening meal was often grey. Potatoes, carrots, peas, chicken, and ham were all the same color, distinguished by the size of the lumps. I learned to eat quickly. When eaten cold, the lumps wouldn't stay down. Salads were green. They appeared with brittle and bitter leafy things topped with an acrid vinegar and oil concoction. By comparison, broiled liver and scorched broccoli were a welcome treat.

I stared at the stove for hours, willing it to reveal its secrets. At age ten, I was tall enough to reach the burners without a step stool. I haunted the library searching out cookbooks, copying recipes, memorizing techniques. After school, the kitchen buzzed as I tested recipes, discarded failures, and devoured successes. During summer breaks, I baked, roasted, pan-seared, and steamed my way to a healthy weight. Sauteed chicken cutlets in wine sauce with mushrooms replaced broiled liver. By age 12, I cooked breakfast for the family and dinner was ready by six o'clock.

When I turned 16, Mother handed me a grocery list, the keys to the family car, and cash to shop. The kitchen was officially mine. Mother assisted. I taught her to assemble a salad, the proper proportion of vinegar and oil, and how to steam broccoli. She cleaned while I cooked. We chatted and laughed together while we worked and caught up the details of the day.

Our kitchen activity settled into a comfortable routine. I cooked and served the meals. Mother washed the dishes and scrubbed the sparkle back into the kitchen.

Dad ate out less often.

With her husband and five dogs, Michelle Ferrer lives in Texas just far enough north of Dallas to breathe fresh air and bask under open sky. She writes short fiction and is currently working on her first western novel, The Yellow Rose of Someday.

Bee Futures

Vaughan Stanger

Having counted his thirtieth bumblebee corpse of the morning, Farmer Giles could no longer deny that the Battle of Sheldon Farm had begun.

He trod the scorched remains into the turf while gazing at the nearest apple tree. By rights, its blossom-laden branches ought to be thick with bees. Sadly, today's inspection of the orchard had revealed none; at least none still alive. At this rate there would be hardly any Braeburns for his pickers to harvest come September. And the same would hold true for his pears, raspberries, tomatoes and courgettes.

Until now Farmer Giles had given little credence to the local rumour mill's mutterings about laser-equipped robo-wasps. But faced with the destruction of his genetically optimised pollinators, he could no longer deny the reality of the situation. Now that GM wheat production had ceased throughout the UK, the bio-Luddites were turning their firepower on the Weald of Kent's fruit and vegetable growers.

Why do we bother?

His inadvertent broadcast over AgriNet brought an instant reply, buzzing deep inside his head.

Because farming's what we do, brother!

As usual, Farmer Jones spoke the truth.

Amen to that!

If the people of this increasingly brown and unpleasant land were to enjoy their usual cornucopia of foodstuffs, farmers like him would have to find a way to win the war.

#

After finishing his day's labour, Farmer Giles liked to relax by watching wartime documentaries beamed directly into his head by the History Channel. From these he understood that determined attack usually overcame stubborn defence.

Still, he had quotas to fulfil, with heavy penalties from Asda if he failed to deliver. So he ordered a new batch of pollinators — this time an artificial variety equipped with laser stings.

#

The bee did not stir when Farmer Giles brushed his toes against it. On this occasion he could discern no signs of scorching. Given the absence of a diagnostic data feed, he concluded that an EM pulse had fried the robot's tiny brain.

Alerted by a motion detector flashing red in his peripheral vision, Farmer Giles strode out of the orchard. As he approached Sheldon Farm's eastern boundary, he discarded his stealth cloak. A gangly, shaven-headed man and a stouter, dark-haired woman, both dressed in camouflage gear, looked up from their mil-spec tablets.

"You'll never stop me farming," he told them.

It was what he did. He knew no other purpose.

The pair gawped at him. Perhaps it was his nakedness that startled them. But why wear clothes when one was sustained by sunlight?

And why grow food for people who didn't deserve it?

The man shrugged. "Your wheat-growing friends in Norfolk said the same thing."

"I can always buy more pollinators."

Now the woman chipped in. "And we'll destroy them, too. We won't give up until you *stop* planting GM crops. You'll run out of money long before we do!"

Which was doubtless true, Farmer Giles mused. Plus the local police had long since given up any pretence of defending his land. Was this a war really worth fighting? Faced with a financially ruinous escalation in insectile hostilities, he nodded his acquiescence.

"Okay then; I'll think about it."

"Well, all right!" The woman looked startled at the ease of her victory.

Farmer Giles turned away from his persecutors.

He would just have to find another way to turn a profit.

#

The truth was unpalatable, but could not be denied.

Growing non-GM fruit and vegetables made no financial sense. Non-GM plants cost too much; the required fertiliser levels were illegal; the yields too low.

Farmer Giles gazed at the meadow daisies, flourishing despite the heat.

I think I'll try flowers.

With continental growers struggling to maintain supplies due to summer droughts, he felt confident he'd identified a profitable new niche.

Farmer Jones snorted his contempt. *Well, I'm switching to biofuel maize. There's profit in that, for sure. Good luck with your blooms, though.*

Good luck to you, too!

Farmer Giles suspected his neighbour would need something a lot stronger than luck to repel the swarms of pests migrating from the Mediterranean, but he decided to keep his counsel.

In any case, he had seeds to order.

#

After depositing two baskets of freshly-cut flowers on a fold-up table, Farmer Giles leaned against Sheldon Farm's main gate and waited for the next group of refugees to arrive. His bee count had reached ten before a 4x4 parked up.

Biofuel supplies remained plentiful, evidently.

Two people got out of the vehicle. A gaunt-faced, dark-haired woman clutched the hand of a whimpering child. Farmer Giles realised he'd seen her before. He guessed that the anti-GM campaigner's partner had deserted her shortly after the supermarkets closed their doors for good.

The woman stared at the flowers before turning despairing eyes on Farmer Giles.

"Haven't you got any food?"

Farmer Giles shook his head while sliding a tulip stem above the boy's left ear.

The woman frowned. "What's *that* for?"

"Something for the journey," he said.

The boy had started munching on the offering even before his mother could drag him away from the baskets. Farmer Giles gave a sorrowful shake of his head. He had hoped people would choose to die wearing flowers in their hair, but that rarely happened.

These days he didn't have the heart to ask for money.

Bee Futures was originally published in Nature volume 497, page 152 (02 May 2013).

Vaughan Stanger trained as an astronomer before working in the defence and aerospace sector for many years. Now a full-time writer, his published fiction is collected in Moondust Memories and Sons of the Earth & Other Stories.

Ding

ML Willard

It's a little piece of plastic, a thin strip of resin coated with chemicals. Quite nondescript, really. It could double as a tongue depressor. Not that I would put *that* in my mouth! Not that I wanted to pull it off the shelf in the first place. Such an innocuous slip of nothing with the power to change a person's world in two short minutes.

The timer on the windowsill is really loud. Why did I pull it out again? It would have been easier to use my phone. I could have set an alarm and then gone to let the dog out. Hung the load of wash that's been sitting since morning. Picked up the mail. I mean...well, I could have used my phone but I didn't. The timer kept in the back of the kitchen cupboard seemed more appropriate. The steady tick as it counts down from 120 is weirdly comforting. As if someone is sitting in the room with me. Waiting as impatiently — fearfully — as I am. Tick: a hand in mine. Tick: two fingers brushing a stray lock of hair off my forehead. Tick: a warm palm patting my back. Tick, tick, tick, tick. It. Will. Be. Fine.

I stand in front of the window with my eyes closed, letting the sunlight bathe my face through the glass. It is warmer, finally. Spring has arrived in defiance of a persistent nip from the north. A month ago this same glass radiated cold. Made me shiver whenever I stepped out of the shower. Now I can almost smell the lilacs starting to bud in the yard below. The thin skin of my eyelids is rived with tiny blood vessels glowing crimson against a cherry backdrop. I focus on those vessels. Try to follow them without moving my pupils, without cracking my eyelids. The heat and the steady ticking lull me. A jagged sigh escapes my pursed lips. The plastic strip is sitting behind me in the shadow of a flower vase. Almost but not quite hidden from view should I choose to turn and look. I don't. I lean on the windowsill and touch my flushed cheeks to the glass. I breathe out and feel the damp condensation expand from my lips. My respirations sync unconsciously with the timer. Inhale, tick. Exhale, tick. Inhale, tick. Exhale, DING!

No! I'm not ready! How can a little piece of plastic dictate my destiny? This isn't right. This isn't fair. This is just...stupid! I was stupid. A little whiskey, a little wine, a little jazz, a little dine. I am smarter than that. Well, at least I thought I was. A little lust and no fuss. Condoms? What are those? What do you mean expired??? No! I'm not ready! But DING!

The breath rattles in my throat. I clutch the sill and shake my head against a dark, dizzying wave of nausea.

DING! It's not the sound everyone says you'll hear. It's anticlimactic. A little like the act itself when your partner rolls over like a bloated corpse and burps. No fireworks or sparklers. No cheers or luxuriant shudders. Just burp and

DING! Followed by a little strip of plastic lying on a shelf. My only companion the cryptic silence of an empty and oddly expectant house. There is no point of waiting any longer. No point in regrets over out of date prophylactics and one too many shots of Black Velvet.

I turn from the window and open my eyes. Cast a quick glance at the timer sitting in silent anticipation on the windowsill. Thanks...I think...for keeping me company. A deep breath and I reach out. Snag the strip from the shadows. Ready, set, DING.

Wife, homemaker, fierce mama bear and determined author. ML Willard writes for enjoyment, personal therapy and to explore the human condition. At this moment she is polishing her skills with short fiction while plugging away on her first novel, "Choices of the Heart".

Temper and Temperance

Paul Cordes

Felip was furious. He hated the old barracks, hated the man who ran it, and hated the mercenaries who bunked in it. More than any of those, he hated waiting. He was the boss of a Ripper war gang. He didn't wait for, he was waited on. He didn't ask, he demanded. He didn't buy, he took. But he couldn't do that here. He needed a favor from the man who had the power to destroy either Felip's gang or the killer they had provoked. So he spent his time pacing, growling, and hoping this would work.

"How long is Jonathan going to make me wait?" Felip snarled at the guard who opened the door. The guard was unmoved. She motioned for Felip to follow her and lead him up a splintered staircase, past a pair of guards wearing newly forged armor, a second pair in chainmail that was obsolete a decade ago, and entered an office that was so far out of fashion it had circled around to antique. Jonathan, the man he had come to see, was sitting on the far side of a desk holding a mug of tea. A second, steaming mug waited in front of an empty chair. Lit candles stood in ancient sconces mounted on the walls. Felip was shocked to see that it was well past sundown. He tried to disguise his shock as a glare at the man who'd appointed himself the magistrate of the city's Outer Commons. Felip sat and gulped his tea. Jonathan sipped. Both men waited for the other to break the silence.

"It's about your daughter-in-law, sir," Felip spat the last word as if it were painful to say. "Charity. She's declared a vendetta against us."

"That's one way to say 'Winning a fight I was stupid enough to start.'" Jonathan said. He was a talker. A blowhard, by Felip's standards. The direct response had caught him off guard. He clenched the mug in barely restrained fury.

"Could you call her off?" Felip asked through clenched teeth. His grip on the mug was so tight his knuckles were white. He could feel the pins and needles in his fingers. He emptied his mug and slammed it down on the desk in an ineffectual display of determination.

"Why?" Jonathan asked. He reminded Felip of the teachers he'd blown off as a child. So calm and collected. Except this teacher could erase him in a heartbeat.

"Because she's out of control! Because you play the wise man and a wise man would know this is bad for everyone! You set the rules! Hold her to them!" Felip roared. His chair clattered on the floor behind him as he leapt to his feet, mug in hand, and prepared to fling it at the older man. But he froze as the guardswoman's hands seized his wrist and shoulder.

"Sit. Down," Jonathan commanded. The guard didn't release Felip until he did so. "The rule is that a line drawn in blood cannot be crossed."

"Right. She has to ignore us." Felip said. Trying to look out the scarred glass of the window was better than meeting Jonathan's gaze.

"That goes both ways," Jonathan said. The glare he levelled didn't remind Felip of a teacher anymore. It reminded him of his father. Quick to point out Felip's faults and quicker to anger. "She quit your gang years ago. The line was drawn with whatever ritual your predecessor forced on her and she had to stay on her side. But last week you lost your temper and tried to kill her. What did you think she would do when she survived? Roll over and die?"

"I had to send a message, sir," Felip said. He swallowed and looked at Jonathan. This time he meant the honorific.

"What message? You're too angry or stupid to keep from picking a fight that will get your entire gang killed?" Jonathan pinched the bridge of his nose. He looked down at the desk, the empty mugs, and finally at Felip. "I couldn't stop her from killing you even if you didn't deserve it. But I will grant your people a favor."

"What's that?" Felip straightened in his chair.

"This started with your order so it ends with your death. If Charity finds you on the roof of the old spice market at sunrise I promise your gang will survive." Jonathan said. He refilled his mug. "I'm afraid the tea's gotten cold. You should leave and spend the night thinking."

Felip stood and bowed silently to acknowledge the dismissal. To his surprise Jonathan returned the gesture. The guardswoman didn't bother leading him to the exit. He knew the way. Sunrise found him facing his fate head on.

Paul Cordes is a network security analyst from Virginia with all of the nerdy interests that implies. His only previously published work is Gold and Glass in volume 2 of Sojourn. He lives in Virginia with his wife, son, and two cats.

The Dansari

Melissa Gale

This is the last of it, the water that is. I shuffle toward the lake edge with the others from my village. It's the last for my people and our animals. That's why *she* came... The Dansari.

"Sabina!" my friend whispers excitedly. "Look at her! She's so *young*!"

Bare feet make a shushing sound on the dry ground as everyone shuffles solemnly toward the edge. The leaves of the pettle tree crackle when the breeze touches them, and the sound of bees buzzing around the water, louder in this unnatural quiet, is mesmerizing.

"Mailys, you have to be quiet!" I hiss. "We can't make any sound. You know what happened last time!"

Last year a small boy stepped on one of the bees near the water and cried out. During the ceremony his father stood with the boy in front of him, covering his mouth and nose to keep him quiet. I still wasn't sure if the boy's death was a punishment for the offense, or if the father had caused it. You do *not* insult the Dansari.

She comes once a year, near the end of harvest as the plants and water are drying up, to perform The Supplication. The ritual that puts the plants to sleep, protecting them from the darkened days and cold nights, and opens the sky allowing the water and snow to fall again.

"She's supposed to be more than a hundred wintercress harvests!" Mailys whispered, a little quieter this time.

"That's just what our parents tell us. They've been saying that since I was five harvests, and when the snow falls this time, I'll be 16. They say that because they think the fear of being chosen as the next Dansari will keep us quiet." I look fondly at my friend. "And clearly that doesn't work on you."

"Don't you think it would be amazing? You know, to be chosen as the next Dansari?"

Her eyes sparkle as she covers her mouth, trying to conceal her excitement.

"Leaving your family to travel to other lands to bring the sleep and rains? Living a hundred harvests and watching as your family ages and dies before you? No... not amazing."

"But that's just it! You get to live longer and see all the lands that are forbidden to us!"

Mailys looks longingly at the woman in the center of the pool. The Dansari's long, dark hair cascades over her shoulders and breasts as she looks down, avoiding eye contact with any of the approaching villagers. Not that the villagers would try to make eye contact.

"No one knows when the last sleep will take us, Dansari or not," I whisper, "and nobody knows how the Dansari are chosen."

"Well, maybe this really *is* the year," Mailys whispers. "You're just into birthing years, like me, and also never lain with a man."

"That's because no man will have us!" I laugh. "Ow!"

The sound of father's hand slapping my arm is loud enough to make the other villagers turn. Looking at my feet, I rub my arm. Feeling the heat rise in my cheeks, I don't need to look up to feel the anger on father's face. The Supplication is an important ritual. Probably *the* most important ritual, and I was disrespectful to the Dansari. I will pay for the shame I brought my family.

We arrive at the edge of the water. The pool is pretty shallow this late into harvest, deeper around the edges, but there's a small island of sand in the middle that's just under the surface. That's where the Dansari stands. Watching from the edge, I see her wiggle her toes. It gives the unsettling illusion that she's standing on top of the water.

The Dansari looks up and makes eye contact with the village elder, focusing only on him, and nods. He starts to bang his stick on the ground, *bang... bang... bang... bang...*, creating a tempo for her. His wife sits to his left and begins to circle the bronze bowl in her lap with the leather-wrapped mallet. The sound is hollow and numbing, it paralyzes all thought.

The Dansari clasps her hands at her chest, closes her eyes and tilts her head back. Praying to Vetur for the safe transition of the plants to their sleep, and for the rains to be sent here once again. Listening for his answer.

The villagers bow in unison. They stand and begin to rub their hands together, making the sound of dry paper being rustled.

Bang... bang... bang...

My head spins as the air is permeated with bees, ringing and static. Grabbing the sides of my legs to steady myself, I watch the Dansari drop her arms and slowly roll her head in a circle as she starts to dance. Her movements are slow and beautiful. As fluid as the streams in early spring.

Bang... bang...

Like a tapping inside my head, the beats come faster now. A few villagers have started to stomp in time to the rhythm as they rub their hands. The earth vibrates under my feet as I watch the dancer move gracefully, stepping lightly across the island while lifting her arms to the sky.

You never know when the last sleep will take you. It's the same for everyone, and everyone needs the water. I look up at the sky searching for the rains, willing the skies to open and release their water. I close my eyes and feel the vibration of my people. I will the rain to come to me — to my people. They're all *my people.*

Bang... bang...

Faster still. All the villagers have joined in the ritual now. The first drops of rain begin to fall, wet drops on my face, as I begin to sway. With my eyes closed I reach out to her... and surrender.

Melissa Gale is a paralegal by day, but story-teller at heart. She has another flash fiction story, "Well You Know Maybe It Was" published in Flash! A Celebration of Short Fiction" and also writes erotic fiction for myerotica.com.

Feet

Helen Carothers

It was just a digital camera. My Gramma gave it to me for my twelfth birthday. We had moved to a new town and I didn't know anybody. Who or what did she think I was going to take pictures of? Gramma is weird.

I started fiddling with the camera and took a picture of my feet. Better than nothing so I took pictures of my feet bare, feet in socks, feet in shoes. I took pictures of my feet on the bed, on the rug, in the kitchen. Maybe Gramma isn't the only weird one.

I sent some of the pictures to Gramma. She wanted to know where the feet would go next. Good question. I took my feet and my camera outside. Feet in the grass, feet on the dirt, feet on the gravel.

"Whatcha doin'?"

Scared the bejeebers out of me. I didn't know anybody was around and I couldn't see anybody when I looked.

"Whatcha doin'?" This time he poked his head above the fence.

"Just taking pictures of my feet." What else was I going to tell him?

"Cool. Can I help?"

I didn't get a chance to answer. He was over the fence and in my yard before he even finished the question. We spent the rest of the afternoon photographing our feet all over that yard.

The next morning, I woke up to find Billy waiting in the back yard. I poked my head out the window and asked what he was doing.

"Hurry up, sleepy head. We got work to do."

By "work" Billy meant photographing more feet. He knew everyone in the neighborhood and wasn't the least bit shy about knocking on their doors to ask if I could photograph their feet. I wasn't sure which was worse being the new kid alone in my room or being the new kid with the camera on everybody's porch. It turned out okay as most of the old ladies gave us cookies and the old guys gave us advice.

We even got to spend a lot of time with the girls across the street. Kathy and Sue are not sisters but they act like they are. They live in the gray house and the yellow house but I'm not sure who actually lives where. They are the same age as Billy and me so now I know at least three people that will be in my grade at school.

Maybe Gramma giving me that camera wasn't so weird.

Helen Carothers is a newbie writer capturing images with words rather than a camera. Just a little weird.

Tea with Death

Frances Pauli

Death takes the fit as surely as those in need of sit-ups. It's not personal, he assures me, as we drink our tea. There's no avoiding him. His victims include the health food nut, the jogger, and the raw food juicer just as surely as the donut aficionado.

"Last week I stopped a woman's heart while she drank a kale smoothie." He grins and his eyes go black as tar. "Trust me."

"But it's personal to them, you know." I add bee pollen to my matcha and he rolls his eyes. "It's always personal."

"I don't pick favorites," he insists. "I'm not like Fate."

We both turn our heads and spit on the ground over Fate's shenanigans. Death shrugs and cracks a smile. I've been meeting him for tea every Saturday since my mother's passing. It's a friendly arrangement... even if he lies. He knows damn well it's personal.

Her death is coming for me, after all.

"I blame Time, the old Fart."

"I'm sure he blames *you*."

"Maybe." He swirls his cup, squints at the contents. "You can die of anything, a bus, a fall, a clot of blood in the wrong place."

"Even if I live well." I nod. I get it, but we both know this thing is real. We both sat with her while the disease ate her organs. "Lose weight, get fit, cut out the sugar."

"It can't hurt." He smiles a shiver right up my spine.

"It can hurt."

It *does* hurt, in fact. All the doctor's medicines couldn't hide that. But he's a fine companion for a broody tea, and I let it go this week. I nod and drink my green, detox, pollen-boosted tea as if it were a lifeline, the miracle cure that doesn't exist.

Maybe, it shouldn't exist.

"I blame Fate," Death says with a sage nod. "That bitch never did play fair."

He takes his tea black, unsweetened and dark as an abyss. If you look into it, sometimes, you can see the future, a twist, a hint. An ancient scrap of magic. I don't have to peek today, I keep my eyes on the sun filtering through the windows, the patterns that glow on the carpet under our little corner table.

I don't need to look because we both know it's my face shining in the bottom of the cup, my reflection, dark and personal, in his future.

Deaths sets his cup down and clears his throat, a sound like an ambulance siren, like a heart monitor droning. He pushes back his chair and shrugs. "See you?"

"We'll see, won't we?"

He walks out first, and I pay for two cups of tea even though the waitress gives me a funny look. You never know with Death. That's his whole point. He's still lingering on the sidewalk when I drift out, but we ignore each other now, strangers until tomorrow.

So when he steps into the street, I react on reflex. When the taxi blares its horn, I lunge for him without thinking, drag him backwards to the squealing of brakes that would never have been in time.

Not like he could have died anyway.

We both know it. We both stare for a moment, as the steel monster screams past and the sea of pedestrians washes like a tide around us. Then he shakes himself and laughs.

"It doesn't change anything, you know?"

"Sure."

"Nothing can."

"Right."

"Makes no difference."

He is made of lies. I see it in the way he walks from me, in the way he looks both ways when he crosses the street. It changes everything. And tomorrow, I'll be taking my tea alone, not looking.

Because it does no good to know.

Frances Pauli writes speculative and anthropomorphic fiction. You can find her list of published works including the upcoming Hybrid Nation series on her website at: http://francespauli.com

Time In A Bottle

Chris Hussey

Cerulean, malachite and alabaster swirls rolled within as the vial bobbled and bumped across the uneven pine table. The grooves and splits of the dry, unsanded planks spoke of heavy use and shoddy craftsmanship. Each moisture-starved miniature crevice tried to serve as a trench to capture the glass cartridge as it wound its journey to the other side. The eventual victor was a knothole, working in conjunction with an adjacent bump. The bump lifted and angled clear the cylinder, redirecting the momentum to slide into the natural hole. The knot, in turn, moved the vial just enough to point the cork stopper like an accusing finger toward its interrupted destination.

A shimmering, black, silken glove crept forward, eager to help the vial complete its journey, but a throaty grunt stayed the hand within. "Not quite so fast."

The glove's owner twitched his manicured moustache. Gray and fading black hairs flinched toward his left eye. "Is there a problem?" The man's lips moved as if he'd just eaten bad lemons. "You've been paid."

The vial's roller nodded, and with a gloved hand of his (worn, chestnut and leather), tilted the brim of his hat (pinched front and slightly dirty) back. "True, but only half."

Another unified chorus of hairs twitched. "With the remainder upon completion and veracity of," slightly bulging eyes looked with lust at the settling swirls, "the item." The voice dribbled annoyance.

The man produced his other hand (also gloved) and removed the first, laying his hand flat and wide on the table, as if it was capitulating to the liquid. The ring and little finger of the hand were wrinkled, the knuckle joints bulbous and arthritic. The other three fingers bore the signs of a man fitting the age of the roller. "Is this veracity enough for you?"

A slight gasp parted the hair-lined lips of the silk-gloved man. The rounded eyes flitted from the partially withered hand, to the vial then to the hand's owner, then back around the circle once again. "It's wondrous." The words flowed as if uttered by a venerable woman seeing the naked, muscled form of a man half her age.

"Depends on your view." The other man flinched as he spoke, returning the glove to its prior place.

Silkened hands vanished into the breast pocket of a tailored and striped suit, soon producing a billfold and a glass vial of his own, this one with a luminescent ivory fluid. Crisp bills and the bottle gently settled close to the first. The gloves hesitated before securing the first vial.

"I trust you." The other man said. He leaned forward, scooped the money and the glowing glass, thrusting them into the breast pocket of his dirty town coat. His tongue clicked. "But your father shouldn't."

The moustache twitched again. Lips trembled. Slightly. "I don't know what you mean. My father... is dead."

A pessimistic tilt of the other man's head. "Well he will be once he gets a drink of that liquid time."

"I am merely a collector of rare items, sir. You've been paid. Your money and your liquid light. Good day." The moustached man rose.

"You're also Reginald VelJohnson, oldest son of Dominic VelJohnson, the patriarch of Direwald Rails. And contrary to your previous statement, Dom is an old fart who simply hasn't seen fit to die, allowing his aging son to inherit the family business."

Reginald's moustache twitched in guilt, his lips making the same sour motion. "This is unfortunate."

"Yeah, for me." The other man tilted his chair on its rear legs, left hand reaching toward the pine beam behind for support, right hand moving low for balance. "There was a chance you wouldn't have me killed after this mission. Liquid time isn't easy to steal. Now that I know who you are and shot my mouth off about it I know for sure you'll have me killed."

"You could have stayed silent. I would have been none the wiser."

"Yeah, but though Dom's a bastard of the highest order, his railroad helped a lot of people close to me. In a weird way, I feel I owe your father. Hence, my dilemma. Do I let you go and look over my shoulder the next few years, or do I kill you, then worry about a vengeful father, whom I'm trying to save here and now, coming after me?"

Reginald let a small grin cross his slim lips. "Perhaps I can make it worth your while."

"Perhaps." He tilted his head the other direction. "And I'm a betting man. Hence why I took this risky job to begin with." His head straightened and eyes locked with Reginald's. "But I'm going to bet on your younger brothers being cutthroat, just like you. I'm betting they will be sad their brother is dead, but also happy to see that line of succession shorten. Daddy might come after me, but I can be patient. More patient than you."

"Mister Whittaker. Let's be reasona..."

Steel slid from leather in an instant followed with a clap from Whittaker's pistol. Just as quickly, the weapon returned.

Reginald spasmed for an instant, then slumped forward onto the table, dislodging the vial of liquid time from its knotty home, setting it rolling in a new direction. Whittaker rocked forward, launching from his seat, while his two-fifths aged and gloved hand lunged for the vial.

With a scoop, the vial was secured. Whittaker continued to move, gliding from the room, the door latching with a clink behind him. Reginald VelJohnson remained, laying upon the table, blood pooling about him, staining his gloves and providing the dry and cracked face of the table with much needed moisture.

Chris Hussey has been writing for role-playing games and fiction since the early 90's. Active in the RPG industry, Chris is a self-described "Podcast Journeyman," having been a co-host on Fear the Boot, Gamerstable and others. He currently runs and produces the Deadlands Actual Play podcast, "The Adventures of Young & Holt." Chris lives in Alaska, where he spends his Real Life as a Marketing Director for a local television station. He is currently considering a career change to becoming a full time career counselor for a college bound moose.

Game On!

Elizabeth K. Pratt

Their silver whistles gleamed by fluorescent tube light, casting bright reflections on the gloss-polished concrete floor. They walked in triangular formation, all six mindful of their status within the pack. Across the back of the spearhead, the special needs teacher took center position with the cheerleading and girls' volleyball coaches at the corners. The three pillars of machismo took the fore: football coach Ferrell, flanked by the baseball and basketball coaches, always took the point.

The men sported bushy moustaches but were clean cheeked, hair buzzed with military precision. The women of wore matching pony tails, their big bangs bouncing in hair sprayed uniformity against scowling brows.

Each coach carried a red or blue rubber ball, the same as used in kickball every spring. But this was mid-winter. It could mean only one thing.

Coach Ferrell halted the parade between the fifth and sixth grade lunch tables, where a fearful hush had befallen the smallest students. Some froze in place, sandwiches and fish sticks held at half-mast.

The coach chomped audibly on his wad of pink Hubba Bubba, letting fear spread through the herd before he spoke. "Let's head for the gym, kiddos. Time for a tournament. We'll take 4th and 6th grade with us," he gestured with his red ball to his left and right. "5th and 7th, you're with them," and he nodded over his shoulder. On cue, the women raised their balls in salute. "Sudden death. Last man standing wins for his team. Any questions?"

Jimmy Wilcox, new that week from a school in Chicago, raised a hand, apparently oblivious to the terrified stillness of his fellow 4th grade classmates. "Coach? What kind of tournament?"

Stalking forward like a panther on the prowl, Coach Ferrell fixed his sights on the small city boy. For Ferrell, football was king, and the tournament was a drill with one goal: eliminate the weak. These matches determined the future athletic fate of these flimsy children. Who would be water-boy and who would be quarterback?

Looming before Jimmy, his polyester jersey and shorts blazing in bright white and cobalt blue, he bounced the red ball in one short pop from the top of the boy's carefully gel-spiked head. "Jimmy, the game is dodge ball. And, son, you are already out."

Elizabeth's stories and essays have been included in "In the Words of Olympic Peninsula Authors" Volumes 1 and 2, and her articles have appeared in the Peninsula Daily News, Sequim Gazette, and Compass & Clock magazine.

Aunt Clara's House

Karen Eisenbrey

"So who was Aunt Clara again?"

"Great-aunt, actually. Grandma's youngest sister."

"And you were close?"

"Not really. We mostly only saw her at her annual Christmas party. But we moved away when I was twelve, so I missed all the parties after that. By the time I moved back, she'd stopped entertaining."

"Then why did she leave you her house?"

I wondered as much as Dave did, so I didn't even try to answer. Aunt Clara had always sent generous birthday and graduation gifts, but she had no children or grandchildren of her own. I assumed my cousins received the same. But only I had received a house. No, a mansion.

I unlocked the front door and stepped inside.

"Bet it's haunted!" Emily nudged her little brother. Jacob's eyes went wide.

"No such thing as ghosts," I said. "Go and explore. Pick your rooms."

Grinning, they thundered up the stairs in a race to the top. I wandered into the big front room. This was where Aunt Clara had held her parties. I could still picture the enormous Christmas tree in the window and the elegant food on trays. A rosewood grand piano dominated the room, eight feet long if it was an inch. Aunt Clara was a concert pianist and recording artist, one of those glamorous performers in evening gowns or smart pantsuits. I'd had lessons as a child and always played a few carols at her parties, but I'd stopped playing by high school.

I lifted the lid from the keyboard and plunked a few notes. The instrument was in miraculously good tune for having been untouched for months.

"Honey, why is there a piano in the dining room?"

I found my husband across the hall in another elegant room. In the place where most people would have had a china cabinet stood an antique upright piano. I plunked out a melody. It was in nearly as good tune as the grand.

"I guess Aunt Clara never knew when she might want to sit down and play."

Discordant notes drifted down from the next floor. We exchanged a frown and climbed the stairs. We found the children in the first bedroom, banging away on a spinet.

"I want this room!" Emily cried.

"No fair!" Jacob complained. "Why does she get the room with the piano?"

But upon further exploration, we found the room next door also contained a piano. As did the master bedroom. What I at first took for a writing desk in the kitchen turned out to be — you guessed it — another piano.

Dave scratched his head. "Who has six pianos? Was she a hoarder?"

"Come on, the house is immaculate! Maybe she was... a collector? Or some of them could be rescues."

"I guess I should be grateful she wasn't a crazy cat lady."

Once we'd settled in, we did a full piano census. Total: eight, including one concert grand, one baby grand, one upright, one console, and four spinets. I had a sentimental attachment to the big one, and the children loved theirs, but we did not need eight pianos. They had to find new homes. But have you tried selling a piano these days? We managed to give away the upright from the dining room to someone willing to pay moving costs. The next day we found an even older upright in a previously undiscovered pantry. We moved it to the dining room. A pantry was useful space, and it's not like we had a china cabinet.

On the bright side, both children were eager for music lessons. I started playing again, too. Our piano teacher traded lessons for studio time in our unused, piano-occupied rooms for students without their own instruments. A couple of those families eventually decided to adopt "their" spinets. We rented other rooms to students from the local arts college — dorm and practice room in one. The elegant front room found new life as an intimate recital venue. Aunt Clara's house — our house — was once more a home to music.

For months, I opened doors with a mix of eagerness and dread, but the spirit of Aunt Clara must have been appeased. We haven't found another piano in over a year. We can live with six.

Karen Eisenbrey is a Seattle-based fantasy novelist. Wizard Girl (coming in 2019) will join Daughter of Magic (2018) and The Gospel According to St Rage (2016), both finalists for the Wishing Shelf Independent Book Award.

Kippers for Kipling

Craig English

"What kind of fish is that?"

"That?" The shopkeeper, a ponderous Hindu, scratched his enormous nostrils. "Maybe anchovy."

The anchovy was mounted on a wooden plaque.

"Strange color," I remarked.

"Maybe painted? Welcome to Burning Tyger. You looking or buying?"

"Looking."

"Bah." He lumbered off, leaving me alone as I had hoped he would.

Yes, I was looking. And if I found what I was looking for I would be rich. If not, I was ruined. And quite possibly facing prison.

The Burning Tyger ran riot with exotic and mostly worthless flotsam. I set off down an aisle, on the hunt for a tiger or a tea set or a Masai warrior.

For a moment the smell of books and dust disoriented me, made me think I was back at home and not in a questionable quarter of Bombay. You see, I am a research librarian. From Winooski, Vermont. I like my New York Times crossword with my morning coffee, and my tuna sandwich precisely at noon. My name is Phillip Dustmoor. Yes, I know, a librarian named Dustmoor — ridiculous. When my wife, Anna, ran off with the CPA, she explained that it was because I am boring.

My uncle, on the other hand, the late Dunston "Dusty" Dustmoor, was not boring. He wrote mystery novels featuring a Pittsburgh steelworker named Gus and his mangy dog. Old Gus, with his beer-gut bonhomie and beer-nut wisdom, was a hit, a cash cow that made Uncle Dusty wealthy. Dusty was always traveling abroad, Sri Lanka or Katmandu or Cameroon, places that sound delicious in a book, but which, in person, I was certain, sported large carnivorous insects and unfortunate toilet facilities.

I received word of Uncle Dusty's death one week after my divorce. He had been shot in the back in a bar in Mozambique. When I returned home from the funeral, I found an envelope, postmarked a mere day before Uncle Dusty's death. There was a poem inside, along with a note. "My time is up. Solve the puzzle, lad, and all of it is yours. Don't forget what Gus says!"

Now, pacing the Tyger, beneath the whisperings of prayer flags, I extracted the poem from my pocket.

There's a Legion that never was listed,
That carries no colours or crest,
But, split in a thousand detachments,
Is breaking the road for the rest.

It went on like that for a bit and then:

To go and find out and be damned
(Dear boys!),
To go and get shot and be damned.

Well, dear old Unc had certainly got himself shot. The poem I recognized as Kipling; the second stanza was filled with exotic place names — the Oil Coast, Wallaby Track, and The Fly. It took me two months to screw up the courage to leave Vermont, and two years of traveling to visit each location. At each I found a clue that led me to the next. I'd lost my job and I was a quarter of a million dollars in debt. But, as Gus says in the best seller, The Bratwurst Incident: "First the worksky, then the brewsky!"

In a dingy corner of the Burning Tyger, I came upon an alcove hidden by hanging wooden beads. I parted the beads and jumped back. A tiger glared at me, its fangs bared in a snarl. This must be it!

I referenced the poem.

And some share our tucker with tigers,
And some with the gentle Masai,
(Dear boys!),
Take tea with the giddy Masai.

"Tucker" means food, and I wondered what might be in the belly of the beast. I looked around. The shopkeeper was blocked from my sight by rows of fat-bellied wicker baskets, so I reached into the tiger's mouth. There was something down there, all right, something cold and hard, but it would not fit through the teeth.

I'm afraid I acted badly then, but understand that I was desperate. I pulled out my Swiss Army knife and set to the tiger's desiccated flank. Inside, I found a teapot and, yes, emblazoned on its side, a grinning Masai warrior. It was a worthless piece of British imperialist kitsch, but within, I was certain, was my fortune.

With trembling hands I removed the lid and peered in. I had been expecting perhaps a key to a safe deposit box or a bag of gems — but not a cockroach. The horrid creature waggled its antennae at me.

"What have you done?" the proprietor screamed in my ear. I dropped the teapot and it smashed into a hundred pieces.

"Stupid American! You pay."

"I've got no money," I squawked.

"No money?"

He grabbed the back of my collar and my belt, dragged me to the door, and threw me into the street. The knee of my left pant leg ripped open and my skin did the same.

I got up and started back toward the shop. "I'll make it up to you –" But something hit me square in the head. When I came to, I was on the ground and lying next to me was the mounted anchovy.

There was no use. I was friendless and destitute in Bombay. My hopes were broken into more pieces than the teapot. Maybe it had all been a goose chase. Maybe Uncle Dusty was laughing in his grave.

I picked up the fish and staggered away from the shop. Blood rolled down my forehead. When I wiped my eyes, I noticed the tail had broken off the painted fish and something was sticking out — a slip of paper tucked inside clear plastic. I retrieved it.

On the paper was a procession of carefully printed numbers and a note in a familiar hand. "Well done lad! I recommend Zurich in the spring. Any Swiss banker should be able to help you."

Only then did I remember what that lunch-pail-toting sleuth, Gus, said to his dog in every book.

"There's always a red herring, Rudyard, never forget that!"

Craig English's novels include: Black Swan, a tale of Wall Street greed, dragons, and a mild-mannered Shakespeare professor; The Anvil of Navarre, a swashbuckling tale of love, revenge and sexual identity; and most recently, Dark Net Wolves, in which a young cat-burglar/hacker plots her revenge against a hideous cyber troll. His nonfiction includes Anxious to Please: 7 Revolutionary Practices for the Chronically Nice.

Drinking and Driving

My Air Force Years

Larry Danek

I was in the Air Force during some very trying times and there were a lot of interesting things going on. Some of those would have included the building of the Berlin Wall, the Bay of Pigs, the Cuban Missile Crisis, the Assassination of our President John F. Kennedy, and the Vietnam War. I often think about that great Chinese curse, "You should live in interesting times".

This story, however, is more about the novelty of strange rather than the anxiety and fear that permeated the 1960's. This event took place in the year 1963 and represented only one of the many oddities that I encountered over the four years I served in the Air Force.

I was stationed at Ellsworth Air Force Base near Rapid City, South Dakota and was assigned to the 43rd Munitions Maintenance Squadron. The base was and probably still is a SAC (Strategic Air Command) installation and the 43rd was in charge of storage and handling all the munitions for the base. I was one of the lowest ranking members and had the duty of storing the munitions and maintaining the area around the bunkers. The base was the permanent location for a fleet of B-52 bombers and the associated KC-135 refueling tankers. It was also the location for receiving and preparing the warheads that were to be installed on the minuteman missiles that were being deployed at that time. I wasn't part of that process and didn't have much to do with the missile set up at all. I was, however, assigned to receive the warheads and place them in storage for the team that would eventually ready them for installation.

In order to fulfil my part of the operation I had to have all the clearances necessary to get the warheads off the C-124 aircraft and into the bunkers for safe keeping until they were deployed. I also had to have my military driver's license stamped for the use of a fork lift to move the warheads. The unit I was in was referred to as NWS (nuclear weapons supply). It consisted of one supply officer (captain), two clerks (sergeants), and four airmen of lower rank.

I didn't like having the job of signing for the warheads as the shipments always came in at about four in the afternoon. The time it took to get to the flight line, sign for the warheads, load them on to a truck and take them to the weapons area, ate into my personal time as well as the time that the chow hall was open for dinner.

This particular day, with a shipment coming in, it was a hot mid-summer afternoon. Our forklift had been used by base supply and I had to go retrieve it. I was returning to the squadron with it and spotted a Jimmy Jingle truck. I stopped and bought a milkshake and proceeded up the road. The rules for driving a forklift on the road required one to be going backwards so the back wheels would be going in the forward direction, or is it the front wheels going backwards? Anyway, this was to keep the chances of losing control to a minimum. I held the steering wheel with my left hand and turned my body with my right arm hooked over the back-rest of the seat. I was drinking the milkshake through a straw while holding it with my right hand. The motor pool office stopped me and informed me that 'drinking and driving' was not allowed and he pulled my military driver's license. He told me to sit there and finish my drink, then return to the squadron with the forklift and don't drive any more.

I thought, this couldn't be all bad, as I wouldn't have to miss dinner at the chow hall and could get off with the rest of the squadron. I guessed wrong. When I informed the captain of what had happened it didn't seem to bother him at first. He was just going to send someone else to get the warheads. Things escalated rapidly after that as he found out that 'somehow' I was the only person on the whole base with all the proper clearances. Don't ask me how that could have happened. My guess would be that the previous holders of those clearances had either shipped out or left the service. The supply officer and clerks failed to notice the problem until too late.

When the motor pool officer refused to give me back my license as requested by first my Captain and then my Squadron Commander, he relented after the Base Commander got involved and ordered him to do so. Of course that left me on everybody's list. I ended up going out to meet the plane and get the warheads. This caused me to miss another meal at the chow hall and required spending some of my own money on what little food I could afford. I would have been okay with that but I was then required to attend five night classes for drivers training. That was another loss of personal time that I never got over.

The Squadron Commander paid me back in spades later when I came up for promotion as he traded my potential stripe to another squadron. I think the supply office may have lost his commission because of what had happened, I never knew for sure.

I never regretted my time in the Air Force as I saw many things that were both good and not so good. I had made the commitment to serve my country and I learned a lot about myself and how other people saw the world around them. I had to deal with people of different backgrounds and attitudes. I often thought that made me a better person and hope I helped others to see the world the same way.

Author Larry Danek was born and raised in western Pennsylvania. He has been an ardent reader and only began writing after he retired. This story is from his memory of what he went through while in the Air Force but he has published books of fiction; notably the Nomadic Ghost Series.

The Wicked Lovely Orchard

Orin Melvin

Manzek and Shevas Tenpails, a gnome couple, lived in a burrow under a rusted Chevy Luv pickup that sat without wheels on the hard dirt outside the town of Wenatchee. On one side ran the canal while a small, overgrown orchard bordered the other. Manzek noticed that most humans just stared at tiny boxes, while Shevas commented that kids didn't play around their home like they used too. Still, they took precautions.

He kept a plump patch of goat heads growing around the pickup. They had two escape tunnels, but only one actually led anywhere. In the other he kept treasures he found such as rusty spades and half smoked cigars. Shevas knew that humans didn't like rats, so she kept a rat room where one or two could stay with a promise of daily kitchen scraps. The only stipulation was that, should a human approach too closely, they would run straight for them. Shevas enjoyed talking with the rats, and they kept her up on the neighborhood gossip. The problem was the cats. Last week during May Day a gnome boy came wandering into the festival holding a bloody rat tail. It had belonged to her last tenant. As it was, she was having difficulties recruiting lodgers. She had an idea.

"I think we should get a dog to scare the cats away. One of those cute little ones."

"Our German ancestors never kept dogs," he said as he put on his hat.

"Yes," she replied, "but our ancestors didn't live under a pickup either."

"True. But with the goat heads a dog just isn't practical. The dog will scare away the cats and eat the rats itself. Think about it."

"I have thought about it, a lot. I love talking to that old fluffy black one. He tells me about all his squirrel adventures while I scratch his chin. Poor thing can't run anymore or else I'd invite him to stay. Let's invite one of the little ones to stay when they sneak out of their yard one night."

Shevas's smile matched the sparkle in her eye but Manzek didn't say anything and went out of the burrow.

*

On a late Tuesday afternoon in June the gnomes wandered into the orchard to pick dandelions for salad and tea. They checked on their mushroom patch, a spreading mix of shaggy parasols and glistening inkcaps. After picking a few, they headed back to the Chevy Luv. At least, they tried to head back.

The fifty-year-old apple trees had not been trimmed in the past five years, and the grass grew as it wanted to. Shadows blended and danced, and hid all sorts of creatures from robins to rabbits to the occasional raccoon. It also hid hungry, lice-laden tomcats with stenchy breath hissing between pick like teeth.

The Siamese stray shot itself into Shevas's stomach and tore her dress with his razor claws. It grabbed her neck. Shevas kicked and punched but the more she fought, the harder the teeth clenched and the more she felt the claws dig into her.

Manzek rushed the cat only to be met with a flash of claws and a slashed face. Blood trickled and soaked Shevas's dress. The cat began to lick her face as it held her down with a claw. She looked into the icy eyes of the cat and felt the bristling whiskers on her cheek. The cat's sticky fur brushed along her neck. Her wet eyes pleaded at Manzek.

"Be at peace, my dear, stay at peace."

And with that, he bolted away.

The cat stopped licking her, and Shevas shifted to watch the clouds float along the baby blue sky. The leaves sparkled green in the slanted light and she focused on a blue copper butterfly flitting about. She felt a fang press in. He said that he loved her, but he simply left. She had watched him save baby swallows and half-poisoned mice, but when it came to her, he had just left. She focused again on the butterfly, the leaves, the sun, and the sound of a bee. The fangs pressed. In her death, she would remember life.

"No you wicked thing. Here. Here."

The top of Manzek's hat appeared and then a snowball from hell jumped through the grass. The cat sprang off Shevas. It hissed and arched its back at the lightning streak of a Jack Russell Terrier. The dog growled and yapped and forced the cat back into the shadows where it finally turned its tail and ran. Shevas rushed into Manzek's arms. The terrier bounded back and stole his hat. She ran in circles through the grass, up to the canal, back through the orchard, and finally laid at the gnomes' feet. All the while, Manzek tore his shirt and bandaged her wounds. At last, they embraced in a bloody hug.

"I'm going to figure out how to light that cigar when we get back," he said.

She looked at the snowball from hell and gave a little smile.

"Can we keep her?"

"What? The wicked thing? The family down the road got her for Christmas. I've been trying to train her since you told me you wanted a dog. She was meant to be your Summer Solstice present. You can have her if you want her, but fair warning, the best name I can come up for her is Wicked."

"Wicked will do," she said, and gave him a long kiss.

Orin Melvin, an elementary teacher, is passionate about preserving planet Earth and truly believes love conquers all. He centers his writing in the fantasy genre for both adults and children.

Harry, Harry, Quite Contrary

Ahmed A. Khan

Come nearer, dear boys and darling girls. Your very own storyteller, Kai Lung II, unrolls his mat and tells you a tale of wondrous deeds, intriguing wisdom and confusing morals.

Once upon a time, there was a young man named Harry. He was quite ordinary in every way imaginable. His looks, his intelligence, you name it. He had quite ordinary parents. He went to quite an ordinary school. At school, his teachers were ordinary. And so were his friends. In short — get the picture — everything about him was ordinary. Except for one quality that he possessed. His one distinguishing feature was his contrariness. He had a curious habit of always trying to do just the opposite of what he was asked to do. At the time of his birth, the doctors tried their level best to deliver him but he would not emerge. In despair, the doctors finally declared that a caesarian had become compulsory. Out popped Harry the very next minute.

One day, when he was a kid, his father told him to be truthful so he went to his mother and informed her that his father had kissed their maid. Mother had a big fight with father. It was all very interesting. The most interest thing about the incident was the probably insignificant fact that there never was any maid in their house.

When Harry was nine, his parents took him on a tour of Europe.

"Don't go too far into the water, Harry," his mother instructed him when they were at the Dover beach.

That day, Harry became famous for being the youngest boy to swim across the English Channel.

On another day, in his school, one of his teachers said that education was important in the current times and no good jobs could be had without a proper education. Promptly, Harry quit school, ran away from home, joined a gang of juvenile delinquents, and, at the age of twenty four, was elected as the president of the country — the youngest president the country ever had.

My dears and darlings, come closer and pay heed as I tell you about perhaps the final episode of Harry's colorful life.

One day, Harry became privy to the fact that it was impossible for a physical body to cross the speed of light. What did he do then? In his room, he started running in circles around his bed. Faster and faster he ran. Faster and faster and faster faster... and he neared the speed of light... and he crossed it... and he vanished from our universe and popped into the tachyonic universe where no physical body can move slower than light.

Serves him right.

Ahmed's works have appeared in Boston Review, Strange Horizons, Interzone, Anotherealm, etc. His stories have been translated into German, Finnish, Greek, Croatian and Urdu. Check out his works at http://ahmedakhan.blogspot.ca.

Mary Got Hanged

Chris Karr

1916.

Two thousand mountain folk gather into the railroad yard to watch Mary die. She's unaware of her crimes, obliviously standing amidst a cluster of circus employees given the more-difficult-than-it-sounds task of carrying out her death sentence.

Mary is a murderer.

This much had been proven yesterday at her trial. Half a dozen eyewitnesses testified that she threw Red Edler into a drink stand and proceeded to crush his skull. Since Red was too dead to speak for himself, she was convicted by her peers. But a problem remains: how do you execute her?

The rookie headsmen brainstorm with their best ideas. One says they should just hang her. Another says he knows a blacksmith who can shoot her. "Shootin's *real* dramatic," he says. Another suggests electrocution. One of the more bashful fellows mentions they could squash her between two railroad cars. And the first fellow again says that they just need to hang her and be done with it. But he's outvoted and they fetch the blacksmith.

They lead Mary out to the center of a field and allow her a few final words before she's shot. The audience collectively leans forward, too rapt with tension to munch on their popcorn. The little kids are shushed and settled upon the shoulders of their parents.

The blacksmith fires but she still stands.

He fires a second and third and fourth time.

Mary is unmoved.

He fires a fifth at her face.

It appears she cannot be killed.

The blacksmith shoots her five more times but she's unfazed.

As he loads another round into his rifle, Charlie Sparks, the maestro of the Sparks World Famous Circus, appears onstage and asks the executioners why this isn't working. Mary tries to break away but she's subdued by the crew. The blacksmith asks Charlie if he should shoot again but Charlie can't understand why they can't just hang her all dignified like. "Ain't lynchin' quicker anyhow? These people paid good money to see Mary die!"

The hangmen don't want to point out the obvious: Mary's too heavy to be hung.

Charlie barks "figure it out" and leaves.

He's hysterical right now because he's losing the only asset his circus ever had aside from the painted dogs and a clump of clowns that scare the kids.

His show is currently being obliterated by two crowd-sucking titans named P. T. Barnum and James Bailey. How can you compete with tigers and freak shows and people getting shot out of cannons? And who can rival Poodle Hanneford, a setter of world records for leaping on and off of a running horse? You *can't* compete with Poodle! You just *can't!*

As Charlie watches his show wither, he wonders how he could have done things differently. His first mistake was hiring that boozehound Red to take care of Mary. He didn't feed her properly nor as often as was needed. And now, because Sparks Circus hired a former hotel janitor to look after the crown jewel of his fading spectacle, and because the news of Red's termination spread like brushfire through the surrounding territories of Tennessee, thereby causing the leaders of these towns to declare no circus harboring a convicted killer will be allowed into their open fields, Charlie was forced to execute a five ton elephant worth twenty grand. His heart was pricked to see the animal die, but his brain blistered at the thought of losing such a costly mammal.

Hence the idea to sell tickets to see the Death of the Biggest Elephant on Earth. This tragedy ballooned into a one-time publicity event in order to recuperate a fraction of the cash.

So they string Mary up on a giant crane.

When the chain snaps she falls and breaks her hip.

The children sitting in the dust scatter like cockroaches when they hear the agonized moans of the beast.

The executioners find a chain with tough enough links to hang her high. She swings suspended in death, mouth frozen in an open horror death mask cast from her final gurgled gasps.

How torturous and deceitful is the heart of man, thought the fellow who proposed death by railroad-car-squashing. *The desperate wickedness and windings insidious. Who can know the unlit labyrinths of the human heart.*

Chris Karr is a filmmaker, playwright, poet and author from Kentucky. He is the co-creator of "Server Life," an independent TV series on Vimeo and his reviews, articles, and interviews have appeared in "Highbrow Magazine." Mr. Karr currently lives in New York City.

The Bell Tower

Dani J. Caile

I bent low, holding onto the side of dear old Bob Brandle's gravestone as I paused to catch my breath, damning the years I'd spent polishing the silver in the vestry instead of keeping myself in the good shape I'd held when only a mere choir boy. Oh, those happy moments with the pastor in the pulpit on a cold, winter evening, warming our posteriors with the help of the small, hot, rusting radiator installed to keep his Holy toes from freezing during a frosty sermon.

The church bells rang again, breaking my recollection. Who would be ringing them at 2 am? Being the sexton and verger of my small parish church, it was my responsibility to find out who the culprit was. No one except Pratchett rang those bells, and as far as I knew, he was in hospital with an inguinal hernia.

I fumbled through my keys and opened the thick wooden door which led to the bell tower. A whiff of smelly cheese flew by my nose as I saw a pair of feet fly up into the air. There was a small man pulling on the bell rope, without success. He'd grabbed it too high and was going up and down with each clang of the bell.

"Archibald Scratch?" asked the man between rings as he rode the rope up and down, his voice being lost in the gables.

"Yes! Get down from there! How dare you ring the bells! And at this time! You'll wake the whole parish!" I grabbed hold of the end of the bell rope, and helped slow its momentum until the man was almost back on solid ground and the bells had stopped ringing.

"Are you Archibald Scratch of 27 Bottoms Avenue, Worthington-on-the-Wold?"

I had a hold of his trousers and finally the rope stopped. "Yes, yes, I am."

With a hop, skip and jump, the small man let go of the rope, grabbed my hand and placed what looked like a letter into my palm.

"We must not make a scarecrow of the law, setting it up to fear the birds of prey, and let it keep one shape till custom make it their perch and not their terror," quoted the man. "Angelo, Act 2 scene 1, *Measure for Measure*."

"What? What is the meaning of this? Why are you here? How dare you...!" I looked at the letter.

"This..." He pointed to the letter. "...is a summons for non-payment of the annual subscription of Tickle Me Pink, Clergy Edition, and you have been summoned to appear in court at the end of the month. Good day to you, sir." With that, the small man picked up a grey Fedora resting on the cushioned seat in the corner and left by the door.

156

Dani J Caile is not only a respected author of cracked masterpieces such as "Manna-X", "How to Build a Castle in Seven Easy Steps" and "How to Sink a Ship (in eight long, excruciatingly terrifying, stinkingly evil nights)", he is also a fantastic editor and proofreader. Check out http://danijcaile.blogspot.com/

The Fourth Silo

R. J. Drury

Jake didn't get many visitors, nor did he want them. In the year since he'd taken up residence in the aging ranch house, he'd found that solitude suited him. As the sole beneficiary of his late uncle's will, he now owned this isolated ranch.

Two irritants marred the tranquility of Jake's new life. Both centred on the four silage silos dominating his yard.

The first problem derived from the art work on the silos. Sometime in the past, his late uncle had allowed a group of local artists to paint murals on the silos. The murals depicted local ranching as it had been before a changing climate turned this marginal agricultural area into a near desert. Cattle, sheep, horses, and a lone dog ambled across the empty silos. Those animals, thought Jake, looked a lot healthier than the scrawny goats now under his care. The art imposed itself as a glaring reminder that this ranch had once been prosperous.

The most annoying aspect of this problem centred on the way the occasional artsy-fartsy tourists, agog over the art, took the murals as entitlement to drive into his yard. The intruders always seemed affronted to find that Jake had the temerity to tell them to leave.

Until he sat down to work out the cost to paint over the murals, Jake had thought that might be a solution. It wasn't.

The second irritant was the fourth silo. Unlike the other three, it presented no entry of any kind. This challenge to common sense outraged Jake's concept of a sensible universe. A silo that couldn't be opened would have been useless even before cattle ranching ceased to be viable here. This silo presented a nagging question without an answer. It loomed over his yard — an affront to logic.

A few months after moving in, he'd taken a pick and tried to cut an opening through the outside wall of the silo. The pick scratched the paint to reveal gleaming metal. His efforts produced one other result. The pick handle cracked.

Next, he nursed his wheezing pickup into town to rent a propane cutting torch. The torch scorched some paint but otherwise showed no effect. The exposed metal gleamed defiance.

The dark Humvee now trailing a cloud of dust into his yard seemed different than the usual annoying intruder. The doors were emblazoned with some kind of government logo. This, thought Jake, looked worse than the artsy-fartsies.

The vehicle halted a few metres away. In silent defiance, Jake stood his ground as the Humvee's dust plume drifted over him. A tall man in military uniform unfolded himself from the vehicle. Unfamiliar with military insignia, Jake couldn't identify the man's rank but, because the man had a fringe of grey hair, Jake assumed he must be an officer of some sort.

The officer carried a folder from which he extracted a colour photograph. He presented it for Jake to see the head and shoulders of a muscular young man.

The officer asked, "Have you seen this man?"

Jake felt relief. So this wasn't about his unpaid taxes. He studied the photo.

"Naw, I don't git many people out here and if I seen someone with a scar like that across his cheek, I'd recollect."

The photo retreated back into the folder. The officer handed Jake a card.

"If you see him, please telephone this number."

Jake grinned. "Ain't got no phone, but if I see 'im, I'll give 'im yer card."

The officer grimaced. "He lived around here forty years ago. He's dangerous. If you see him, find a way to get in touch."

With that, he returned to the Humvee, wheeled around, and rejuvenated the dust plume. Jake stood silent, insistent questions in his head. The man in the photo looked about twenty. If the photo was from forty years ago, what would he look like now? Wouldn't the officer have realized that a forty-year-old photo might be useless?

In less than an hour, answers arrived in the form of another dust plume visible through Jake's kitchen window. This time, the plume came not from the road but from a dirt bike churning its way across country. The bike stuttered into the yard as Jake interrupted his lunch to meet it. He ambled outside, his jaw set, to confront this new intrusion.

The rider removed his helmet. He had a scar on his cheek. Jake froze. This man looked exactly like his forty-year-old photo.

The man tossed the keys for the bike to Jake and announced, "It's yours."

He strode to the fourth silo. A sliding door opened; the man entered; the door closed. Jake's mouth hung open.

A minute later, Jake felt a rumble beneath his feet. The silo ripped itself out of the ground and rose ponderously into the air in a deafening roar. Jake turned his back against a torrent of dust. The rumble escalated into a local earthquake. He lost his footing and fell. The shaking ended. Jake regained his feet and looked up to see the silo vault into the sky.

The other three silos, in ponderous motion, crashed into the ground crumbling into rubble as they did so. In the settling dust cloud, Jake grinned and spoke aloud, "Takes care uh that problem."

He looked up to see the fourth silo become a distant speck and vanish into the sky.

As his eyes fell upon the dirt bike, Jake's grin widened. He wheeled the bike into a shed and, with a jaunty saunter, returned to his lunch.

R. J. Drury is a retired Math and Physics teacher who writes in Stony Plain, Alberta, Canada. His mind roams the universe of space and time. You are welcome to come along for the ride.

The Back Room

Thomas Headley

John Carol was afraid of the room at the end of the hall in a way that could not be explained by rational thought.

John was your typical American. He worked hard at a local machine shop at least six days a week, paid his taxes, and went to church on Sunday. He was happily married and blessed with two young children (both boys). John lived in an everyday house, in an everyday kind of neighborhood, with two bank owned cars in the garage. It could easily be said that John's life was at least a little better than average but everything is also not necessarily as it appears when dealing with something as complicated as the human psyche. Such was the case with the back room of his house.

They had bought that house nearly two years before, mostly upon the urging of his wife, Janet. It was a safe neighborhood, close to both of their careers, (they had been lucky in that respect), it put the boys close to their school and friends; how could he say no? John remembered that his initial opinion of the house was fair to neutral. It was nice enough and he wasn't too particular. He could not even remember looking through the back room at the end of the hall. In fact, in two years he had never set foot in that room, he had not even risked a quick peek to see what was inside.

The boys were roomed together, which was their choice, and he and Janet shared the second of three bedrooms. The room at the end of the hall was a "guest room". Janet had offered to make it a study or even a "man-cave" and John would just smile and politely brush off the notion. Every time that she would clean or go in the room for any reason, John would have to walk away and brace himself as butterflies fluttered in his stomach the entire time until she was finished.

The door to the room remained closed, and if it was ajar, John knew it. He could feel it, almost like an extension of the soul. The room was fashioned in an "L" shape from the doorway, apparently, as John had once actually leaned in to pull the accursed thing closed, but he had never dared lean inside the door-frame. Nothing could be seen but the opposing wall from the doorway.

John awoke one night in a cold sweat, feeling that the door must be open. He could see the clearance of the door-frame in his mind's eye as plain as the ticking clock hung on the wall. He could envision very vividly the door hanging open like the mouth of some gigantic demon, waiting to swallow him in one gory bite. He lay awake in the dense black of night, feeling like a full-grown man had perched upon his chest, making it hard to breath and forcing him to labor for each rasping breath. His heart beat quickened and a bitter chill raced through his body from head to toe at a frenzied pace. He walked slowly out of his bedroom to look, from a safe distance, at the room down the hall. His breath returned to him and the surging adrenaline subsided like a basin of water swirling rapidly down a drain as he looked upon the white, six panel door, pulled securely shut. John turned back toward his bed, and he could almost hear a type of low, mimicking laughter as if the room had somehow gotten one over on him. John knew that the room had been open before, and someone or something must have closed it. He had been around that back room for too long to mistake such a feeling: He knew.

One of the kids had probably left that door open by mistake. Or maybe his wife. She meant well, but maybe the back room was overpowering her somehow. Maybe that could be the reason why she insisted on going in there. It could be that the evil force inside that back room was strong enough even to *control* his wife and his children. His children, just young boys, had always wanted to play around that room, despite firm warnings from their father. His whole family could be conspirators under the spell of that malicious evil. John shuddered at the thought, and wanted to shy away from his responsibilities but he knew what he had to do next to ensure that the back room and its presence, its very influence, could not be spread beyond his home. He did what had to be done.

That night, after darkness had enveloped the town, John walked on toward the river bridge in the cool of the night, illuminated only by the faint and subtle starlight. He had left his home burning to the ground behind him like a deep regret that one tries to abandon. He hoped to silence the evil of that back room and prevent it from spreading its wicked influence. He cried bitter tears of grief at the loss of his family, but he knew that he had really lost them long ago to the back room. The bridge ahead was a watery blur as John viewed it through the distorted lens of his warm tears. He shook violently as he climbed the rusted railing and looked down at the wavy water of the river flowing beneath. He could never be sure that the room, now ablaze, had not infected his brain too. He had just killed his family, a mission of mercy he had thought, but maybe that was the room causing him to fulfil its evil desires. He could never be certain, and this is why he stood atop the side railing of the river bridge and sought to end his own existence to save others. A smile formed as he considered this righteous sacrifice.

John swallowed as much of his fear as he could in one gulp and stepped off the rail.

Thomas Headley lives in Cincinnati Ohio with his wife and three children. He is the author of several short works of fiction, usually featuring strange characters or mysterious circumstances. His writing often explores the more dark and troubling aspects of the human heart and mind.

Pitchforks

Kevin Rabas

One: Those Democrats are gonna come with pitchforks.

Two: The only Democrats I've ever seen with pitchforks were composting.

Mom: When Jane Fonda came to Fort Hays State, the farmers did come into town with pitchforks. It was kind of a joke. She was touring the country and made a stop, a peace protest. And Dad was already in the reserves and had to stave them off. And when we moved to KC, he had to guard the 18th Street Bridge, during the protests. In industrial arts, they were wanting to make knives and brass knuckles because of the race riots in the schools. It's a wonder why he didn't stay teaching, eh? The industrial arts trash cans were often on fire, and they were filled with wood and sawdust. Built a pretty good fire.

Poet Laureate of Kansas (2017-2019), Kevin Rabas teaches at Emporia State University. He has ten books, including Lisa's Flying Electric Piano, a Kansas Notable Book and Nelson Poetry Book Award winner.

Jalopy Racer

Stace Johnson

There's nothing quite like the flathead V8 under the hood of my '41 Ford. It lopes and surges, eager to lunge. The big fenders quake and rattle in symphony with the rolling exhaust note as New Mexico dust blows across the flattie's cooling fins, exposed because I removed the engine's side panels for better airflow. I rev the motor and the body shrugs, then resettles on soft springs as I wait for the go signal, the scent of hot oil and grease wafting back to me from the engine bay. I see the flagman on the stand through my scratched goggles, his white coveralls caked with dirt and oil, feet spread wide, looking like an out-of-place Norman Rockwell figure. The green of the flag pokes out from beneath his fingers, wrapped around the stick in his raised hand, ready to drop when he's sure everyone is set. It's a standing start this time. Last week it was my turn to flag, and I chose a rolling start. Everybody pitches in.

I look over into the stands, behind the split rail catch fence. I can barely make out Winnie through the dirty, scratched lenses. She has her hand over her eyes, horn rim sunglasses peeking over her fingers. She tells me she's just keeping the dust out, but I know better. She doesn't want to see another rollover. I'm safe, though. I had a buddy weld me a roll cage after the last one, in exchange for half of this fall's venison. He knows I'm good for it.

I blow Winnie a kiss, like always. She doesn't see it, like always. The kids sit next to her on the makeshift bench, excited, eating their cotton candy laced with racetrack dirt. I wave to them and they jump up, yelling "Go daddy go!" as best they can over the idling engines. The ever-present westerly wind blows the starched hem of Mary Ellen's gingham dress and she nearly drops her cotton candy trying to hold it down. Gordy laughs at her and she punches him in the arm.

I chuckle and look to my left, at McIntyre in his '32 Deuce. He wears his usual Kaiser helmet and aviator goggles, and bright yellow streamers dangle from the suicide door handles, a strong contrast to the overall rust color of the car. His helmet pokes out of a hole in the roof, a matching yellow streamer tied to the point. I gotta admit, he's a showman. Winnie is giving out the trophy tonight; I bet he thinks he's going to steal a celebratory kiss.

He's stripped the fenders, making the car lighter. That's probably how he got pole position today, and he won't let me live it down. He's running a flathead, too, but I can hear he doesn't have it tuned right. He throws me a one finger salute; I answer with a nod and turn to look at the flagman.

The rumble behind me says the rest of the pack is ready to go. I rev the engine to redline with my heel, pressing the brake with my toe and holding the clutch until I can feel the Ford tensing, ready to spring off the starting line.

The green flag drops. I drop the clutch and the rear wheels spin, then bite, and the car lurches forward, roaring like an enraged tiger. McIntyre is right with me as we head into the first turn, side by side. He has the inside line and gains a little ground coming out of the corner, so I drop back behind him. His skinny tires throw track clay at me as his Deuce fishtails under acceleration; he's made the car too light. It's fast, but he doesn't have the weight distributed very well. I grin and settle in, pacing him, letting him think he's got the race won.

My Ford's flattie barely has to work to keep up; I know how to tune it. His Deuce is all over the track, sliding back and forth whenever he hits the gas. Yep. Not enough weight in the rear. He keeps looking behind, checking where I am, and I'm always there.

The race is ten laps, and by the ninth, we've passed everybody else. McIntyre is racing dirty, bumping other cars to the high side of the track, making them lift off the accelerator or go over the bank. He's done it to nearly everyone, and I decide it's time he gets a bit of his own medicine. I ease down on the go pedal, creeping up behind him, my big fenders nearly blocking him from view as we bank around and begin the final lap.

He gets on the gas when he exits turn three, and the rear of the Deuce steps out, throwing a rooster tail of dust. I press the accelerator gently and nose forward, barely touching the back of his car just behind the left rear wheel. What little traction he has breaks, and the '32 does a graceful pirouette up to the high side of the corner, McIntyre's helmet streamer coiling like a barber pole. I give him my own salute as I roll by, leaving him to face the other the drivers as they point and laugh.

I cruise past the checkered flag and take my victory lap, then park in front of the flag stand and cut the engine, crawling out of the welded door and taking off my goggles, a happy raccoon grinning away as my family crawls through the fence.

Winnie walks my way with the trophy, a smile, and a fresh coat of red lipstick.

Stace Johnson is a Colorado writer and musician. His recent written work has appeared in Star*Line, Martian Magazine, and Edward Bryant's Sphere of Influence.

Playing Stalker-in-the-Night

Tais Teng

Castle Sharroq was a thousand years old. Her buttresses and crenelations had been carved from the living granite. Feast halls and corridors honeycombed the interior: structures as elaborate as any termite hill.

King Harold Goldenhair had once brandished a two handed broadsword. His arms had been like tree trunks and he was the only one who could draw the Magic Bow of Ivriel. Harold had married no less than three queens and none had reason to complain about his prowess. A thousand more beautiful girls had loved him and shared his bed. He sired seven sons and more bastards than marigolds in a fallow field.

For little Prince Hames these things were only tales and tall tales at that. The king's flowing locks and beard had long since turned silver and then white as snow. He now tottered through the trophy rooms and argued with companions long since dead. No more broadswords and battle axes for King Harold: he could barely lift a butter knife.

It was clear the king wasn't long for this world. Soon he would be joining his queens in the Wall Halla, the Great Hall beyond the Rainbow Bridge.

Which would leave his throne vacant.

Hames saw his older brothers eyeing each other, fingering their daggers. When King Harold first sat down on the throne no other contenders had been left. Not a single brother or uncle. Not even a third cousin twice removed.

As a toddler Hames had played the game called Stalker. Children sat in a circle, their eyes tightly closed. One, who was the Stalker-in-the-Night, walked around and touched a boy on the nape of his neck.

He next cried "Morning has broken! Awake, awake all!"

The touched one would fall down face first, dead. He would be the next Stalker to circle and claim a victim until no boy was left. In the end all would stand up and walk singing to the end of the rainbow.

When the oldest brother returned from a boar hunt with a quarrel firmly lodged in his left eye socket, Hames understood his brothers had started playing Stalker-in-the-Night. The quarrel had been unmarked, but he didn't believe for a moment it was from some outlaw in the woods.

Now one boy had always been excused from playing the game. Jessurun had hobbled around, dragging his left foot. One eye looked to the right, one to the left and he would start laughing when no joke was told.

The next day Hames started dragging his left foot. He giggled, talked to cats who studiously ignored him. He wrote his own name in excrement on the wall of his room, but decided that was excessive. Pissing his bed was enough.

Soon Hames became almost invisible. He was too high born to taunt so ignoring was the best option for all courtiers. He most certainly wasn't in the running as the next king.

A second prince was found in the middle of the rose brush labyrinth, his throat cut. The third one tumbled down the stairs and ended up on the landing, with his neck broken.

King Harold took his own sweet time dying.

Three brothers were left.

Then only two.

Finally one, Lencelaud. That brother was as handsome as an archangel, with the golden hair and beard of his father. He would make the perfect king.

Hames had just turned thirteen by then and he felt kind of impatient. He put one of those little black spiders from Tuscany in Lencelaud's left boot, a scorpion in his right.

#

A sister woke him the next morning. He wasn't quite sure of her name. Caitlin? Cassilda? Sisters didn't count and there were so many of them. At least a dozen.

She handed him a bowl of mulled wine.

"Drink up, dear brother. You'll need it."

He took a big swallow. The wine was pleasingly hot, with an aftertaste of cinnamon and something astringent.

"What is it?" Hames said and he forgot to gibber for a moment.

"I have some sad news and some even worse news. Our father the king died at cock crow. That is the bad news. The worse is that Lencelaud was found dead, too. His face was swollen like a pumpkin, his tongue black as cuttlefish ink."

Hames threw the heavy fur blanket off, sat up. "So I am king now!'

"Yes," the sister said. "For now."

He frowned. "What do you mean, for now?"

"We sisters, we always shared. Now Cassilda, she is very good with a crossbow. She can hit a sparrow at sixty paces. Little Yonica is always leaving her toys in inconvenient or downright dangerous places. Like the winding stairs of the Northern Watchtower. Me, I studied with the Witch of Brookhill for seven years. She taught me how to dig up a mandrake, ways to steep belladonna flowers. All the best poisons."

Hames stared at her, tried to speak, but his tongue had become a dead weight.

"Queen Caitlin," she said, "Doesn't that have a nice ring?"

Tais Teng is Dutch writer, illustrator and sculptor. His novel Phaedra: Alastor 824, set in the universe of Jack Vance, will be published by Spatterlight in 2019.

Contingency Plan

Steve Pease

Amongst the test tubes and incubators in laboratory sixteen of The National Child Development Center, it was kicking off.

"What in hell are you doing?" asked Mary.

Tossing her curls, Frankie responded like some hormone-fueled teenager.

"Well, duh, I'm trying to have some fun."

"This," replied Mary, pointing at the growth tank, "is not fun, it's lunacy."

"Girl child after girl child — monotonous!" said Frankie, still in teenager mode. "The perfection and sameness we have now is just boring."

The body in the tank was growing visibly by the minute.

"Anyhow," she said, "I've done my research; before the plague, 21st century women had some fun. I want to enjoy a dinner date. I want to try dancing. Without being indelicate, I want to find out if something warmer is better than the frozen variant we're using."

Mary looked at her in disbelief.

"We women invented and spread that plague for very good reasons. Some might have seemed trivial; like hairiness, belching and snoring. But others were serious; I'm talking domestic slavery and abuse, job inequality. I'm talking rape and warfare."

"Look," said Frankie, "if, just for a minute, you stop being a do-gooding pain in the ass, I'll fix you up with a guy too. But, whatever you decide, I'm making myself a man."

Tears and fear appeared in Mary's eyes. "Don't you understand the danger? You're talking about resurrecting a threat that held us back for millennia."

Frankie laughed, and produced a vial out of her pocket. "Look, I have a contingency plan. This is plague plus one; just in case you're right, and he turns out to be an asshole."

Steve Pease enjoys life in Northern England; writing, dog-walking, and playing poor guitar. He once had a 'proper job', drafting press-releases and briefings for British politicians — an ideal apprenticeship in crafting fantasy.

Starseed Unicorn: The Literature Dimension

Lisa Love

Pages upon pages upon pages...stacks and towers and rivers of printed papers...mountains of pages on grounds of pages...some gold...some white...some with pictures in colored ink, some with lines and many words...

Fonts for days: curly kinds, more straight-edge loud kinds (all capitals, like YELLING), and some so miniscule and narrow that no naked eye could sort them out! Some of the fonts stretched far and wide...alllll theeee waaaaaaaay aroooooooooouuuund...and some just paused gently in a sea of space.

The covers ranged from hard to soft. And some of the binding materials surprised and awed, like one thinly sliced rosewood, another one cork, a glass one, and a metal one. Those were rare, though. Mostly, papers rumpled and rippled here, there...everywhere.

Whenever Starseed Unicorn hopped into a book, she landed in some kind of magical portal! This one was the natural waterslide that whirled all the way down...and dropped into a great underwater lagoon...

"Oh, I see...this is the *Goonies* novel!" Starseed became aware...

...and then through her awareness she was able to switch which book she experienced in...

The Literature Dimension.

She swirled and whirled into a secret dresser and all the way through to the forest of *Narnia*, which was much more beautiful than the movie did justice. She enjoyed long gallops in the snow, and when she tired, she whizzed right out and into the in between part of this dimension, where all the pages rippled, and because she looked at so many at the same time, she just began to sink where she was, like in quicksand...

Oh, she had been brought into the fire swamp in *Princess Bride*! Westley and Buttercup hopped on her back and rode her safely out.

Then it was all dark...pitch black...in *The Neverending Story* in the uncertain part when the world is being saved, and she was in the closet with the Empress who needed a name (a unicorn and a princess in a closet, can you imagine?!). Thankfully, Starseed called her Lotus, and the whole universe bloomed, safe and sound. Phew!

This was all well and good, but Starseed realized how sticky these seemingly harmless bits of literature could be if she selected a particularly engrossing one of a subject matter that did not exactly manifest...well...the best.

Starseed had always known better than trying to manifest, because she knew the very best would always be manifested for her when she simply felt Loved...However, she also knew that she could not help but manifest sometimes, in conscious and unconscious ways, because while she is a spiritual being, she does sometimes have a body that has something of a mortality to it, and that's one of the blessings of God, Which Starseed did not presume to know.

Starseed had proof of manifesting: she noticed synchronicities in relation to whatever literature she consumed...

...and truly, that is the crux of reading: it is an act of consumption more than an act of creativity...and for many, it is an act of escape more than an act of true, heartfelt connection. However, it all depends on the literature...

Something called to Starseed from across the way: she teleported over and melted into...the storyboards for the movie *Spirited Away*, which lived more fully than the other literature, perhaps because they weren't scripted and flowed out organically during the making of the movie.

There is Love here, Starseed felt.

Amazing, I can feel the Love in the ones that are made in Love! She realized fully, with a great sense of relief. She was saved.

She played in the spirit dimension represented in the scene over the bridge, and she flew over the water with No-Face and took the train with a ticket she dreamed up for herself. She even flew with the paper dragon and took a salt soak. She tried a starry bite of the coal workers' sprinkle food, and it tasted like *fizzle fazzle WOW!*

And because of the nature of the literature, she learned deeply of her spirit lessons. She realized she can always be a heroine in all dimensions, regardless of her age or form or reputation, and everyone can. She realized that as long as she tries her best and works hard, she will always be safe and nurtured and guided. And, maybe most importantly, she realized that help, guidance, miracles, and relative success all flow in organically in ways that cannot necessarily be predicted but are truly dependable because the Divine Source Loves us every moment and offers every dream come true and solution in infinite ways always.

After sweetly waving farewell to her new dear friends, Chihiro and Haku, who became smaller and smaller in the distance, and she swam deeply into all the pages in the middle part again, comfortably this time.

She felt something calling to her and beheld a glowing, almost like a glow she had seen before, or maybe not (she did not know). Something deepmost within her glistened and opened gently, spilling out sweet, cool, white light to all and everywhere in beautiful swirls and twirls.

She came to it, slowly and calmly. The cool blue colored book shined with one word bigger than the rest, or more important at least: *Heartfelt*.

What relief! It is her life guide! Not for just this lifetime, but for all lifetimes! And it is best for everyone and somehow best for her, and it is somehow both for her and from her.

In such close proximity to *Heartfelt*, Starseed dissolved into Stardust and merged with this spiritual guide. She became the spiritual heart lessons, the epiphanies, the metaphors, the Love in action, the poetic verse in rhythm. She became — simple, fully and completely — Loved.

It's why she'd come here. And it's why this place was made. It's what we've all been hoping for.

She felt gratitude, fully and completely, as her heart experienced the expansive shift from outside of the connection to within. The portal for *Heartfelt* led to...Home.

Author of novels Heartfelt *and* Starseed Unicorn, *Lisa Love just published an anthology of true stories by people with special abilities called* We Are The Gift...and why we're here.

Locked In

Kimber Grey

At first, it was good, innocent fun. Just a quirky role-play to pass a water-logged spring break. It wasn't my first time volunteering for one of the psych department's social experiments in an effort to fold a couple of extra bills into my pocket. Play make-believe prison in a moldy basement, get three square meals a day for free, and earn some good karma with this cute shrink-in-training, Sandra. Not like the time I had to face my greatest fears and let them put tarantulas on my face.

Easy money.

We were all given uniforms, told our roles, squared away into 'cells' or 'barracks', and locked in. Immediately, it was obvious who would enjoy 'doing time' more. The guards had nicer clothes, better beds, more freedom to move around, T.V., and even better food. The prisoner's uniforms were itchy, the beds stank, and I thought I saw mold on the bread.

In spite of that, there was a sense of equality in the beginning. The basement leaked, and we were all damp and cold, prisoner and guard alike. We would joke about the dichotomy of our squalor verses the apparent luxury of an extra sheet. We would wax philosophical about how perception made even the tiniest of things seem grand. Then we would all go to bed shivering.

As it should have been expected, the playful taunting and teasing devolved into darker play. Two days of poor sleep on foul beds made the prisoners irritable, and the often over-exaggerated mockery from the guards began to grate on the wards' nerves. It was still a game. We were still getting paid. But the fun had run out.

I'm not sure when I realized some of the prisoners were really struggling, or when the taunting had become so vicious that I began to tune it out. I was watching prisoner 38 through the bars, Billy-the-back-talker. Two guards prodded him with unfolded hangers. They weren't breaking the skin, but they'd been doing it in shifts for nearly twenty-nine hours. 38 had stopped begging them to stop two shifts ago. He lay on his bed, back turned to the guards, quietly crying.

Then it happened. Billy wet himself.

It should have triggered something in all of us, a human's ability to recognize the true wrongness of what had just occurred. But none of us were who we once were, none of us were human. Instead, the guards laughed and cheered. The prisoners looked away, none offering 38 any support. None wanting to be the next victim of the guards' malicious pastimes.

I looked away, too, and found the gaze of Sandra-the-guard. She was smiling, looking to me as if she had just discovered a new world. Surely, 38's incontinence would be the fodder for several award-winning papers, and she was expecting me to share in her triumph. It was disgusting. I smiled back.

It's hard to explain the real sense of quiet terror we were all enduring and the twisted survival instinct that took hold of us. The guards had bonded and fed off of each other's spite, no longer recognizing themselves, afraid to deviate from the horde. They had passed some ambiguous point of no-return, and to keep from assimilating the crimes against humanity they had already committed, they escalated to the next 'prank' designed to run down the hours of the clock.

The prisoners all showed signs of sleep deprivation and stress. Prisoner 12 had vomited every-other-meal for the past two days. Prisoner 27 hugged and rocked herself whenever she was taunted. Prisoner 8 had begun sleeping all day and scratching hatch-marks in the wall whenever dinner was delivered through the faceless opening of the basement door. Their misery was palpable. At some point, we somehow forgot we were students, not really prisoners or guards.

Sandra didn't participate in the pranks, but she inspired and encouraged them. It was her idea to begin adding hatch marks to 8's wall when he was sleeping. She documented his growing anticipation of the end of the experiment, glowing with pride every time he awoke and failed to discover the deception. Apparently, it was easy to lose track of time if there were no clocks or windows. He was so consumed with his need to be free of his cell, he stopped communicating with the other prisoners, creating his own form of solitary confinement. When 8 added the last hatch that was meant to represent the final day of his imprisonment, he laughed and threw his dinner onto the ground.

Peter-the-guard hosed him down, but 8 just laughed and pretended to take pleasure bathing in the icy water. Peter had become the worst of them. He had taken the longest to settle into the guard-cult, hanging back awkwardly and watching the cruelty escalate. Sandra finally brought the dictator out of him with her quiet coaxing, and he made up for the delay with a true dissociation from the person he once was. Peter had been fun-loving, easy-going, slow to anger, and quick to forgive. Peter-the-guard was a malicious robot. He saw it as his duty to force the prisoners to submit to the guards' wills and ensure the integrity of the pranks.

8's hysterical joy combined with Peter's robotic delivery of cold justice somehow elevated everyone from the misery of the experiment for the rest of the evening. The guards laughed on and off about it long into the night, and 8's humming earned a few reprises from his fellows. Still, we all knew what would follow.

The next day, 8 refused to eat, looking at each plate of unappetizing food with a queer smile of expectation. When dinner arrived, he stared at it for a full minute before he rushed to the wall to count his hatch marks. He began doing math on his fingers and counted his hatches again. He began to mumble that he must have counted one dinner twice.

Sandra smiled at me, and I returned it, woodenly. I knew she would spend hours writing her notes that night, regardless of how 8 reacted. In the end, the distraught prisoner went to bed without eating.

The next morning 8 stared at the hatches on the wall, rocking and waiting. Every day a new prisoner had been selected to endure the hanger-poking torment for 24 hours; today, Sandra insisted the victim be 8. The guards shifted their chairs to cell #8 and began to prod. Three shifts passed, lunch came, and the prisoner barely seemed to notice the torment. Sandra took her notes, and Peter took his turn with a hanger. He showed no mercy, finding a single spot he could target reliably, and jabbed away till specks of red seeped through the filthy fabric of 8's uniform. Still, no reaction.

That was when dinner came. 8 shrieked the moment he saw the plates and ripped the hanger from Peter's hand, drawing an angry line of blood across the guard's palm. For the first time, Peter's mechanical execution of his duty devolved into rage. He jerked the hose from the wash-sink and cranked the water to high. At first, no one realized what he had done. The cold water rocked 8 to a gasping silence. Abruptly, he screamed and shrank from it. He ran from one side of his cell to the other. Then everyone noticed the steam that was rolling off of him and roiling up from the scalding water.

Even Sandra stared in shock.

8 wailed. Peter bared his teeth. The door to the basement opened, and professors poured down the stairs. They were drawn into the prison by the desperate cries of 8, who was trying to hide behind his scant bed. All of the volunteers came out of their daze and became students again. They shouted at Peter, their expressions twisted with horror.

"Peter, stop!" Sandra screamed. "You're hurting him!"

Then she slapped me.

The last to succumb to the hysteria of the experiment, and the last to awaken from it. I watched the hose fall from my suddenly numb fingers.

Kimber has authored nine fantasy books and two anthologies. She appears in multiple anthologies, and her work can be found at Patreon.com/KimberGrey and amazon.com/Kimber-Grey/e/B00BU84D7W

Kansas Morning

Ann Vigola Anderson

Winter's morning long ago...with nature's tiny Christmas decorations hanging like ice tinsel everywhere this morning, I lingered under my covers and thought about the times my grandma would bring me breakfast in bed. This was a winter only event and when it was only me staying at my grandparent's house. To have my grandma all to myself was like hanging out with Glinda from OZ as everything was happy and warm and I seemed surrounded by a pink bubble.

I would sleep in the spare bedroom with its goose down mattress and crisp white sheets. I don't think color sheets existed back then (and my grandma would not have approved of them) and my grandma's sheets always were bleach white and soft. The quilts were mounded on me, some handmade cotton quilts made by my grandma and a soft wool one she made out of old sweaters and soft felt. My grandpa would go to the basement and load shiny blocks of coal into the furnace before bedtime and sometimes in the night if it were extra cold.

On very cold days, my grandma would carry a worn wooden tray in, covered with a flour sack dishtowel, which somehow, she made look elegant. I would sit up, rub my eyes and she would say, "Good morning, sunshine." The feast would be set on a pillow on my lap. It was usually her pancakes, as thin as paper and stacked four inches high, each layer hiding a teaspoon of butter that the day before had been fresh cow's milk, and cane syrup that ran happily over the edges like a tiny waterfall on the plate. If the chickens were in the mood, she would add a fresh egg sunny side up with a yoke that was the color of daisy centers. A glass of orange juice and a cup of milk coffee rounded out my breakfast in bed.

My grandma would ask, "Would you like to go on an adventure after breakfast?" Yes, yes, of course and I would eat so quickly and throw on my warm clothes. She would already be pulling on her heavy black coat and had my mittens and hat ready. We would walk out to the barn and she would gently wrap her apron around the neck of one of their sweet draft horses. He would nuzzle her shoulder and she always had a piece of carrot or apple to give him. With only an apron for a halter, she would hoist me onto his broad warm back and grandma would lead us down the dirt path to the pasture.

Our destination was almost always the windmill that I loved. It was so tall and I loved to hear the blades whir in the wind. The tank would be full of water and if we were lucky, there would be some of their cattle getting a drink. One time, the calves were there and though they were skittish still, grandma talked to them and they let me pet their soft brown fur and stare at their beautiful eyes.

And then grandma would swing me back onto the horse with the apron strings and we would head back to the house. The horse went straight to the barn and another piece of apple or carrot was a reward for being such a good ride.

My grandma was the last of the pioneer women in Kansas who knew how to work hard, never complained, always put others first, and watched over her family like a Rhode Island red hen.

She always had time for me and to take me on an adventure to see the windmill spinning circles in a Kansas blue sky.

Ann Vigola Anderson is a writer and tennis coach at Jayhawk Tennis Center, University of Kansas. She's married, has three cats, and lives in Lawrence.

Snuffy, the Amazing Cat

James Bartlett Parry

Snuffy was found wandering outside St. Joseph's Care Center, dirty and hungry. Staff members began setting out dishes of food for him, and soon he was allowed inside for his daily feedings. Eventually, he, of course, worked his way in permanently. Once he decided to adopt the staff, he became the official 2nd Floor Companion Animal. The second floor consisted of single-room apartments for lifers – those in need of assistance as they lived out the final months of their lives. This was his domain; Snuffy was in charge of the second floor. The first floor was devoted to rehabilitation of those recovering from injury, stroke, or surgery. (Another cat, whom Snuffy held in contempt, took care of the first floor patients.)

Snuffy roamed the hallways ignoring staff, looking for food and, at the same time, waiting for that call or whisper from one of the human residents in need of company.

As if his special ability to love and be loved by the sickly and elderly wasn't enough, Snuffy had an even more amazing talent. Sometimes, these codger-lodgers did not have to verbalize their need for companionship. This cat – which apparently is true of many animals – could somehow detect that need through a sixth sense. He was particularly adept at sensing the imminent passing of any patient who was all alone. Whenever Snuffy picked-up one of these signals he would pick-up his pace, and with a determined look, high-tail it to the appropriate room.

After months of duty, staffers realized that Snuffy had purrfected his amazing ability. He never erred. Whenever nurses or aides entered a room and found one of their patrons had crossed over, there was Snuffy, curled up against the person to whom he had brought comfort during those final hours.

Years went by. Snuffy became the stuff of legend. He was the subject of several human-interest stories, be it television or newspaper. There was once a small piece on Snuffy near the end of NBC Nightly News with Tom Brokaw.

Several more years passed, and Snuffy was becoming a bit elderly himself, but still maintained his amazing power, and kept his flawless death-vigil record intact.

Nadine, a newly-hired aide, had, of course, heard of this famous cat. In fact, he was the primary reason she had applied at St Joe's. She had been an animal-lover all of her life, and was especially fond of cats. She was fortunate enough to be assigned to the second floor, and now could meet this famed feline figure. She was unfortunate enough to be assigned to night duty, being the newbie.

Second floor policy was to take patients' vitals every four hours on the dot; at 8 P.M., midnight, and again at 4 A.M. during this – forgive me – graveyard shift. However, Nadine came to realize that night duty was actually a blessing-in-disguise, for it allowed her some quiet time with Snuffy near the start of her shift. She would give him an extra treat or two, an extra pet or two, and occasionally would roll a small ball which Snuffy loved to chase down the main corridor.

One sleeting evening near the beginning of the second month of Nadine's St. Joe's employment, she, for the first time, had not a single problem during her rounds, and, so, arrived at Mrs. Landers' room several minutes early for the midnight vitals. (Now, Mrs. Landers had been in poor health for over a month, and at the age of 94, was not expected to live much longer.) As Nadine entered her room, there was Snuffy climbing off the face of the no-longer breathing Mrs. Landers, and curling up next to her.

Yes, Snuffy was an amazing cat.

Jim Parry was born in Boise, Idaho, but somehow found his way to Spokane, Washington at age four, where he still resides. His book, BOOK ALL THE TEACHERS, can be found on Amazon or in most bookstores.

The Bellenfants

Dean Anthony Brink

Odd and hypnotic, they totter about ignoring onlookers. Some call them remnants of a golden age best forgotten, others call them drifters captive to their own inertia.

Groomed to exude propriety and rise to the offices of their now-fallen parents, their rhythm itself seems to parody their pasts.

They wander from the Port of Tacoma over the flatlands of Federal Way and as far north as Marysville, steering clear of what is left of their homes long ago on Mercer Island.

One might think diehard reformists would want to track them down in some form of unsportsmanlike class revenge. Nothing could be further, as I hope you will see for yourself on your visit.

A new spirit of modesty and giving prevails in our potlatch economy up and down the Puget Sound.

Nor have any of the poor Bellenfants been tagged for any crimes — the fate of their parents.

Though hardly aging, as advertised in the marketing campaigns, what the sun does to them makes up for it as they must scavenge to eat hand to mouth. Many have the thickened skin of old age pinned to their faces already in their 20s.

Thus they remain as visible to anyone as the ubiquitous Scotch Broom blooming fluorescent shades of yellow along the pot-hole plagued I-5 corridor.

They are certainly stained, but not by their own greed as much as by that of their parents and the misplaced pride they placed in them. They remain silent bearers of this burden, this scab not healing, yet so very ripe and ready for some entrepreneur to pick up their story and run with it, playing the humanitarian card to the hilt.

#

I'm not really sure how much you know about them, but it all began as a bet among Mercer Island Lion's Club members. They held dreams of perfection for their children and paid for the beta-testing using them. But their ultimate aim was to assemble a cocktail of patents to bring to market and make themselves even richer.

In a cruel twist of fate, many of the Bellenfants barely survived, being so overloaded with implants, vitamins, and gene-tailored injections and meds.

Yet their curse had just begun.

In the spectacle of wars concocted in part by a few of the same men and women, the more successful Bellenfants were designated national treasures so as to spare them from military service when they turned 18.

That, for ordinary folk, was the last straw. Bellenfants became the epitome of inequity and omens of pending adjustments.

#

I think many of us are ready to put such rancor behind us.

In fact, one only hears kind words of concern and sympathy for them as they rummage through dumpsters in back alleys. No one has the heart to chase them off. Things have changed.

Now, in hindsight, in a way they seem not only products of eugenic experiments gone awry, but even more like harbingers of the great transformation that came to pass.

After the reforms, Bellenfants flocked to the lab in Bellevue, seeking refuge, redemption, and, mostly, cures to their growing ailments.

They still suffer on many levels. For starters, they seem to live in their minds and are visibly driven to nomadism.

Though as a percentage of the population miniscule, being homeless and thus exposed, they seem to pop out of every park or alley in the region.

Some say their intellectual breeding led to gradual implosion, like Nietzsche. They turned so far inward they lost the very breadcrumbs leading back to their place in our shared world.

Organizations like yours can try to help pull them out of this limbo of lost, fuzzy selves.

#

You also asked about their parents. Most surviving parents abandoned them not out of brute cruelty as they escaped to Argentina but simply in hope that they might survive by blending in with the other children. I know it sounds absurd. Indeed, they are reminders of how uneven the distribution of resources was, and as such are kept at a distance. If spotted carrying on as of old with their entourages of bodyguards brandishing AR-15s, they certainly would not have survived a week. It would be an outrage, drawing out vigilante militia squads.

Withdrawn from others, they seem to have no connection to anyone, not their lost parents, not even each other. No form of life in any of its networks or ecosystems seems to suit them.

They were the last victims of the free market, its final blind thrust toward perfection.

Still, there remains something charming in them, the way an antique brings the patina of a lost paradigm to an otherwise unremarkable room.

#

And you asked how so many came to exist.

180

By the time the faulty genes became fully expressed in the children (during the tail end of puberty), it was already too late. A whole generation had emerged.

Some pundits blamed a gene sequence thought to have been copied from a koala — certainly too cute an explanation to be true.

Yet, indeed they seem to crouch in silence, frozen in some anticipation of drastic punishment, as if caught in the vortex of a world caving in on itself.

This gives them an air of transfixed timidity and humility reinforced by their perpetual filthiness.

They conjure our deepest fears, and as such would seem perfect for fundraising.

They have a spooky look we can bank on. It almost always elicits a deep response in onlookers. Run a search for the old Bennington Colors ads, especially the one in which a half-naked eunuch is running around in a Dr. Seuss-style top. That sort of thing works, though heaven knows why.

If you like, I can help you track some down to interview, if they can still talk. At least I could help you take pictures for a cover story. I'm sure your work will be a hit and earn support from the larger corporations dotting the coast. We can work out the percentages later.

Dean Anthony Brink's science fiction has appeared in various anthologies and magazines. "The Threepenny Space Opera" is forthcoming in Space Opera Libretti and "The Scarlatti" in Helios Quarterly Magazine.

Snot

Russell Smeaton

My eyes are itchy, my nose is bunged up and I'm forever sneezing. Don't get me wrong – I love summer. I'm just sick of hay-fever. Judging by the amount of red eyes and sniffing in the office, I'm not the only one suffering.

The weather forecast last night reported that there would be even higher pollen counts. I've stockpiled a load of nose spray. I'll be fine.

Another day over, another bucket of snot. The office was half empty today. Several called in sick, but some we didn't hear from at all. Not even email.

When I got home I had a crazy sneezing fit. I hawked up a great glob of snot. That wasn't too bad. What was bad was the creature squirming inside. It looked like a foetus or a shrimp. I flushed it down the toilet before puking. Maybe I was mistaken. I mean, it makes no sense, right? My skin still crawls thinking about it.

Waking up this morning, I couldn't breathe. My nose was totally blocked. I didn't sleep well, either. Dreams of that snot-thing kept waking me. I tried to call in sick, but no-one picked up so I just sent an email.

I sneezed out another one of those things. Don't ask me why, but I've put it in a jar. I guess I wanted to prove I'm not going crazy. The thing flopped about pathetically until I filled the jar with water. Now it's swimming around. It looks a bit like one of those sea monkeys. You know, the ones that look cute on the picture but are just fleas or something? I wonder if I should feed it. It comes to the jar wall when I tap it.

The weather forecast says the pollen count tomorrow is going to reach record levels. I've ran out of nose-spray, and my nose is locked solid with mucus. Every time I blow it another creature slithers out. I know it's not normal but that's what happens. I've been putting them in the jar with the first one but it eats them, growing rapidly. As it grows "it" is becoming a "she", and she is beautiful.

This morning I was woken by a smashing sound. She had somehow fallen off the shelf, shattering her jar. As I came into the kitchen she sat in a puddle of broken glass and water, pleading at me with those gorgeous eyes.

There was no weather forecast today, only static from the radio. I've not seen or heard from anyone in a while. It's just her and me. She continues to grow so I've moved her into the bath. When I touch the water, visions fill my head of a place that is not on Earth. It's the most beautiful, relaxing place I've ever seen. Unknown stars swirl in an indigo sky and all around is warm blue water. It's just her and me forever.

She keeps inviting me to get into the bath. Tonight I'll join her.

Russell Is published in places such as Ravenwood Quarterly, Planet X and the Occult Detective Quarterly.

The Priest's Curse

Aditya Deshmukh

Lord Bronor stormed inside the throne room and bowed before Queen Righnara. He opened his mouth to deliver the bitter tidings, but his voice failed him. He simply stood gaping at the queen, his jaw shuddering.

Righnara rose, digging her nails in her palms. Her nostrils flared as she waited. "What is it?"

Lord Bronor's eyes wouldn't meet hers. "With all due respect, I don't think the news is fit for a lady's hearing, my Queen."

Righnara clenched her fists, but forced a calmness on the edges of her twisting mouth. "Tell me," she commanded in a sharp sword-like tone. She wondered when her subjects would take her for a queen, and not just the king's wife. No, it was time they realized who she was. "The king might have treated me gently, but he always respected that I had a warrior's blood. Dare disrespect me again and I'll rip you into pieces."

"I beg for your forgiveness, your Highness. But I'm old, and these old eyes still see you as you were on your wedding night – a nervous, fragile beauty. Now I'm starting to see a lioness roaring just beneath this delicate face.

"But what can I do? I'm bound by a command, my Queen. Before the illness took him, the King had asked me to keep any grave tidings from reaching your ears. I promised him, my Queen, I promised him his wish will be followed until the day I die."

"My husband loved me deeply, and you did well by guarding his final wish. But these are hard times. This glorious land of Almora is dying and I can rest in blissful ignorance no more."

"Indeed, my Queen." Bronor bowed again. "I now realize I should never have obeyed the King's command in the first place. I've watched you take charge when the King collapsed. I've watched you swallow your tears and harden like quenched steel. Never again shall I disrespect such a strong, honourable woman."

"What honour, Lord Bronor?" Righnara went to the window and stared hopelessly at the volcano – a monster marching on her crumbling reign from the south – spurting fire in the air and painting the sky in shades of red and orange. Her eyes turned glassy. "Parts of my kingdom are breaking and falling into the volcano." Tears began trickling down her cheek. "And I cannot save my people," Righnara whispered, sobbing. "Tell me, Bronor, why won't God grant me a moment of peace? Why must he steal away every source of my serenity? What is my sin?"

Conquering Almora had cost Righnara a thousand men. It had cost her her husband. Even when she strangled the Priest – the leader of the old Almora – she couldn't satisfy her hunger of blood. She had every native killed. But nothing could grant her the sweet sensation of revenge of her husband's death. *Fire will come for you, and you'll burn for the rest of eternity,* the Priest's corpse had then said.

And it had. The volcano had bloomed to the south only three moons after her men occupied the empty city of Almora.

"Not your sin, my Queen. Men do wrong deeds all the time. God is simply cleansing this land by taking those who sinned."

"It's the poor who live to the south. It's the poor who are dying. Sins of the poor are nothing compared to those of the rich. This isn't God's justice, Bronor." Righnara started pacing around the throne room, thinking. "I just wish there was something – anything at all – that can hold the city together."

Lord Bronor looked away.

Righnara caught his hesitation. "What is it, my Lord?"

"We found a seed the size of a dragon egg in the ruins of the Priest's Temple. The natives had a unique name for it: *Virarme Maya* or the *Tree of Life.* Its roots hold the world, its canopy shelters from the terrors of night, and its fruits are believed to be stars, bringing light, warmth and riches."

"I've heard of the Tree of Life long before I came to this land. I had no idea the Priest and his men had the Seed in their possession all these centuries." A smile dawned on Righnara's face. "It seems like God has answered my prayers after all."

Bronor looked straight into Righnara's eyes. "But my Queen, the Priest had a reputation. He belonged to a strange religion. He worshiped strange Gods."

"There's nothing we can do to fight the elements of nature, other than surrendering to other powerful forces. I don't care if this God is the Devil himself. I'll do anything to save my people. I believe this will work. In fact, the Tree of Life will make us stronger, mark my words."

The sapling grew into a massive tree within just three moons. Its humongous bark quadrupled in size – so that now its trunk looked like the feet of a hundred elephants joined together – and its roots slithered deep into the ground, conquering every inch of earth, until they reached the volcano. These roots held the city together and kept every building from falling into the monstrous hell-like opening of the volcano. The fruits were coconuts full of fuel. Trading it overseas brought gold and silver and other riches.

A smile grew on Righnara's face and stayed there for months.

But a night came when Righnara awoke from a nightmare, drenched in cold sweat. She ran to the balcony and saw her kingdom burning. The roots had touched the lava, and the fruits of fuel helped spread the fire. As flames licked her castle, Righnara felt the Priest's chilling curse strangling her very soul: *Fire will come for you, and you'll burn for the rest of eternity.*

Aditya Deshmukh is a mechanical engineering student who likes exploring the mechanics of writing as much as he likes tinkering with machines. He writes dark fiction and poetry. He is published in over three dozen anthologies and has a poetry book "Opium Hearts" coming out in June, 2019. He likes chatting with those who share similar interests, so feel free to check him out here:
https://www.facebook.com/adityadeshmukhwrites/
https://www.instagram.com/deepcrazyshit/

They Followed Us Home

Diana Hauer

Dasher wagged his tail and pressed his nose to the window. When the car door opened, Dasher streaked out like a brown-and-white blur, pausing only to raise a leg and mark a corn stalk. The Russell terrier's white coat soon had mud splatters in addition to the tan markings around his head. Suzie stepped out of the car warily. With German Shepherd gravitas, her gray muzzle tested the evening air. Her feathery tail waved slowly as she lowered her nose to investigate this unfamiliar setting.

The dogs weren't bothered until the car drove away. They chased it down the dirt road until it sped out of sight.

Suzie gave up before Dasher. The old dog sat panting in the center of the road, head lowered and shoulders slumped. She'd been abandoned before. Dasher eventually ran back and sniffed her all over. She smelled the usual pain and soreness that comes with age. He didn't have that problem yet.

Suddenly, a wide streak of light tore through the sky. The dogs shivered and huddled against each other as it shrieked overhead. A few seconds later, it crashed in the middle of the cornfield. After a few seconds of cacophony, silence ruled. Golden light shined through the corn stalks.

Curiosity overcame caution. Light meant house, house meant food and sofas. Tails wagging, the dogs trotted over to see what had landed.

\#

"Our progenitors will kill us." Xiadz moaned in ultrasonic whines. Black, bulbous eyes set in gray skin reflected the bright warning lights. She glared as if shet could dim them by force of will.

Crear growled and barked in deep, rumbling tones: "The vehicle just overheated. We'll add coolant, everything will be fine."

In a flash of yellow scales and whip-like tail, Crear scampered to the supply compartment. "There isn't any. The parentals must not have stocked it yet."

Xiadz clutched her head and crouched down, moaning louder. "Our privileges will be revoked for crashing their new vehicle. We must call them before the native inhabitants come and investigate. I don't want to be imprisoned and dissected."

"No, we wait calmly," growled Crear. "It should cool down soon, then we can leave and put the vehicle back with no one knowing."

An alarm buzzed. "What's that?" asked Crear.

"Proximity alert! Two native life forms approaching," squeaked Xiadz. "We're doomed!"

Suzie and Dasher circled the hot, metal house. Dasher bounced up and down, tail wagging. Suzie approached cautiously. She was confused by the strange smells. Dasher paused to relieve himself on the silver surface, then bounced around some more.

Suzie laid down to wait and watch. If it was a house, or a car, a door would eventually open and let them in.

#

"It just anointed the vehicle with bodily fluids!" screeched Xiadz.

"Perhaps it is some sort of welcome ceremony," growled Crear. "I'm sure it will wash off."

Xiadz paced the small interior compartment, rubbing her smooth, gray head. "This is not happening. We are not stuck on a strange planet, surrounded by hostile natives who squirt bodily fluids on my progenitors' vehicle."

"I'm not sure they're hostile," Crear chirped, pointing at the screen.

Xiadz leaned over to examine the view. "They are showing teeth in our direction."

"But they haven't attacked. Maybe they're curious. Do you think they might help us?"

Xiadz rippled her skin. "I'm not going out to ask. Let's wait in here, where it's safe."

"I'm going outside."

"Crear, no!"

#

A seam appeared in the smooth, silver wall, expanding into a door. Dasher ran for it, but stopped short when he smelled the creature standing in the doorway.

The terrier sat down and craned his head up and back to take in the tall, scaly, yellow creature. He saw its tail was wagging slowly. Dasher didn't know if it was a nice wag like a dog's or a thoughtfully cruel wave like a cat's.

With a clicking growl, the creature stepped out of the vehicle. Suzie sat, frozen. In her thirteen years, she had never encountered anything like this.

Dasher yapped happily and ran circles around the tall, yellow thing. He paused only to piddle before slipping past Crear into the ship.

#

Crear stood still as the small creature performed its greeting ritual. It seemed friendly.

"Crear, help!" whined Xiadz. "It's coating me with saliva!"

"Probably not poisonous," growled Crear. Her nostrils twitched. Something smelled familiar. "I don't think it's sentient."

"It's covered in hair and now it's on my lap! Help!"

Crear crouched to sniff the puddle left by the small creature. "Bring me the chemical scanner." Crear looked up to find herself snout-to-nose with the brown-and-black quadruped. Its big, brown eyes met hers fearlessly. Crear jumped when its pink tongue extended and painted a long line of dampness on her snout. Chuckling, she flicked her tongue out to do the same. Its rear appendage moved back and forth and its mouth mirrored her open-mouthed smile.

Xiadz stomped out and slapped the scanner into Crear's hand. "That creature is sitting in the spare pilot chair." Xiadz sneezed and wiped her nostril slits. "And its fur has invaded the vents."

Crear poked a probe into the damp soil. Her scaly crest rose. "Xiadz, this fluid is chemically similar to engine coolant! If we can get a pure sample, we can restart the engine cooling cycle."

"There's a big puddle on the compartment floor. Will that do?"

#

It took two tries and one more urine contribution from each canine before the engine hummed back to life.

Crear pointed at the open door. The two dogs (according to the planet's broadcasts) made no move to leave.

"You should go," crooned Xiadz. "We are grateful for your donation of excretions, but we are leaving your planet."

"They don't understand," said Crear. Suzie leaned against Crear's leg. "They have imprinted on us. It would be unkind to abandon them."

"What will we tell our progenitors?"

"We'll say they followed us home."

Diana Hauer is a mother and technical writer by day, a dreamer and role-playing geek by night. She lives in Beaverton, Oregon, with her husband, son, and dog.

Post-Lies

John Houlihan

The day they abolished lying, most people still believed it would never work. Then the nano-drones arrived, and we entered a new kind of reality.

It began with the very best of intentions of course. Over there they'd endured a president who redefined the term mendacious and just before his impeachment, couldn't even tell himself when he was lying anymore. Then came the catastrophic sundering of Europe based on more lies, the combined deceptions of a self-interested horde of charlatans, liars, plutocrats and billionaires — and the self-deceptions of so many prepared to believe them.

After that double catastrophe, people had had enough of fake news, alternative facts, truth isn't true, and foreign actors meddling in their affairs (and their feeds). The whole world was crying out for someone to do something, anything, but we never quite guessed what that certain someone had in mind.

Still, people were willing to embrace change, open to it, ready for it, but perhaps not expecting it. Then, one otherwise unremarkable Tuesday evening, warnings began to appear across every imaginable media outlet and across every conceivable social media feed, eight words in bold neon type:

"The end is coming. The end of lies..."

Most people still thought it was a hoax. A clever one mind, otherwise how else could it infect every single broadcaster, site, platform and other source of information, and translate itself into every language across the known world?

Besides people may yearn for truth, but truth is a hard thing to define: your truths are true for you, but for me? Well, they might make as much sense as a symphony of Mongolian nose flutes.

But lies? Ah, now lies you *can* detect. There are tells, pupil dilation, autonomic responses, subtle changes in expression or breathing, that skilled interrogators and sensitive equipment can perceive. Sensitive equipment like billions of autonomous self-replicating micro-drones which had been released out into the world with but a single purpose.

But who did the releasing? Well no-one knew and no-one ever stepped forward to claim the credit — or perhaps that's the wrong word — either. The smart money was on some Silicone Valley techpreneur with a messiah complex, but if nothing else, they at least had a sense of humour. In the initial release when someone lied, the drones just formed a big red flashing exclamation mark above that person's head, bleating an unmistakeable visual warning.

Version two-point-zero went even further. When mankind's unknown benefactor deployed that update, the drones began to behave differently. Every time someone lied, the drones swarmed and the person's nose grew an inch. With every subsequent falsehood, it would double, expanding exponentially until birds could perch on it. You're familiar with the fairy tale I take it? No wonder people dubbed it 'Pinocchio Syndrome'.

Imagine that, instant visual feedback on when someone's being economical with the *vérité*?

The changes were instant and most profound. No more half-truths, no more evasions, even the noble and ancient art of good old fashioned bullshitting went into a steep and terminal decline.

People became a lot more guarded about what they had to say, if they said anything at all. Questions became weapons, answers were either truthful, or risked instant exposure and humiliation Trying to sound sincere when you've got an ever-expanding proboscis? Never a good look.

Personal relationships suffered too of course, those dozens of little white lies, half-truths and minor fabrications that oil the daily machine swiftly vanished and people became too afraid to ask.

"I love you" quickly became the most loaded of all statement-questions.

The question that dare not be speak its name was pretty much all of them, apart from the blandest of observations. The world woke up to — and suddenly wholeheartedly endorsed — Britain's eternal and ongoing fascination with the weather.

There were some winners of course, the legal system swiftly cleared its backlog overnight, and an open and shut case became the norm, easily resolved at the plea stage with the simple question: "Are you guilty or not guilty?"

Estate agents and used car salesmen suffered (to everyone's obvious delight) but politicians, well, they were the worst hit. Your heart bleeds? Yeah everyone else's too, for all of a nano-second. The first prime minister's questions post-Pinocchio was incredible, a constant stream of unvarnished truth that issued forth in manner never been seen before, and will never be seen again.

Truth became weaponised and it was wielded with a laser-like precision.

But then someone spoiled it all, one of those media bastards, asking that question, that terrible question, the one question that should never have been asked, the one to which we were all better off not knowing the answer.

"Prime minister, how long has mankind got? Climate change, pollution, poisoning the environment and the suffocation of the oceans. Have we reached a tipping point whereby our species has doomed itself to extinction within the next fifty years?"

The echoing silence spoke volumes and then... well then, the world really went up in flames.

I'm a British science-fiction and fantasy writer, perhaps best known for my Seraph Chronicles and Mon Dieu Cthulhu! series including recent novel, Feast of the Dead. I've also contributed to anthologies like The Hotwells Horror and FLASH!. More info at: http://www.john-houlihan.net

The Fifth One ended up in France

M Earl Smith

"It's rather breathtaking, isn't it?" said the first priest, his head barely turning as the second stared at the nun, floating above them in the air.

"Quite astonishing, really. The Order has given long service in the church, though, so should it really be a surprise that they would be the ones who are actually the subject of a miracle?" The second priest nodded at the nun. "I doubt, however, that Sister Agatha will see where she has ended up as such."

Both of the priests laughed. Sister Agatha, the headmistress of the parochial school in this province, was universally loathed by her charges, past and present, for the way she administered the school. She ran it, it was said, with an iron fist. Children were often *thwapped* across the hand with a ruler for even the most minor of infractions. There were rumors to the fact that several had abandoned the faith because of the punitive nature of Sister Agatha. She was, in a word, mean. Not that any of that mattered.

The first priest, decked in his new scarlet robes, laughed once more. "Should we get her down?"

The second stared for a moment, removing his hand from his own robes long enough to glance at the scars on the back of his hand. One too many *thwaps* from a ruler. Ignoring his comrade for a moment, he looked up at the nun, smirking. "How ironic for you, Sister Agatha. The fifth chair in a prayer circle, all seeking intervention from God to escape the Deists and their revolution against your shallow, imperfect God. How ironic that the fifth one ended up in France, back in the midst of the revolution you so feared." The priest noted the wide eyed look of terror that came across the nun's face, and grinned.

The first smiled as well, realizing that, by the nun returning to France instead of being rescued by her prayers, their thoughts on her were confirmed. "Now, now, Pierre, we are simply followers of the Supreme Being. It is not our job to decide on punishment. Although, if you could choose one, what would it be?"

The second glared at the nun, floating high above them, his countenance betraying the utter hatred he held for the woman. "Well, Jacques, it would bring me, and The Supreme Being, much pleasure to remove her tongue with flaming tongs, much as they did in Grimm's Fairy Tales. And how about you, comrade?"

Jacques pulled his hands from his robes and stared at his own scars. He was a little better at Pierre at containing his anger. However, there was nobody listening except, for, perhaps, The Supreme Being, so what harm was there in a little venting? "Me personally? I'd love to take the poker from the fireplace in the kitchen and burn her eyes out with it. However, the Jacobians would have our hide if we meted out the Republic's justice for them, so perhaps we should let them know about the return of Sister Agatha, hmm?"

Pierre sighed. "Very well. Although I am glad the other sisters got away. They were wholesome, and not everyone deserves to lose their neck on Robespierre's guillotine. Shall we?"

Jacques grinned, and waved a dismissive hand at the nun, whom, with a shriek, started to plummet towards the floor.

After all, all they had to do was turn her in, alive. And alive meant a lot of things.

M. Earl Smith is a writer that seeks to stretch the boundaries of genre and style. When he's not studying, M. Earl splits time between Philadelphia, Cincinnati, and Boston, with road trips to New York City, Wichita, Kansas, and Mystic, Connecticut in between.

The Great Unknown

Russell Nohelty

"Do you know why I hate Santa Claus?" I asked with a deep gasp. Technically, I couldn't breathe, but that didn't stop me from gasping when the occasion arose.

"I have no idea," Doctor Trevor replied from across the room. Humans didn't take kindly to my presence, even though I never did anything malicious to them. He was bald and rail thin. His hand shook uncontrollably as he scribbled illegible notes.

I had been seeing him for over a month to help with my crippling jealousy of other supernatural beings. He had yet to get comfortable with the fact that I was Death, that it was my job to take people to their final salvation, or that I spoke so casually about it with him.

I lay on the red couch next to a bay window that looked out on the park across the street. I dangled my bony feet off the end of it as the light shone on my pale face. The couch was clearly made for a much smaller man than I, though I'm not sure I had ever been a man, or human at all.

"People idolize that jolly fat man for delivering presents once a year," I said to him. "Yet, here I am, the last, final comfort in their loved one's lives, and most of them fear me. He works one day a year, but I don't get one second off, not even one. I even work on Christmas."

"And yet, you are here," he said.

"Am I?" I replied. "I am in so many places at once these days that I'm not even sure which is the real me."

"That must be hard for you."

"It's never been harder," I replied, tilting my head toward him. "Every day there are more and more of you people, which means there are more and more people dying, and I am tasked with ushering you all into the afterlife."

"May I ask you a question?" he asked, mumbling under his breath.

"I should hope so. I've been coming here for weeks and you haven't asked me anything of import yet."

"Did you...shepherd my mother?" he asked.

I smiled. People didn't think Death could smile, but the idea of death was so laughably ridiculous I often couldn't believe I did anything but grin at the thought of it.

"I did. She was a lovely woman."

"And my father?" He asked without another moment's hesitation.

"I have shepherded every member of your family for a hundred generations, dating back to when you could barely be considered human at all."

The doctor lowered his pen to the pad in front of him. "Does it hurt?"

I pushed myself up and turned toward him. "I'm not sure. They never say it hurts. Usually, they are scared, or confused, but they are never in pain. On my best days, my job is to relieve people from pain."

"Where do you take them?" he asked, tears welling in his eyes.

"Beyond," I replied.

"That's not a very good answer," he said, scoffing through gritted teeth.

"I know," I replied. "I wish I had something better to offer, but I only play a small part in the grand design. I am only the conduit which transitions you into the next phase of your journey. When you reach the end, I return."

"What is the meaning of all this?" he asked me. "It feels so pointless."

"That is the question people ask me most of all, and the one I am most unqualified to answer."

"Try," he said, venom bubbling in his throat.

"From what I have seen, the meaning of life is to love and be loved, to laugh and cry, and come to peace with your existence, so you can welcome death as an old friend."

"You're saying all of life is just to become comfortable with meeting you? That sounds like an overinflated ego to me."

"Perhaps, but you asked my opinion. I am as prone to myopic thinking as anyone."

"Do they welcome you? The ones you shepherd."

"Some do. Others curse me. It varies. The happiest are the ones who have found some peace in this life."

He placed his paper down and stared at me with watery eyes. He choked back what remained of his emotions and took a deep breath.

"Why did this have to happen to me?" he said. "Why did I get cancer? I'm only thirty-six."

"Now we come to the crux of it," I replied. "Bad luck, I'm afraid. No, that is not exactly correct. Random chance would be more appropriate."

His whole body convulsed in sadness. "I had so much to do, so much left to do."

"We all do."

"Not all of us," he replied. "Some get to live long, full lives. They accomplish everything they set out to do. It's not fair."

"And some die at birth, without accomplishing anything. You're right, though," I said, standing. "It isn't fair. None of this is fair. It is just as it is, and that's all we can do."

He looked up at me. "And it won't hurt?"

I shook my head as I moved toward him. "Not even a little bit."

He dropped his head into his hands. "Then do it already."

I held out my hand. "It has already been done. You have been dead for this past month. I have kept you here until you grew accustomed to it and accepted me willingly." A white light grew above me until it filled the office. "Come, let us away."

Doctor Trevor grabbed my hand and stood up. Together we were enveloped by the light. It is not fair that Santa Claus gets all the glory, when I bring people to the greatest gift of all; a warm hand to travel with into the great unknown.

Russell Nohelty is a USA Today bestselling author, publisher, and speaker. You can find him at www.russellnohelty.com.

Endgame

Mikey Mason

Gregor had been a vampire since before the Battle of Hastings, but preparing his weekly game of Dungeons and Dragons was easily becoming one of the fiercest challenges he'd ever faced. It's hard enough, he thought, running such a game for humans, but running for other immortals...? He shuddered.

He loved the game. Of course he did — he was immortal. If you've ever wondered why games came into being in the first place, well... Stop wondering. It was likely a very bored, very long-lived, supernatural creature. Games alleviated boredom and no one experienced boredom on such epic scales as immortals.

It was the mummies who invented Senet, which was too old even for Gregor to get a taste for, despite Ahmose-Meritamun's insistence that he learn to play. Never again will I date a mummy, he thought. And never again will I game with one of my exes... She did play one hell of a wizard, though, when she felt like it.

The Daevas of Persia created Backgammon, which was interesting enough for a century or two, though he understood implicitly why they were "the gods to be rejected." They cheated. Compulsively. That's why Sarwar was no longer in their gaming group. Bastard never failed a roll, ever. And always, always played a bard.

The Lilin, succubi and incubi, invented Checkers and Ur in Mesopotamia. Entertaining for a decade or two, but it was plain to see why they — and likely the Mesopotamians, in general — preferred sex. Ninsun was a Lilin, and played a rogue to boot. Her character, Anunit, carried a crossbow in one hand and a wine skin in the other. If whatever she faced wouldn't drink with her, she'd just as soon shoot it and rob its corpse.

The venerable ghosts of China invented Go, which was far too linear and reeking of pure logic for Gregor. He wanted a story now, though he'd spent quite some time playing Go with Shun Ling after Ling surreptitiously made his way out of Fēngdū Guǐ Chéng in the 19th century. Oddly enough, although Ling espoused the superiority of the tactical nature of Go, he played a barbarian. Rage, charge, attack, repeat.

Gregor had been consumed with other games before. He'd spent years playing Nine Men's Morris, a few centuries playing chess. Then the card games: Karnöffel, Gleek, Noddy, and Maw. Reversis, Ombre, Penneech... even Piquet. He'd gladly learned Poker and Euchre, Hearts, Spades, and spent decades playing Solitaire of all sorts.

There wasn't a board game he hadn't tried at least once. He'd even played Monopoly back when it was still the anti-capitalist propaganda known as

The Landlord's Game. Once, in a fit of boredom in the late 1930's, he'd suggested they make the game "more interesting" by putting money on Free Parking, and no one had ever played the game right ever again. If he wasn't damned to hell for being a vampire, surely he'd burn for that.

But then, in the '70s, he'd heard about this Dungeons and Dragons game. Certainly he'd taken part in a few weeks of tabletop miniature war-games set in the Napoleonic era, but he'd never heard of such a game where the action took place entirely inside of your head. It was addicting. He started running games for college students, high schoolers, anyone who would play. He didn't know what kind of creatures this Arneson and Gygax were, but he stayed away out of deference for the game. It filled a longing in him that he hadn't realized was there.

He took a long drink from the goblet to his right, steeling himself for the long night of preparation before him. Game night was tomorrow and this campaign was a monster — forgive the pun. He'd laid the groundwork for intense political intrigue since session one, carefully hidden in subplots and small details: the names of an important character briefly mentioned once and heard again in tavern chatter a few sessions later, rumors of unspeakable, treasonous acts near the borders, faint but growing signs of conflicting factions forming in the kingdom, right under the players' unsuspecting noses. Hints. Clues. Intimations. Subtleties. None of it had mattered.

Ahmose-Meritamun's wizard favored the fireball, lately, and every problem looked like kindling to her. He suspected she did this on purpose and simply to annoy him — she was far more perceptive to court intrigue than most. He wished once again that they'd never dated. Ninsun's rogue was too busy picking everyone's pockets, from the city watch to her own party members, or offering non-player characters a drink and then shooting them and looting their corpse. Ling's barbarian... well... Rage, charge, attack. Repeat. Ugh.

Tomorrow night, one way or another, he'd drag their characters on board the plot train, writhing and screaming if need be. He almost wished Sarwar was still in the group. He was a cheating bastard, certainly, but he could at least name an NPC or two. But, no. One night, after a session of perfect die rolls that he mysteriously snatched off the table before anyone else could see, the other players had enough and sold him out to a sect of bizarre cultists in Montana. Gregor could still hear the echo of screams and curses in ancient Zendish as the cultists bound his soul into a jar and sealed it with virgin wax and the blood of a bull.

Wiping a single crimson rivulet from the corner of his eye, Gregor returned to his notes and set back to work. Gods only knew what his players would do to him if he failed to deliver...

Mikey Mason makes his living writing and performing music of all types for geeks. You can learn more at MikeyMason.com.

Jack of Diamonds

Tyler Denning

An Ace of Hearts and a Jack of Diamonds. That was my hand, and appropriate for me as I'm Jack. I had already earned twenty dollars, a small fortune to a former farmhand like me. Poncho got knocked out two hands ago. He stood near the bar, drinking something fierce. He apparently was spending his third-place winnings early.

John was sitting across from me after knocking out Poncho. Calling a desperate bluff by Poncho earned him some more money, about the same as mine. At this rate, the game would continue for several more rounds, maybe an hour or two. But, this was a good hand. "Call your dollar and raise...10 cents."

John eyed me and the cigar lit up as he inhaled a deep breath. He moved his calloused hand up to his weathered face, grabbed the cigar, and blew the smoke directly in front of him. Into my face, that is. The hot smoke combined with the desert air, and it was brutal. My eyes watered, and I tried to hold my breath, but the smoke burned my nose and I had to breathe. I coughed, loudly. Sure, I'd smoked before, but Mama had torn my butt up when she found out. "Waste of money and good air, they are," she said, wagging her finger in my face. Lord God Almighty, I miss her. But, I had to get some more money for the farm.

"Sir, I'm going to have to ask you to refrain from interfering with the other player. Once more, and I will have to disqualify you." I'm not sure how a small town saloon got a fancy dealer from Dodge, but I could kiss him at this very moment. John scowled, but that seemed to be his normal face.

"Alright, boy. Let's do this. I'm ready to leave this hole of nowhere. You go ahead and give on up. You don't need this money. Second place isn't bad. Take the money you've gotten and leave. Trust me." I looked into his eyes. Did he look...frustrated? Angry? Confused? Pissed off was probably the best bet. Definitely someone I didn't want to tussle with after the tournament. It took me all yesterday to earn my way here. And the second place of another twenty dollars isn't bad. We could get a new pair of cows or even a good plow horse! But...first place would get me fifty dollars! That along with whatever I earn here would change everything.

"I'm sorry mister, but I gotta keep playing." I checked my cards again. Ace and Jack, same as before.

"Hell, I don't feel bad for taking this money from ya then." He put his cigar back into his mouth and shoved all his chips into the middle of the table. "All in. You wanna learn the hard way that the world is a cruel place, fine. I'll be your teacher." A quick count and I saw that he had put in a little over twenty-one dollars. Sweat dripped from my face.

I've tried to be a good person. I've gone to church. Mama taught me to read, and I've read the Good Book. Pa tried to instill some morals in me before he lost his. But, all those clay chips in the middle of the table were worth more money than anything I had the right to. My own pile of chips was the only thing close enough. Greed is a sin, and it took me right at that moment.

"Alright, sir. I'm all in." I pushed my own chips in the middle. The dealer nodded to both of us, and took the top card of the deck and placed it to the side. Then, with a skilled and practiced hand, he grabbed the top three cards, placed them close on the table and flipped them all at the same time.

Ace of Spades, Two of Clubs, and Ten of Hearts. Another card placed to the side. The next card turned face up: A Queen of Diamonds. A final card discarded. The last card placed down...

It was a King of Hearts. My heart skipped a beat. I had a straight! I looked over to John's cards. He had the Ace of Clubs and the Ace of Diamonds. Three of a Kind against my Straight. I won!! The dealer looked over the card, moved the two and the ace in the center down, showing my straight. "Mister Jack wins."

I reached out with my hands to scoop the chips back to me when a large knife slammed down near my hands.

"You cheating bastard!" He threw the table to the side, the chips scattering across the bar. He closed the distance with a single step and grabbed me by my shirt. With a heave, he threw me out the window into the street. The glass shattered easily and I went tumbling. By the time I had my senses about me, he was already out in the middle of the street, hand hovering above his holster.

"No one makes a fool of John Donahue. Pull yer iron, boy!"

I stood up, my knees shaking. I'd gotten into a fight before with the ol' Johnston boys, but they threw punches, not me. This was the first time I'd been tossed around by another person. "Mister! I'm sorry, but it was a fair game." The sun was blazing, a much different scene from inside.

"Pull yer iron! Last chance!"

Pa's old service pistol hung at my side. He left it with us before he left and I took it just in case. It was about to see some use. I'd only ever fired it a few times, and that was a week ago when I left. My hand hovered over the gun.

"Draw!"

Tyler is an avid tabletop role player and game master. He hasn't made books more valuable by dying yet.

A Gift to Kali

M. K. Martin

We found Emily along the road. She was wrapped in a dirty bed sheet and clutching a Zippo. Three months and she's still not really talking, but she doesn't flinch whenever we get near her, so progress, right?

Jen and I sit on the roof of the van as the ragged red sun slinks away. It's afternoon but night comes early under the ash clouds. Skeletal trees stretch bare breaches towards the rainless sky. The sky hoards her moisture and the earth lies barren.

Emily stands in the field, the faded green of her sweatshirt stark against the straw yellow of the dead grass. A dust devil dances across the road, a twisting funnel of ash and topsoil. Both Jen and I look over our shoulders towards the west. Most of the dust storms come from the scorched graveyard that used to be Los Angeles. It's already too dark to see much other than the lightning flashes.

I call Emily. She doesn't respond. I jump off the van and trot over to her. "A storm's coming. We gotta scoot, kid."

#

The wind catches up with us, shaking the van as we pass the junked out shells of cars. No telling why people pulled over and left their vehicles here. The world is too full of mysteries and we have few answers, so we make uncomfortable peace with ignorance.

We exit the highway at the town of Castle. Most of the buildings have already been scavenged, windows smashed.

"Over there." I direct Jen to a Victorian sheltered by a windbreak of browning pines, the kind of place where historical societies used to meet.

As we exit the van, the wind slashes us with needles of sand and powders us with ashy dust, soft as talc. It gets into everything: ears, mouth, collects as mud in the corner of our eyes. The wind is so strong we have to push off the side of the house or be crushed.

The inside is cool and clean. The wind rattles the windows, demands to be let in under the doors and through the cracks in the foundation, screams down the chimney. Jen and I laugh as we shake out the dust. Emily brushes a hand through her shaggy hair.

"Don't shoot."

We jump at the man's voice. Jen and I both draw. An elderly man steps into view, holding his hands up.

"Name's Jerome," he says. "The boy and I have been here since, well," he shrugs, "since they evaced the town. Said there was a collection point back east, but we were waiting on the boy's folks to come back."

200

Jen and I exchange looks. We know how this story ends.

"Will you stay for dinner?" Jerome asks and I can't help but laugh. He smiles, too. His smile is quick and easy, not rusty like ours or missing like Emily's.

"We've got peaches," Jen says.

#

I can't remember the last time we sat at a table with real plates and silverware. The boy, DeWalt, helps himself to seconds of the sweet, slippery merrygolden peach crescents.

DeWalt wants to go look for his folks, he tells us. Jen and I make noncommittal noises and Jerome pats the boy's dark, fuzzy curls.

After dinner we spread our sleeping bags on the living room floor. We give Emily the couch. Jen insists on searching the house and I stay with Jerome and keep the boy in sight until she comes back.

Jerome doesn't seem to mind our caution. He lights lanterns and gets out a book. DeWalt joins him on the couch and Emily leans against the arm. Jerome reads aloud about the goddess Kali and her consort, Shiva. Kali brings destruction but also brings new life into the world after she's calmed.

After Jerome and DeWalt go upstairs to bed, we listen to the cacophony of the storm. Jen reaches over and slips her hand into mine, our fingers intertwined. With so much gone wrong in the world, we steal a moment of bliss, our own eye of the storm. Around us, the dark house groans and the wind sputters out the last of the storm's fury in gasps and gusts.

#

I don't know if it's the light or the silence that wakes me. The storm is gone and there's nothing but the ticking of Jerome's grandfather clock from the hall. The ticking and a crackling.

I sit up. Red-orange light flares outside. Not lightning. Raiders! I shake Jen and scramble up. My pistol holster hangs from one of the couch's armrests.

The couch is empty. Emily is gone.

I don't think. I run. I'm barefoot, but I don't feel the gravel in the drive as I spin and spin, searching for Emily, for the raiders.

The firelight flickers from the side of the house and I sprint that way. At the corner, I stop.

Emily and DeWalt stand hand in hand before the conflagration. The windbreak trees burn.

I'm drawn, moth-like, to the flame; the heat caresses my face. The fire reaches for the sky, the smoke and embers dancing up to join the clouds.

"We're making an offering to Kali," DeWalt says. His eyes glow like coals and he watches the destruction with hunger and curiosity.

"Why?" I hear the rustle of Jen's footsteps and wave to let her know we're all fine.

"To bring the rain." Emily's voice is soft.

"Oh, kid, listen…"

Thunder crashes. Something hits my face. It's small and cold and wet, but I'm not crying.

We turn our faces to the heavens as the rain falls. Jen screams and dances in ecstasy and I join her. We cup our hands and drink, anoint ourselves with water from the gods.

In the morning, Jerome and DeWalt pile into the van with us. Emily hums as the miles fall away behind us. She puts her hand out the window and swoops it through the air and smiles.

M. K. Martin is a motorcycle-riding, linguistics nerd. A former Army interrogator with a degree in psychology, she uses her unique knowledge and skill set to create smart, gritty stories that give readers a glimpse into the darker corners of the human mind.

Beach Patrol

Guy Ingram

Eduardo's bicycle patrolled at leisure across the beach sand. This was his favorite time of day. The end-of-summer exodus had begun. With his security duties lightened, Eduardo had time to appreciate his surroundings of spectacular beauty. Tourist season meant weaving through a maze of sun-baked bodies laid out like roasting ears of corn. Or playing Dodge with frolicking kids squealing with pleasure as they chased weary sea gulls and terns. This morning he could enjoy the sight of a sun shattering the undulating ocean waters' surface with splinters of gold. Only a lone deck chair pulled up close to the water's edge disturbed the serene setting.

Ah, the lovely Madame Bonary is still with us. Out for her regular early morning swim. He pedaled toward the chair, noting how the woman's pink robe draped across its back billowed in the morning breeze. As he rode, he faced the water and searched for a sign of her presence. His view encompassed only an expanse of soft whitecaps swelling and lapping to their demise on the sandy shore.

An unsettled feeling stirred Eduardo to pick up his pace. He halted beside the chair, his bicycle falling as he stepped forward. He scanned the damp sand and made out the indentations left behind by her footsteps, just a single track, headed for the water.

Once again he peered outward, this time moving his now intense gaze in slow motion from one edge of his view to the other. All the while, he prayed for the sight of something besides water. Several sweeps back and forth disclosed nothing. Hands on hips, he shook his head in an effort to dispel the sinking feeling in his gut.

Madame Bonary has left us also.

Gay Ingram writes from her cabin in the piney woods of East Texas. For over twenty-five years she has been entertaining and informing readers. Her love of American history is reflected in such novels as Troubled Times *and* Twist of Fate. *Her most recent publication,* George Washington: Boy Surveyor to Soldier, *shed light on how pivotal events affected our first president's life choices. Information about all of her books is available on her Amazon Author Page:* https://www.amazon.com/author/gayingram

Locked In / Writing is Wrong

(With love to Ray Bradbury)

Linda Mercury

"What we have here, gentlemen... Oh, and lady," Doctor Roth inclined his head to the lone female student, "is a rare and disturbing case." He slid back the viewing pane in the armored door to reveal a barred window. The medical students, a mixed group of one woman, older returning students, and eager youngsters, crowded around, creating a small knot of movement in the long sterile hallway of the sanitarium. They clutched their voice recorders and jostled for position to look inside the room.

A tall red-haired woman, wearing the uniform of asylum whites, sat at a table in the small cramped room. As opposed to the other patients they had already seen this morning, her clothes gleamed in the early morning sun. Unfamiliar machines crammed the limited space. "Hello, everyone." Her deep, robust voice shook the door.

Every student stiffened when she made eye contact. Dr. Roth frowned. This batch needed better self-control if they wished to work with the mentally disturbed. Patients could smell fear.

"This patient is the sole surviving case of the Midnight Disease," he proclaimed, his words echoing off white walls.

They all swallowed. The one with the freckles put the back of his fist to his mouth.

"What are those things on the wall?" a voice asked from the back of the group.

"Those are Books." He spat the word out, trying to keep the taste of it from his tongue.

The eldest student shook his head. "Disgusting! Reading and writing are illegal! People get ideas that way." He shook his voice recorder in Dr. Roth's face. The little machine squealed. "Ideas kill. She should be in jail with the rest of the monsters who make society unfit to live in."

"Just as we prescribe illegal drugs for people in pain, we prescribe illegal material for her. Before, she'd slice her finger and use the blood to write on the walls, floors, everything. It was uncontrollable."

The patient kept quiet, studying their faces. She stroked the tip of a strange item across a white surface on the table, leaving a black, winding trail behind it. The female student turned an alarming shade of green.

Dr. Roth gestured to the shelves lining the tiny room. "The courts ruled this is the best way to keep the patient calm and comfortable."

"That's the most ridiculous ruling I ever heard. Those rebels in the woods would have a field day with this. The courts should have euthanized her!"

"Are you a judge or a doctor, Johnson? Are you suggesting your personal feelings are more important than a patient's needs?" Dr. Roth snapped at the student. He leaned and peered at the young man's face. "Do you presume to argue with our learned government?"

Johnson paled. "Not at all, sir! I would never –"

The female student stepped to the window. The two women studied each other while the men faced off. "She's intelligent, is she?" she asked into the tension.

Dr. Roth turned towards the question. "Yes, and there's the rub. She makes her own materials since there are no other ways to manufacture what she needs. She designed and built all those strange devices you see. This is the only source for paper and ink in the country." He rested his hand against the door. "This case has been both my greatest triumph and my worst heartbreak. Can you imagine what she could do for our glorious society if she weren't mentally ill?"

The woman stood, strode to the door. Her long red hair and tall body filled the small cell. The walls barely contained her vitality. She placed her hands against the metal of the window sill, exactly opposite Dr. Roth's hands.

"You know I forgive you for putting me in here, Father."

He wrapped his fist around the bars. His daughter reached for him.

"Don't touch her!" screeched the female student.

"I thought it was genetic. It can't be spread by contact, right?" Finally, a timid one spoke.

Dr. Roth shook his head. "There might be a genetic component, since it sometimes appears in a family line. Nobody knows for sure, though. It is completely unpredictable."

The patient went on tiptoes to squint at the class. "I see a familiar face. Is that my youngest brother? The one born before I came here?"

The quietest student stepped forward. His wide serious eyes peered out under a thatch of unruly red hair. He put his voice recorder in his pocket and placed himself in front of the door.

"It's nice to meet you." Jacob reached through the bars to greet Rebekah. A hush fell over the hallway as the two rubbed fingertips and whispered endearments to each other.

The students glanced suspiciously at Dr. Roth. One whispered about suspect activity into his voice recorder and how Idea Enforcement should investigate the Roth family.

The patient snorted. "Oh, stop that. All the members of my family are law-abiding citizens. Now, if you would excuse me. I have a deadline to meet." She nodded to them, her eyes lingering on her brother. She picked up her paper and studied it.

"Now, if you would all walk down to room 208, I'll meet you there." Dr. Roth gestured down the hallway. The youngest and eldest Roth siblings exchanged a long last look. The class shuffled off, arguing amongst themselves. Jacob followed behind the rest.

With the grace of the finest pickpocket, the boy dropped a pen his sister palmed to him into the lab coat of the most brutal student. A smear marked the flawless surface of the fabric. The second went into Jacob's own waistband, hidden from all eyes. No tattling dark marks showed on his clothing. Only the one who taught that delicate touch could have seen the actions.

Dr. Roth schooled his face to prevent anyone from reading his joy. He gave his valiant daughter, the one who sacrificed herself for the rebellion, a thumbs-up behind his back.

Hello! I'm Linda Mercury, a writer and creator of really unusual fictional worlds. More than anything, I care about compassion, connection, and intimacy. All of my work is about coming together. Because life is way better when people tell each other the truth of who they are.

The Dancer

Lisa Nordin

The grey-haired woman was sitting on a toilet wearing a dingy white sleeveless shirt when the middle-aged woman walked into the bathroom. "Can I help you, Dorothy?"

"Yes, I called a long time ago and nobody answered my bell."

"I'm sorry, the girls are terribly busy, I'm just here helping them out for now."

"Who are you?"

"My name is Margaret and I'm one of the nurses here. I do paperwork and check blood pressures once a week." Margaret was slender, blonde and she wore black framed glasses.

"Well, I'm glad you're here, I'm freezing, and I need to get off this toilet."

"Of course, what would you like to wear?"

"I guess that would be okay," Dorothy conceded. "There's a pink sweatshirt on the brown chair next to my bed. I want to wear that."

"Okay," Margaret said, turning toward the bedroom. She spotted the sweatshirt on the seat, along with a pair of blue slacks lying over the back of the chair.

"I brought these slacks too."

"I wore them yesterday, but I can wear them again today."

"Okay," Margaret replied. "Do you want to take your glasses off before I put this over your head — just so I don't knock them off?"

"Alright," Dorothy said dully, removing the glasses from her face before setting them in her lap.

Margaret carefully pulled the opening of the sweatshirt over Dorothy's head. The aging woman tried to put her arm in the hole, but her attempt was feeble, so Margaret guided her arm in the sleeve and then did the same for the next. Then Margaret bent over and guided Dorothy's feet in the opening of her pants.

"Can I help you stand up Dorothy?"

"Yes, let me get my glasses on first." Dorothy said lifting the spectacles to her face. Then, fumbling for the grab bar on the wall, she gripped it, leaning forward as Margaret put her arm under Dorothy's.

"Ready?"

"Yes."

"One, two, three," Margaret said. "Just hang on while I pull up your underwear and pants."

When Dorothy was standing with her pants pulled up, Margaret realized she was sweating. "Grab me my walker."

Margaret turned and looked at the metal device. She picked it up, sliding it in front of the old woman.

"There you go."

"Stay until I get to my recliner in the other room."

"Okay, "Margaret agreed, as she walked slowly alongside Dorothy. Together, they reached the chair, when Margaret looked up at a group of black and white photos on the wall in frames. "Wow Dorothy, those look like photos from an old movie."

"They are — I used to be a professional dancer in Hollywood. I was twenty-two years old in that picture."

"Those costumes are amazing," Margaret said staring.

"I worked with one of the best professional choreographers of that time."

"Those pictures are incredible."

"Thank you," she said with a slight smile. "Say, you know what?"

"What?" Margaret said looking at Dorothy.

"You look like my sister-in-law Jo?"

"Is that right?" Margaret smiled.

"Well she's dead now, but when Jo was younger, you look just like she did. She had a big heart, Jo did."

"What a nice way to be remembered," Margaret said.

After Dorothy was comfortable in her chair, Margaret asked if she needed anything.

"You said you take blood pressures while you work here. I've never had you take my blood pressure before."

"Well, there is another nurse that works here — Alice. She probably takes your blood pressure."

"Yes, I know Alice. My blood pressure is always high when she takes it."

"Would you like me to take it while I'm here?"

"If you wouldn't mind?"

"Not at all — I'll grab the cuff and my stethoscope."

So, Margaret left the room, returning with her equipment. Sliding the sleeve up a bit,she wrapped the cuff around Dorothy's bony arm, and then placed the stethoscope directly on her wrinkled skin. "Oh, that's freezing!" Dorothy complained. Margaret smiled but said nothing as she listened with the stethoscope.

"One-seventy over ninety-two."

"Yup, that sounds about right."

"I'll make a note of it, Dorothy. I'm getting ready to go to the office now, so I'll pop in next week to say 'Hi.'"

"Okay." And Dorothy smiled a small polite smile.

After Margaret left the office that day, she drove home in her car thinking about the photos of Dorothy as a young professional dancer. The poses she held, the sleek short hairstyle and the dark, dramatic lipstick she wore. Probably the thing that seemed so unbelievable to Margaret was the strength and beauty of Dorothy's legs in her dazzling costume.

That night after Margaret went to bed, she dreamed she was on the set of an old Hollywood movie. She was sitting next to a man, who was shouting directions at a group of young dancers while clapping his hands. The dancers were moving together gracefully to an unfamiliar tune when Margaret looked to her right. Dorothy was sitting next to her beaming with joy, then suddenly she stood almost leaping to join the other dancers, appearing young and vibrant as in the photos on the wall. Margaret sat gazing at the dancers, until her alarm rang, waking to a new day.

The following week Margaret returned to the nursing facility to her part-time job. Instead of checking the computer for patient updates, she gathered her stethoscope and cuff, to head toward Dorothy's room, anxious to see the old photos again.

Knocking slightly, she walked into the room, where an older man and a woman were packing cardboard boxes. Margaret stopped short. "Hello — I'm looking for Dorothy," she said. The man and woman looked at each other, then at Margaret. "Dorothy was our mother — she passed away last week."

"Oh," Margaret paused. "I'm so sorry." She glanced at the wall where the photos had hung. Her heart sank when now all she saw were a few nails.

"I met her last week for the first time," Margaret said. "She told me I looked like Jo."

In unison, they both answered, "You do."

Lisa Nordin lives in Wisconsin with her husband and three sons. Not only does she enjoy writing but she loves to sing in church. She is preparing her first fictional novel to be published in summer of 2019.

Polymerevolution

John A. McColley

Mei dropped into the water, thankful that this survey was the last of the day. She didn't relish the hour-long kayak trip back to the island, but these corals weren't going to preserve themselves. A sharp nip in her thigh caused her to pull up short, examine the area. She saw only a pin point discoloration on her suit. Manufacturing flaw, scratchy. Lime green flippers allowed her to shoot through the water.

Corals in sight, Mei's forehead wrinkled. They were all the wrong colors. She was struck by the idea of being in the laundry aisle of the grocery store. Bright oranges, reds, yellows, greens, blues, even purples represented colors she'd never quite seen before in a reef. Better than the dying ones I've seen all week. With the acidification of the ocean, the increase in carbon dioxide, the coral was the canary in the coalmine. What was different here?

Collection canister and small hammer in hand, she struck the base of a finger of coral. The formation exploded. Bright orange flakes shot in every direction. Reflexively, Mei dropped her tools, brought her legs forward and kicked backward a few feet. What the hell? Fluorescent chips the size of fingernails fluttered down through the water. After a few seconds, they folded together spasmodically, jetting back toward their perch, the white, skeletal, coral finger.

I've never even heard about anything like that. I need a sample. Mei looked for her hammer and saw only a swarm of yellow flakes settling back down on the coral it had struck on landing. Some of the flakes landed on the hammer itself. Well, I can scoop the whole hammer up in the canister, then pull it out when the creatures pop off. Another stab on her leg made her jerk. Stupid suit. She scanned around for the acrylic jar. Some flakes had dropped onto it, as well. Carefully, limbs jittery, she drew closer. "Ah!" She yelled through her regulator. More nips as on her leg, but across the top of her foot. A swirl of blood like smoke dissolved into the water. Instinctively, she kicked, and spotted orange flecks on the green plastic, each beside a hole where blood flowed forth. The edge of the orange was discolored, blending into the green.

It took a long second for her mind to click to the outrageous truth. Another second and she was rushing to try to pull the flipper off, only to feel another bite. Her leg jumped and she pushed harder to shove the swim aid off. A nip at her side, a bite on her other foot and she was swimming toward the kayak as quickly as possible, writhing and wriggling, casting off her weight vest and other flipper, struggling with the long line to the zipper on her wetsuit.

The line pulled free and drifted in the current as her kayak dissolved into a cloud of orange something and swam toward her.

John A. McColley writes across the SFFH spectrum for magazines, anthologies, and websites from his basement lair at the edge of a 300 acre wood. A wife, three kids, three cats, and the Internet challenge his writing time and keep life balanced. He's a member of the SFWA and currently serializing novels at https://www.patreon.com/JohnAMcColley

No History of Violence

Terri Clifton

She hated the smell of his pipe. Whatever blend of leaves he used created a dense, cloying smoke that penetrated everything. The smell in her hair used to make her cry, as if he'd sunk into her and she was gathered into the cloud of his existence. With nowhere to go, it never occurred to her to leave. She simply existed, in place, like the house, the barn. Rolling hills and thick woodland might be beautiful, but they offered no protection. No protection, she thought, crossing to the window. No protection anywhere.

The beatings had started on their wedding night, enough for her to understand how things were expected to be. Her dowry was his, her body as well. Her hesitation, simply a flinch from his rough hands, was enough to justify the brutality with which he claimed her. In time she learned not to wonder about love, or freedom, or anything at all.

She'd hoped a child would change him, that planting his progeny would soothe whatever demon raged in him. But a swelling belly hadn't stopped anything and long before the proper time her hope had died, and she'd buried it along with the tiny body under the willow tree, just before the first snow.

The tree was now tinted a bright, fresh green. The brook was running high and the foxglove all leaned over from the night's hard rain. Last night had been the worst so far. The things he called her had never mattered. Bruises and bones healed each time, but the laughing about the babe as he did his best to sow another, warning her to hold her legs together this time, lest another one fall out.

Behind her, at the table, he drank his morning tea.

"Tastes queer", he said, just before the cup crashed to the floor.

Terri Clifton received a fellowship for Emerging Artist in literature by the DDoA in 2013. Her work has been published in a dozen anthologies and journals. She lives on a historic farm along the DelawareBay. Find her on Facebook at www.facebook.com/TerriCliftonAuthor

Phone Calls and Lies

Irene Radford

Levi Gilbert stared at the stack of new files in his email. Six he deleted without reading. He really didn't need his sisters and nephew prying into his private life right now. He hated lying to them. Better to leave them in ignorance.

The next eleven messages were from his boss, or his boss's secretary. He moved them to his handle-soonest folder and moved on. Another fifteen looked like they might be spam but could be from customers. He'd deal with them when he had time.

The ones from his children he opened immediately, read two lines each and deleted them. Nothing important, they merely wanted money.

His phone chirruped. He looked at the caller ID and pressed the ear piece to activate the connection. "Sweetheart, how are you?" he said to his girlfriend, coughing at the end of the sentence. God, he wanted a cigarette. The family quack had said no more. If he had any hope at all of living to the end of the year he had to quit smoking. Three damn weeks without a single cigarette and he still craved the hot burn on his throat, the gasp of holding the smoke in his lungs, and the quick hit of energy.

"I'm fine, Levi. But I need to know that you are okay. Have you heard from the doctor yet?"

"No. Not yet. I miss you."

"Can we get together tonight for dinner or after?"

"Oh, sweetheart, I wish I could, but my wife is insisting I spend all my free time with the family. I've only got so much time left..." He coughed again for emphasis.

"Don't I deserve some of that time too? I have been your lover for seven years."

"Sweetie, you know I want us to be together, but I have obligations, commitments. I will make time to be with you. My thoughts are with you always. Just not tonight." He pulled three more coughs from the bottom of his lungs, making sure she got the full effect of the phlegm.

"Don't worry about it, Levi," she said, layers of guilt soothing her voice.

"I've got to go, sweetie. My boss is hovering." They made kissy noises and disconnected. His boss was safely ensconced in his office in the corner.

Levi heaved a sigh of relief and opened the next five emails that looked urgent. He'd just hit the send button on the last of them when the phone rang again.

The screen displayed a picture of his wife and their aging corgi.

"Margie, my dear, hello," he cooed into the phone.

"Levi, darling, has the doctor called yet?" She tried to hide her demanding impatience, but he'd lived with her too long not to recognize the whine of a petulant princess beneath the loving words.

"No, not yet, dear." He skimmed a few more emails. Then he remembered to cough, not too loud or long, just a reminder of his impending doom.

"You'll let me know as soon as he calls? I'm really worried about you."

"Yes, dear. You will be the first to know the diagnosis."

"You should be at home and in bed where I can take care of you."

"I promise to take a nap this afternoon. Then I have a Lodge meeting at seven. I'll be home right after, nine-thirty at the latest."

"Okay. But you make those men go outside to smoke, and don't let them give you cigarettes, or go with them."

"Yes, dear. I know. And they know too, you've made sure their wives control them." He coughed again, for real this time, the long, hacking spasms that started in his gut and spread out until his entire being was caught in the near endless cycle.

Margie waited until he could breathe again before speaking. "Get a glass of water and rest in the employee lounge a few minutes."

He made an inarticulate noise and obeyed. But he was back at his desk with the glass of water before his boss had time to notice he was missing.

Three emails and two snail-mail letters later he noticed his boss hovering.

"Heard that cough, Levi. You okay to work?"

"Of course, sir. I need the money. I'll work as long as I can."

"That isn't necessary. But if you don't mind, I have a new project I'd like you to take over. The last guy got in over his head and mangled the report. It needs your finesse and expertise."

Levi coughed again, just to make sure his boss knew how sick he was going to be.

"I'm terribly sorry, sir. The doctor has ordered me to go straight home and rest, alone and quiet."

"It will mean a bit of a bonus. I know at a time like this you are gathering your resources and getting organized. I want to help you as much as possible, but I also need you to do this."

"Well... how much of a bonus?"

The boss named a figure he really shouldn't ignore.

"Well, I can do some work on it this afternoon, and then come in early tomorrow."

"Fine, fine." The boss slapped him on the back.

Levi wondered if this was a good time to cough again. With luck, he'd untangle the botched report and get it re-organized in half the time allocated, leaving him with more than enough time to meet the dancer he'd hooked up with at the club last night.

Three paragraphs into the weirdest tech language he'd ever read, the phone rang again.

"Levi, good news," his doctor chortled. "The spot on your lungs was a glitch on the X-ray. Your blood tests are close to normal and the MRI is clean. You don't have lung cancer after all, just a touch of seasonal bronchitis. But let's take this as a warning. Don't you dare start smoking again."

"You... you mean I'm not going to die?"

"Not this year, unless you get run over by a truck."

"But... but... the cough?"

"Like I said. Bronchitis. Want me to call Margie and give her the good news?"

"No, no, I'll take care of it."

"Then I'll see you at the Lodge tonight. I'll buy you a drink to celebrate."

And Levi knew that within minutes all of the Lodge members and their wives, including his lover who was the doctor's wife, and his boss who was grand high pooh bah this year, would know the truth. He had run out of lies and excuses.

He almost wished he had cancer rather than find new lies to cover for the old ones.

If you wish information on the latest releases from Ms Radford, under any of her pen names, you can subscribe to her newsletter: www.ireneradford.net. Or you can follow her on Facebook as Phyllis Irene Radford, or on twitter @radford_irene25

Wake Up!

Robert L. Hannah

Wake up!

It must be a dream. They said I could fly, but as I streak toward the unforgiving gray sea of concrete, I realize that it was a lie. The unseen hobgoblins that speak to me in my dreams and haunt my awakening promised me special treats, the power of flight, the ability to defy gravity. In truth, gravity has a firm grasp on me and accelerates my body past the reflective windows of the office building.

Each glass panel is like a celluloid frame capturing my distorted image in a unique pose of desperation while I fight the invisible force driving the concrete up to embrace my flesh and bone. Perhaps the lunatic sprites that so convincingly suggested my departure from the edge above will replay the images for themselves and shriek with demonic laughter at their successful prank, but really, it must be a dream.

I'm told that if you awake from a falling dream before you hit the ground, you will live to dream again, but if not, death will take you into its fold as though the impact forces had a firm base in reality.

Wake up!

My hair is standing straight up as the wind blows at me as though I am a test subject in a wind tunnel. Whistling in my ears nearly drowns out the cries below and horns of the tangled cars on Broadway Street. They're either screaming for me to stop, or they're screaming for me to continue; I can't tell, but in any event, it's beyond my control. I do not remember ever experiencing such vivid sensorial events from a dream before.

Wake up!

Why did I listen? Friends and psychoanalysts have warned me, but the voices were so loud and demanding that I just couldn't refuse. Even though I've never seen the evil tormentors that twist my thoughts, I visualize them in my mind's eye. Their pointed teeth and black leathery lips are twisted in a maniacal sneer, and their beady black eyes are closed tight as they roll with laughter at my gullibility.

Halloween costumes line the street below as they head for Westport or other gathering places for their kind. The closer I get, the clearer their faces become. Many are dead ringers for the imagined faces of my unseen demons. My shadow is starting to shrink as the sidewalk rushes to greet me. A couple of seconds is all the time left.

Wake up!

I take it back! I take back all the wishes for retribution and hateful thoughts that clouded my mind and allowed the goblins in. I swear I take it back! Please help me!

Oh God, it's here!

WAKE UP!

Robert L. Hannah is an author, Mechanical Engineer, 5th degree Black Belt in Kenpo Karate and a devoted family man. "Timber Ghosts" is his first published fiction novel. Others to follow.

The Hill

Johann Luebbering

I cried today.

I did a thing that needed doing.

A drive to a hill. It's a good hill. A view of the river. People visit it sometimes.

I went to see a stone. It doesn't seem like much, really.

I put a D20 in the ground. I don't know where he is now, or if he will get it.

I miss my friend.

Johann Luebbering is an occasional writer from central Missouri. Other published works include pieces in Sojourn (1 & 2) and RPG supplements.

Conventions of the Genre

Jesse Bullington

"If we knew where they came from we could stop them," Gove says.

"Silver seems to stop them just fine," I remind him, funneling the carefully measured metal pellets into the mouth of a yawning 12-gauge shell.

"I mean all of them," he says.

"So do I." I seal the end of the filled shell and get another hollow one from the box.

Every moonrise is another action movie.

I used to hate action movies.

Until they ate my husband and my little boy.

I used to think I just hadn't found what I was good at–what if Wong Kar Wai was born, say, two centuries earlier, before film, before cinema? Would he have done something else, found a different means of crafting beauty? Or would he have floundered, an artist trapped in a world without the tools he needed to flourish?

I was right. About not having found what I was good at, I mean. I could write articles, of course, give lectures, attend conferences, keep the lights on, the internet up, the old 16mm I picked up for a song thrumming along. But I wasn't an artist the way I am now.

I think Gove would have cut out on me a long time ago if I wasn't so good. He stopped bitching about the camera's weight the last time we hit one of their dens, when we must have mistimed the moonrise, when it went from another day at the abattoir to an action movie in the time it takes for bones to break, for fur to sprout, for fathers to realize the sentries were dead, for mothers to realize that their pups have been crushed in their cribs, for all of them to see me framed in the doorway, backlit perfectly, the silver-plated sledgehammer leaning against the wall, the pump shotgun in my hands, my smile shining in the dark the same way theirs used to. They weren't smiling then, and Gove wasn't bitching about the camera's weight, he was doing what I'd told him to, the shutter clicking along with the slide on the gun as the shells were pumped into place.

I would have said my motivations were cliché, that they were pure grindhouse. I would have rolled my eyes when some undergrad argued that any female protagonist was better than none, that the backstory of the heroine was, if not original, at least compelling. I would have told my husband about it later, the wine spicy on his breath, and he would have sided with the student, because he liked grindhouse, he liked action movies, and he especially liked playing devil's advocate.

So I've become a stereotype–an archetype, he would argue–but I'm a stereotype with a silver sledgehammer and a shotgun, a brace of pistols, a nuanced performance (if I might be allowed the vanity), and a cameraman. We burn their dens, we burn everything, but they have good noses, of course, and so I'm sure the others find our presents–I make doubles of everything, so that my personal library doesn't suffer from the film cases full of evidence we leave for any that come after, that wonder at the inferno that claimed their brothers and sisters, mothers and fathers, cousins and friends, spouses and children.

I'm sure I sound like some xenophobic gun nut pursuing the genocide of a people, but the truth, the real truth I don't even tell Gove, is that I don't want to kill all of them–I always want them to be out there. As long as they're waiting in the dark, I have a means of making myself happy, of forgetting the dead, of creating something beautiful, and of having an audience. I wonder when Gove will realize that I'm intentionally timing it so that at least a few rise with the moon to find us in their midst–it would be much, much easier to go in the middle of the afternoon, much, much safer to go then, but it wouldn't be half so beautiful. An artist works with the tools given her, and my tools are made of newly risen moons, the screams of grieving parents, and pure silver.

Roll credits.

Jesse Bullington is the author of three weird historical novels: The Sad Tale of the Brothers Grossbart, The Enterprise of Death, and The Folly of the World. Under the pen name, Alex Marshall, he released the Tiptree Award-nominated Crimson Empire trilogy

Godzilla

Jack B. Rochester

It was a slow Friday at the distribution center, just like every frikkin' Friday at frikkin' UPS. Once the packages goes out on the trucks we just stand around and duck the Super or goes outside and smoke too many cigarettes waitin' for 4:30. So when I goes out for my big wonderful half-hour lunch I says screw it, I'm not comin' back — to myself of course — I'm goin' to the movies. 'Cause I walk past this place every day from the bus stop and the sign out front says this old Japanese monster movie "Godzilla" is playin' today and I know I just gotta see it.

Besides, this little old theater is wicked cool. Popcorn half the price of the big multiplexes, where them little brat teenagers run around screamin' and laughin' at people and who knows what else. I hate those little brats and I hate their mothers for droppin' 'em off for hours of free babysittin' but I hate 'em the most when they actually go in to watch the movie, talkin' too loud and runnin' up and down the aisle and flashin' their goddam cellphones. So, as you can guess, I mostly avoid those big jerkoff expensive theaters.

I buy my ticket, get myself a hot bag of popcorn with real butter and a Coke, and head up to the balcony where I figure I'll get the place all to myself. But just my luck, two minutes after I plunk down this old Oriental lady comes tippy-toein' in — at a matinee for an old sci-fi flick would you believe — and sits down right in the row in front of me. And if that ain't bad enough, a minute later in comes this dumb little teenybop with her long black hair flippin' around and her tight jeans and her little boobs all poofed up in her flimsy top so they stick out like shiny ripe peaches and her cellphone glued to her ear and her mouth goin' a mile a minute in Chinese or whatever.

And wouldn't you know, the brat stops and stares at my boots hangin' over the seat. So I pulls 'em up and she sits down *right in front of me*, about three seats away from the old lady who by now I figure is the mother. *Ain't that somethin'*, I think, *mother and daughter goin' to the monster movies together*. But right away the old woman starts in on the kid sayin' I don't know what but I can tell she's rippin' her good and I'm goin', *right on!* under my breath. So the girl puts the phone away and starts goin' through this great big goddam purse, rootin' around in it like a pig in shit, until the mother hisses at her again. Daughter throws mother a dirty look as she pulls a water bottle out and hisses back and turns away. This makes the mother spew this stream of completely un-

understandable words, except I can make out "Gojira," until finally the girl chills out and hunkers down in her seat.

Ah, man, I think, *I'm in for it,* and get up to go downstairs, but when I look down over the balcony the place is about half full up and all the good middle seats are gone. And if that ain't bad enough, the goddam cellphones are flashin' away like Bic lighters at a goddamn Blue Oyster Cult concert. *Shit,* I mutter under my breath, but the teenybop hears me like before and turns around and glares at me. I stare right back at her and sit down and decide to take my chances right where I am.

I stuff a handful of popcorn in my mouth and take a look at this computer printed piece of paper about the movie I picked up in the lobby. Whadya know, turns out this flick is, like, the American remake of the original Japanese movie, and that was called *Gojira* which I'd heard the old lady say, so I figure maybe they're Japanese and she's brought the daughter to see this classic piece of Japanese sci-fi cheese for some idiotic reason. But it ain't! I mean, jeez, I already know this movie is not, like, *Die Hard* or somethin'. But then I think, I ain't seen it, so what do I know?

Then the previews start up and you know what? The brat pulls out her cell again and the thumbs start goin' nuts textin', as if the mother and I can't tell that the screen is lightin' up the whole frikkin' balcony. I decide I've had enough and lean over and tap her on the shoulder. "Put the phone away, OK?" I say. She looks up, glarin' at me like hell, but for the first time I see she's pretty — actually, like, really a total stone fox. I get this feelin' I don't know exactly how to describe but it's somethin' like, uh, you know, hey, am I messin' up my chances of scorin' on this fox because I'm hard-assin' her? But then I think she's jailbait and I just want to pound her head in the sand, you know? But I could be wrong, maybe she's older than she looks, so I start wonderin' if it's too far gone for me to get somethin' goin' with her. Somethin' like that.

She's still lookin' at me so I reach my hand out again like I want to shake. I kinda smile at her and then it seems like time kinda slows down and our eyes are still locked and she slowly reaches back toward me and slides her fingers across mine. The mother, it turns out, is watchin' this and she snaps somethin' at the girl, so real quick she turns back toward the screen. This really weird silence falls over the three of us, alone together up here in this old balcony. Then the movie starts.

I can't really concentrate on it, even though there actually ain't a lot to concentrate on. I keep lookin' down at the Japanese girl and see her beautiful shiny black hair. Once in a while when the screen is all lit up I bend forward and look down her blouse. It's like I'm totally and completely in love with her but, like, from this distance I don't think I can ever cross. Maybe it's her age, because I figure she's only about 15 and I'm gonna be 22 in May. Jailbait, jailbait, jailbait, I tell myself, but then I think she's not that young, 'cause if she was she'd be in school right now. But still, she's here with the mother so she must be. A kid, I mean. But maybe not. So then I decide if she's not in school then she has to be in college, which would make her old enough to try to hook up with. But then I think, why would a college girl want hook up with me? Because basically I suck.

It all just goes round and round in my head until I can't deal with it. It's, like, just too much fantasy and I just gotta concentrate on the movie and forget she's there. But I can't because she's constantly twistin' and squirmin'. Pullin' her knees up under her chin. Curlin' up in a sexy little ball. Leanin' over on one elbow and then the other way. Every so often tossin' her head back toward me, but I don't look back.

The movie ends. The screen goes black and the lights come on. The girl jumps up and turns toward me and starts to pull her hair into a pony tail, like invitin' me to look her all over. She grabs her bag, digs out her cell and flicks it open, but I wonder if she's really lookin' at me.

The mother says somethin' to her in Japanese and I hear "Gojira" again.

The girl glances at her and says, "Well, what did you expect?" in perfect English. "It said it was 'Godzilla,' not 'Gojira'." Then she glances at me and smiles.

Before I know it I'm sayin', "Yeah, 'Gojira,' that was the Japanese movie. It was before this one." I hold up the story paper I got in the lobby, like I gotta prove it or somethin'.

The girl looks at me and giggles. Then the mother gives her a shove down the aisle and the next moment they're gone.

Jack B. Rochester is author of the Nathaniel Hawthorne Flowers literary trilogy: Wild Blue Yonder, Madrone, and Anarchy. "Godzilla" is adapted from his forthcoming collection of short stories, The Pieces Fit, which will be published in spring, 2020.

Nonna's Bullwhip

Kristine Rudolph

The drab beige blanket hung lower on the right side of the bed than the left. "I should fix that," Louisa thought, but Nonna hadn't stirred in the three hours since leaving the recovery room so she figured she had time. Nonna wouldn't want her bedspread uneven. She was the kind of grandmother who loved having children tear through her house for Easter egg hunts or a game of tag. But she always made sure her crystal and silver had been securely anchored in place with museum wax — just so — before her visitors arrived.

A petite nurse in pale mint scrubs came into the room. "She's still out?" the nurse asked but Louisa knew she wasn't expecting an answer. Louisa smiled a faint smile and nodded anyway.

Lupe — Louisa could see her name in bold print on her badge — took Nonna's vitals with the precision of experience. Her movements were swift yet careful. When she was done, Lupe turned her head Louisa's way and told her everything looked good.

Louisa expected Lupe to leave once she completed her exam but instead, the nurse lingered by Nonna's pillow, gazing down at her like a mother watching with awe at every rise and fall of her newborn's chest. "She's got good hair, this one," Lupe said, stroking Nonna's thick silver strands back, away from her face.

As Louisa watched Lupe arrange Nonna's hair on her pillow, she offered a silent prayer. "Please, Jesus. Please do not let my Nonna wake up right now and call this kind, sweet nurse a 'wetback'."

"Are those your kids?" Louisa asked, pointing to the large photo button on Lupe's scrubs.

Lupe nodded. "That's Alex, that's Max and the little one is Arielle. Did the doctor come and talk to you yet?"

Louisa said he had.

"They got all the cancer. I'm guessing he told you?"

Louisa said he did.

Lupe rested her hand on Nonna's forehead. "She doesn't look like a ninety-year old. I saw her chart, I was expecting someone more — " Lupe seemed to be at a loss for words so Louisa finished her sentence for her.

"Fragile?"

Lupe nodded.

Louisa laughed a polite, hospital laugh.

If only Lupe could have seen Nonna six months ago, before she got the postcard in the mail reminding her of her annual mammogram. She'd celebrated her ninetieth birthday with a huge family gathering at a dude ranch a few miles down the highway. Nonna had drawn quite an audience when she challenged one of the "ranch hands" — a high school kid with a minimum wage weekend job — to a bull whipping contest. The pimply faced teen could barely lift the end of the seven foot long whip off the ground, much less crack it. Nonna hoisted it high and whipped it like her big brother had taught her eighty years prior. It yielded a satisfying "crack" that drew whistles of appreciation from all the patrons of the Long Bar T Guest Ranch and went viral on social media.

Louisa's phone buzzed in her pocket. She'd turned it to vibrate after the surgery ended. Everyone who needed to know about Nonna's condition had been updated and now, Louisa wanted peace. The blaring commentary from the television in the waiting room had nearly undone her. Knowing their audience well, the hospital had set all its televisions to the conservative twenty-four hour news channel. Sitting among the elderly family members of the others undergoing procedures that morning, Louisa had felt horribly out of place. The stiff, starched white button down shirts, the shiny boots and the cowboy hats that came off only for the national anthem — these were the characters who had animated Louisa's childhood. They nodded at the talking heads on the screen — the drumbeat of the angry American — and as Louisa watched them, her eyes welled with tears.

She hadn't cried when Nonna called to say she'd been diagnosed with breast cancer. She hadn't cried when her mother, Nonna's only daughter, said she couldn't make it for the surgery because she'd had a trip to Greece planned for ages. She hadn't even cried kissing Nonna goodbye in the pre-op room. But in that waiting room, surrounded by the familiar that had become hardly so, her tears wouldn't stop.

"You're here." Nonna was finally awake. Her voice sounded weak and scratchy from the intubation.

Louisa reached out and stroked the back of her grandmother's hand. "I'm here, Nonna. I'm right here."

Kristine Rudolph lives in Atlanta, Georgia with her husband and three kids. She is the author of "The Myth of Jake" and is currently working on writing for upper elementary readers.

The Best Policy

Joanna Michal Hoyt

Lisa bit her lip, stared blindly out the rain-streaked window and tried to ignore the churning of her stomach. It wasn't fair of them to blame her, she told herself. It wasn't. She was basically a very honest person. She never lied to herself – well, not really, not about anything that counted. She only lied to other people in justifiable self-defense, the way she'd learned to that summer when she turned nine...

When Lisa's mother announced, smiling, that Aunt Claudia and Uncle Toby and Charmaine were coming to visit and would stay for a whole month, Lisa asked if they couldn't stay somewhere else this year, or if she couldn't go somewhere else when they visited. Lisa's father – Aunt Claudia's brother – grunted vaguely and kept watching the show he'd been watching. Her mother said, "But of course you want to see your cousin Charmaine!'

Lisa, honest fool that she was at the time, said, "I don't! Ever!" She said it loudly and tearfully enough to get her father's attention.

"What's the matter with you?' he asked, turning the volume down.

"Oh, Max," her mother said, smiling almost the way Charmaine did when she was being an Angel Child. "Don't scold Lisa. Poor girl, she's jealous. Don't worry, dear, you can't help being younger than Charmaine. By the time you're her age I'm sure you'll lose your puppy fat too, and you'll be pretty like her and not so shy..."

"I don't want to be like Charmaine!"

"But of course you do. It's nothing to be ashamed of. I remember when I was your age..."

"But I don't," Lisa insisted. "She doesn't even like snakes!" Both her parents stared at her as though she'd stuck her tongue out and flickered it at them.

"Nobody does, dear," her mother said.

Two weeks later they arrived: Uncle Toby sleek and pleased with himself, Aunt Claudia looking as if she was too tired to breathe and it was all someone else's fault, Charmaine smiling a cute little smile that showed off her dimples, and horrible, horrible Miss Muffet like an overgrown rat on the end of her leash, bouncing around and barking. Of course Charmaine scooped Miss Muffet up in her arms and held her out to Lisa as if she was offering her a treat. She and Lisa knew better, but nobody else did.

A year earlier, when Lisa had held a green snake up to Charmaine like that – a beautiful green ribbon snake, the kind that never bites, with smooth dry skin and wise black eyes and a delicate tongue tasting the air (which was how snakes smelled things, as Lisa would have told Charmaine if Charmaine hadn't screamed and kept on screaming so Lisa couldn't get a word in edgewise) – the grown-ups had all acted as though Lisa had attacked her cousin. But Lisa was expected to pat Miss Muffet's smelly greasy fur and be slobbered on by her and smile into her piggy little eyes with their crusty edges. When Lisa was eight she had refused. Her parents scolded her for being sulky. Then they agreed that she must actually be jealous, though she didn't have a very nice way of showing it, and they understood her until she wanted to scream. They might even have gotten Lisa a dog – though they'd have waited long enough to show they weren't bribing her – if Max hadn't been allergic to them.

Allergic. Lisa thought about that. She plastered a smile across her face and said, "Isn't she sweet!" She then stepped forward and reached for Miss Muffet, took a deep breath, and sneezed explosively.

It worked even better than she had anticipated. Miss Muffet thrashed wildly and actually bit Charmaine, who yelped and dropped her. While Uncle Toby bent over Lisa, asking if she was all right, Aunt Claudia bent down to comfort Miss Muffet and ask, "Why couldn't you hold onto her? Poor little Muffy..."

"I don't care! She bit me!" Charmaine yelled in a voice that the grown-ups were more used to hearing from Lisa. Uncle Toby and Aunt Claudia glared at each other. Lisa kept on sneezing to cover the laughter that was banging around inside her, sneezing until she had to sit down, hiding her face in her hands; her shoulders shook so she might have been sobbing, and when she looked up there were genuine tears in her eyes.

"Poor Miss Muffet, poor Charmaine! I'm so sorry! Will they be okay?" Lisa asked, widening her eyes and hushing her voice the way Charmaine had done after accidentally-on-purpose provoking Lisa into a tantrum.

Lisa's father ruffled his hand in her hair. "You couldn't help it. Don't worry." Uncle Toby and Aunt Claudia agreed, and Aunt Claudia looked back at Charmaine just as Charmaine gave Lisa the evil eye.

Lisa didn't smile. She kept her lips quivery and her eyes wide. But behind her eyes she saw a little Lisa laughing and doing cartwheels – perfect cartwheels, even better than Charmaine's – all through the length of that summer and out into the rest of her sweet lying life, leaving Charmaine and her parents and Lisa's parents and everyone else far behind. She wouldn't miss them, she told herself. She wouldn't miss them at all.

Joanna Michal Hoyt lives with her fiercely honest mother and her brother on an upstate NY farm with many beautiful snakes and no dogs. Links to her published stories and essays are online at https://joannamichalhoyt.com/

That Time I Almost Died

Mark Victor King

Sometimes life throws you a curveball.

Sometimes you hit it anyway and score a home run. Other times, it crashes into your life and wrecks every plan you ever had. But that's no reason to quit. Instead you just come up with a new plan.

That's what happened to me late in the winter of 1980. I was 16 years old, a high school student ready to take on the world. My parents were loving, even if my father was busy building a cleaning service empire. I got along with my siblings. My studies were going well. I was reasonably popular. I'd been skiing the week before, and enjoyed the thrill of pushing my limits against an opponent as implacable as a mountain. Life was pretty darn good. I didn't know what was going to happen next, but I felt ready for it the way only teenagers can feel ready for things.

I was not ready.

The weekend of February 9 found me preparing for a regular Saturday night with family and friends. I had teenage sisters, so I was using the shower in my parents' bedroom. I stepped out of the shower, pulled on my pants, applied some pit stick, grabbed my comb, and checked my hair. Lookin' good, amigo, I thought to myself. If I'd been heading for a date, it wouldn't even have been fair.

Out of nowhere, I got a seriously sick feeling in my stomach, like a week's worth of food poisoning hitting me all at once. Then came a headache and dizziness so bad I could barely stand. The toilet was right there, and I thought of it first, but I didn't start throwing up. The nausea just kept coming in bigger and bigger waves.

Using one hand on the wall to keep me upright, I did that bent-over shuffle you do when your stomach hurts. Mom was in her room, only a few steps away. It felt like the last hundred yards of a marathon. I called for her until I was sure she'd heard, then headed back to the bathroom in case my stomach changed its mind about suddenly emptying out whatever was bothering me.

Mom said, "What's wrong?"

"I'm sick to my stomach, and I'm dizzy."

Do you remember the sickest to your stomach you've ever been? You might have had too much to drink. Or maybe it was food poisoning. Maybe stomach flu, or some parasite you picked up while traveling. Remember how you felt terrible, then worse? And it kept getting worse until finally you threw up and you got some relief?

It was like that, only the relief never came. It just kept building until I could barely stand.

"You go lie down, dear," Mom said.

228

I nodded and tried to answer, but couldn't. The headache and nausea just kept getting worse. Every time it reached a point where I thought, "This is the worst I have ever felt, and the worst I could possibly feel," it would crank up a notch and feel even worse.

As scared as I'd ever been in my life, I made my way towards my mom's room. I could tell something was seriously wrong but had no idea what it could possibly be. I had to lean on the wall to keep myself upright. Even without the dizziness, I could hardly stand from the pain and nausea in my stomach and from how my legs were shaking with fear and the exertion of keeping me up.

I made a noise, but it wasn't words. Just an inarticulate sound like a hurt animal. And then I stopped breathing.

Just...stopped breathing.

Do you remember that other time? Probably in grade school? When you fell off the swing, or got a soccer ball right in the gut, and it knocked the wind out of you? Remember how you stood there or lay there unable to breathe until your body remembered how?

It was like that, only my body never remembered how to breathe again. I saw my Mom's face above me, and tried to whisper that I couldn't breathe.

Then things went dark.

What I remember most from that day is the look on my mother's face. She was afraid I would die, and I was pretty sure dying was next on my To-Do list for that day, too. I remember hoping she knew how much I loved her.

A lot of things change when you know you're going to die. You think hard about the things you didn't say, the stuff you never did, the people whose last words with you were angry or hurtful. Since then, I've had a chance to read about Bushido, the code of the samurai of feudal Japan. According to that code, a samurai should live with "death in mind" at all times.

That's not supposed to be some morbid, emo concept where you lie around moaning about death. Instead, it's a way of reminding yourself to live. If you know you could die this afternoon, you won't let some little thing with your wife, or kids, or parents, blow up into a big fight this morning. You won't leave that novel unfinished, that song unsung, that life's work incomplete, because something cool came on Netflix.

"Live each moment like it's your last" isn't exactly a groundbreaking sentiment, but I'm here to tell you it takes on another level of meaning when you've actually done the "Oh God, I'm going to die right now" thing. It's not the life you've lived that flashes before your eyes.

It's the life you haven't.

Mark was told by doctors he had an hour to live...more than 30 years ago. He writes and speaks about disability and inspiration across the country. His book From Snow Skis to Wheelchair *tells his story*

Waiting for Venito

Elizabeth F. Simons

"That's the place, Max. Right there. With the doorman looks like he's from Whatsizham Palace."

"Don't lean in the window like that, you make me look like a john. Get in here. Jesus, I wish Luie wasn't on the inside."

"Okay. Whatever, man. But Venito's in there, just past the dude dressed like an organ grinding monkey."

"Cute. How do you know Venito's in there?"

"I was making a delivery for Cameron, some of that mescaline wine he brews in that basement of his. There's two hard types in the lobby, and a big Samoan motherfucker opening the door of his suite. Venito's right inside, making it with two Korean girls on a leather couch. Fucking couch was so big, they probably needed four, maybe five cows."

"So how do you know he lives there? The man could have come to a party, be holding a meeting. Like that."

"No way, man. Homie was giving orders. He's treating that Samoan like only the man gets away with. That's his crib."

"You're sure?"

"Fuck you am I sure? Why you gonna ask me in the first place, you ain't gonna take my word?"

"Oh for...don't get all swole up."

"I ain't swole up, *pendejo*. You'll know when I'm swole up. I can't believe Luie lets you talk to him like that."

"All right, man. All right. I'm sorry. This is what you do. If you say Venito is there, the man is there. I don't ask the doctor if he's sure I need stitches."

"Damn skippy you do not."

"Don't get all cocky now. Most of the time, you're still almost as smart as wet paint."

"Thanks. Dick."

"Don't mention it."

"Okay."

"So now what?"

"We wait."

"For what?"

"For him to come out, or come in. Ain't doing what we gotta do with him safe up in his crib on the ugly side to two soldiers and a giant Samoan bodyguard. That ain't healthy."

"Could be a long wait."

"Been waiting a while longer than this. Besides, I'm paying you for your time."

"True that."

"Yep."

"So...what you been waiting so long to talk with Venito about?"

"I owe him."

"So pay the man."

"That is the plan, sir. That is the plan."

"Yeah. I can see that. How much do you owe him, and for what?"

"He cut off my ear."

"He what off your what?"

"My ear. He cut it off. You think I keep my hair long because I want to look like a narc?"

"I'll be a son of a bitch."

"That's probably true."

"Jeebus Crow. You wouldn't fuck with me about something like that, would you?"

"Want me to take off my hat, watch you try counting to two?"

"No thank you. Why'd he want to go and do something like that?"

"Wanted me to tell him something."

"And you wouldn't?"

"Didn't see how it was any of his business."

"So he cut off your ear?"

"So he cut off my ear. Second worst thing that ever happened to that ear."

"Seems like he was overreacting."

"Naw. I'd said some pretty choice things about him, his mom, and his cock by the time we got to that point. I likely had it coming."

"You are one strange dude."

"I don't know. Seemed like the thing to do at the time. I'll agree he was overreacting when he fed me the fucking thing."

"Fed you what fucking thing?"

"My ear. Do you even pretend to listen?"

"I listen good. I get paid to listen. It's just that I thought I heard you say Venito fed you your own ear."

"Yes. He. Fed. Me. My. Own. Ear."

"You mean like, *here comes the airplane, open the hangar baby boy*, fed it to you?"

"Not exactly how it went down, but that's the general idea. He sliced it off with a razor like that dude in *Reservoir Dogs*, slapped that bad boy on a skillet with some butter, added mushrooms and a little salt, then made me chew and swallow."

"Hrrrg. Man, that is just seven different kinds of fucked up."

"You're telling me?"

"Oh, man. I don't know if I've even thought about being that pissed off at somebody. Ugh."

"Second worst day of my life."

"Second?"

"Don't ask."

"No. Do not worry about that."

"So you can see why it's important to me that I get back in touch with the man."

"Yeah. Okay. I can see that."

"Okay."

"Hey, Max, can I ask you a question?"

"Is it a stupid question?"

"No."

"Then shoot."

"What did it taste like?"

"What did what taste like?"

"Your ear."

"Excuse me?"

"I'm serious. Between friends, what does a human ear taste like?"

"Ask Mike Tyson."

"I ain't sitting in the car with Mike Tyson doing him a favor."

"Just what in the bright blue fuck are you saying? You want me to tell you it tasted like chicken, something like that?"

"Yeah. I guess. Did it taste like chicken?"

"Sure. It tasted exactly like chicken. Jesus."

"You mean it?"

"Do I mean what?"

"Do you mean it tasted like chicken? Or are you just saying it tasted like chicken the way people do when they don't know what something tastes like?"

"It was my *ear*. Fried in *butter*. With *mushrooms*. I wasn't exactly in a gourmet mood."

"Okay. I can see that."

"Good."

"Was it tough? Gristly? Not much meat in an ear."

"Who dropped you when you were a baby? I had other things on my mind."

"Fair enough."

"It had better be. Damn. *What did it taste like?* What the hell is wrong with you?"

"Oh, be nice. It's a natural...wait. Wait. There he is. Coming out the door right now. Green hat, gray jacket. He's tipping the doorman. See him?"

"Got him. Let's do the thing."

One Last Tale

Michael S. Walker

"More traction," I said. And she said "Yes...Oh yes..." And the five infernal eskimos in her father's bell tower nodded their teeth in agreement.

"Harder, harder," I cried. "That's right," she shivered. And the King of All Pleasure watched as the moon crumbled hard against the bruise of night.

"All things are better in zero gravity," the King winked, dousing us in holy sweat. His fiddlers eight played *My Funny Valentine* and *A Love Supreme*, and for an encore *Do Re Mi* eighteen times.

The country we were in was a strange, wild place, where the robber barons sold anything they could dismantle, and junk hit squads strolled with their bitches around the square of Pottersville, their eyelids tattooed with hate, their muscles iron indifference. They hadn't found us yet, but I was coughing down every morning, getting up, leaving her to go work in a gas chamber parts store on the east side.

"Do you have to go in?" she would ask from the bed, inviting me back in, raising the quilt high as a circus tent. Sometimes, I would succumb.

And the fiddlers would play *The Girl From Ipanema*.

She was so beautiful. Her red hair was the Pentecostal tongue of flame. And her green eyes dreamed a maze of things I wanted palpable. And her legs were ivory. And her breasts were gold...

And the domestic wolves sat by the fire and watched us in surprise as we made love.

"All things must pass," The King of All Pleasure said, on his way to hock his ermine and his crown at the place with twenty and four seeing eye cameras. And his fiddlers eight followed behind him, playing every old murder ballad they knew by heart.

The country we were in was a strange, wild place, where the sons of the poor were fighting wars for the bones of dinosaurs and dying at the age of fourteen. And the bridges were crumbling and being replaced by walls. And the King of All Force stood naked in his new clothes and said: "Well, yes sir, I may be just plain folks...but God told me to do this from his heavenly teleprompter..." It looked like, smelled and tasted of blood.

And the people on the bus rode with their heads down, waiting for the axe to fall, and I watched them in dismay.

"It's gonna be alright," she said. "Come to bed."

And I would lie awake as she slept, my head against her breasts, the five infernal eskimos in her father's bell tower plotting something in their sealskin suits...

Michael walker is a writer, living in Columbus, Ohio. He is the author of two published novels: 7-22, a YA fantasy book, and The Vampire Henry, "a literary" horror novel. He has seen his fiction and poetry published in numerous magazines, including Adelaide Literary and Fiction Southeast.

Kimber Grey

Kimber is a science fiction, fantasy, and horror writer who adores the cranky, urban wizard as much as a repugnant monstrosity. Her books can be found at Amazon, Barnes & Noble, Apple, and most e-book outlets.

The first book of Kimber Grey's fantasy series, *Rise of Faiden*, is available for **FREE** at *any e-book outlet*. You can get the *first two* books for **FREE** simply by visiting:

FaidenFree.GrayWhisper.com

If you liked "Locked In" and want more short stories or some great author interaction (like Q&As, character profiles, and rich background content on all of her books), check out:

Patreon.com/KimberGrey

The Wall of Fame

Annie Carl of the Neverending Bookshop, Author Kimber Grey, Bartt Brick, Cam Mediator, Christine E. Forth, Christine Edgar, Courtney Rogers State Farm Insurance, Daniel Norton, David M. Covenant, Dominick Moser, Douglas & Amanda Sedivy, Helen M. Carothers, Jeb Brack, Jenna, Joan Macbeth, John Samuel Anderson, In Loving Memory of Kathleen Nedrow, Laura Johnson, Laura Petrella, Lisa Schubert May, Mark Lidstone, Mark Seman, Marilyn Trubey, Matthew Johnson, Michael Rosenberger, Nancy Lashbrook Townsley, Pam Dorr, Patrick Whitesell, Richard Clifton, Sally Peterson, Scott Crowder, Seifer Hubbard, Stace Johnson, Steve Fletcher, Terry Steinke, Whatley Family

These heroes backed our project at a level that puts their name (or the name of a loved one) right here in the back of the book. Their names shall live in glory forever!